Look *Right*, Look *Left*, Look *Dead*

by

Anne E. Randell

**Grosvenor House
Publishing Limited**

The right of Anne Elizabeth Randell to be identified as the author of this
work has been asserted in accordance with Section 78
of the Copyright, Designs and Patents Act 1988

The book cover picture is copyright to Inmagine Corp LLC

This book is published by
Grosvenor House Publishing Ltd
28-30 High Street, Guildford, Surrey, GU1 3EL.
www.grosvenorhousepublishing.co.uk

A CIP record for this book
is available from the British Library

ISBN 978-1-78148-985-7

Acknowledgements

Many thanks to Peter for his unfailing support. Sincere thanks to Margaret Lyons whose proof reading was invaluable. Any mistakes remain mine.

Dedication

To Sarah and Chris, for taking my writing seriously.

About the Author

Anne Randell is a retired teacher. She grew up in Manchester and still lives in the North West of England. She has two grown up children. Having enjoyed writing Literacy texts and plays for her students she wanted to continue writing once she left the classroom and completed several writing courses. Anne continues to work in her old school on a voluntary basis, taking reading and writing groups. Having travelled extensively she has had travel articles published. Look Right, Look Left, Look Dead is her second novel.

Previous novel : Next Time It Will Be Perfect.

Prologue

North East Guardian

Father and Son Mown Down by Hit-and-Run Driver

Police are seeking witnesses to an accident which happened yesterday afternoon. The incident took place at approximately half past three on Smithfield Road, a quiet cul-de-sac in the popular holiday town of Seahouses on the Northumberland coast. Joe Nightingale, a single father, aged forty-two, and his sixteen year old son, Peter, were returning from a football practice on Market Garden playing field. A neighbour, Howard Bolton, reported hearing an extremely loud revving noise and said that on looking out of his window he saw a car turn by his property, situated at the top of the road, and travel back at high speed. Detective Chief Inspector Rogers is keen to interview any other witnesses.

The indications are that the pair may have been hit twice. The car did not stop and the police are treating the deaths as suspicious. Joseph Nightingale was pronounced dead at the scene and Peter died a few hours later in hospital.

Mr Bolton added that the car was dark blue and probably a 4 by 4. The car believed to be involved in the accident was taken from a car park in Bamburgh and returned later in the afternoon.

Unable to part with the newspaper, Clara paced nervously around her living room. Dawn had broken several hours ago but the room remained gloomy. Floor length curtains stayed drawn and the only light came from a subdued lamp in the far corner. She seemed unaware of the debris that littered the room, normally so tidy. A plate with the shredded remains of a ham sandwich, the bread starting to curl at the edges, half-finished cups of coffee and several biscuit wrappers gave the room a chaotic look.

She had spent the night trapped in the house, waiting for the paper boy to arrive. He was new to the route and late, the extra minutes adding further tension. At last she heard the newspaper drop onto the mat, the one with three black cats holding up a sign saying *Welcome to Our House*, a purchase that had seemed humorous at the time but which felt inappropriate this morning when no visitor would have been appreciated.

Walking with the paper, which she held as carefully as any mother with her new born baby, she returned to the living room where she slumped down onto the settee, unable to look, afraid to face the possibility that the article she wanted would not be there – that the accident hadn't been successful. Why was she so fearful? It had worked. She knew they were both dead.

There it was! A small item in the Breaking News section at the bottom right-hand corner of the front page, an innovation added recently and proving popular.

An overwhelming sensation of success necessitated movement, however ridiculous her circuits of the coffee table would have looked to an observer. She read the account numerous times, her hands shaking so badly the words blurred. Taking deep breaths she became calmer and reread the article over and over until she had memorised every word. Dead: they were indisputably dead. The previous day she hadn't dared to wait and see how successful she'd been and returning to the scene had been out of the question.

How wonderful! The demise of the first pair was complete: two more duos then the final event with the ultimate victim.

Finally, she sat still. Although totally exhausted she was able to think, to plan and anticipate the magnificent coda. That day was some time off. For now it was enough to enjoy her first success.

The date had been perfect: October 15th. She would allow herself two years before she struck again. Next year would be too soon as accident number two would require far greater planning. There was no hurry, none whatsoever, and Clara knew that anything undertaken too quickly resulted in mistakes that invaded, like unwelcome wasps spoiling a summer picnic.

Unable to sit for any length of time she stood and resumed her wandering. As she drifted aimlessly from wall to wall she recited the words in the report, like a child performing in a poetry competition.

Part 1: Peter

Chapter 1

Unforgiveable.
That is the only word to describe what they did to me,
the people who attempted to ruin my life. I have known
for some time that I have two choices: live with the con-
sequences or take action. I decided that the latter was
necessary and that action meant death. I couldn't carry
on knowing what had happened and not do something,
even if the something was to undertake acts that to
others may seem somewhat excessive.

The camera is not supposed to lie. Clara knew the
phrase well. However, looking at the picture in her
hand she realised that it didn't always tell the whole
truth.

The photograph showed a happy teenager on a
beach, a young girl smiling joyfully at the camera apparently without a care in the world, the baby an unknown
entity and only a few days into its development. The girl
was undoubtedly posing for the young man taking
the picture, someone she had met at the hotel disco on
her first night in Majorca and with whom she had sub-
sequently spent every minute of the holiday. The like-
ness was only able to display one hundredth of a
second's worth of reality and gave no indication of the

events leading up to that instant or the traumas to be played out afterwards. How could it? A photo is merely an infinitesimal glimpse of a life. And it can indeed lie.

Who could have foreseen that such an innocent looking picture would have a direct link to an accident seventeen years later, when the cameraman and his then unborn son would die in an appalling accident?

The holiday, two weeks of Mediterranean sun, had been meant to ease the difficult relationship between Clara and Sophie. They had started life as one until a freak of nature divided their newly fertilised egg and the one became two. For many years they were the best of friends, conversed in their own language and excluded all outsiders. Until their early teens they loved to dress in identical outfits and agreed about everything. They both made good progress at school, Sophie through hard work and Clara thanks to natural ability. Growing apart during their adolescent years had been tough and totally unexpected. Following the end of their A levels they decided to go to Majorca for a fortnight to attempt a reconciliation.

'Are you two having a good time?' Joe was older than many of the men the girls had encountered during their first hours in the resort. Smiling, he added, 'I'm sure I can add to your pleasure.' One twin moved away, the agreement being that they wouldn't cramp each other's style.

His chat-up lines were now aimed at the one who remained. 'Is it your first night here? Not seen you before and I know I would have remembered a pretty girl like you.' The disco had begun at midnight and was in full swing, the music loud and the drinks flowing. It was the last the sisters saw of each other that night or indeed for most of the holiday.

Looking back Clara wondered if things would have turned out differently had she suggested that she and Sophie stayed together.

The holiday failed to reunite them.

However, any need for murder was many years in the future.

North East Guardian

The funeral of Joseph and Peter Nightingale has taken place in St Bartholomew's in the seaside town of Seahouses. Joseph was a member of the family who own the Nightingale caravan parks which have sites all along the Northumbrian coast and he took an active part in the family-run business. His parents spoke of their wonderful son and beautiful grandchild. 'Two bright lights have gone out of our lives – words cannot express the sorrow we are feeling,' said his father, Michael, aged 68.

Joseph and Peter were killed last week in a hit-and-run accident but the police say they are still unsure whether or not the act was deliberate. The car, which was almost certainly involved, had been stolen earlier in the day.

The owner had left his vehicle on the car park near Bamburgh Castle and as he returned, after visiting the attraction, saw it being driven off. He reported the theft to the police. The accident in which the Nightingales were hit occurred an hour later. Mr Jackson's car was returned to the car park and was discovered the following morning in the exact spot from which it had been taken. The police are keen to speak to a young man seen looking at various cars in Bamburgh on the afternoon in question.

Chapter 2

I am not a monster and I am sorry that people have to suffer. Losing a child and grandchild must be truly heart breaking but there was no alternative. Joseph could hardly be considered one of life's innocents, though in all probability Peter was a pleasant young man. He was certainly that the last time I saw him. Thankfully the police are on the wrong track. Looking for a young male: long may that continue.

'I've had the baby so you can collect him whenever it's convenient.'

Joe stood by the phone unable to comprehend the coldness with which the news had been delivered. He had known from the start that she had not wanted the child and had only agreed to continue with the pregnancy on the understanding that he took sole responsibility for him once he was born, but to relay the fact that their son had arrived with such a total lack of feeling was incredible.

'Are you still there? Did you hear what I said?' Joe was almost unable to respond to such indifference. This was their son. A tiny, brand new human being they had, albeit inadvertently, brought into the world. Surely she must feel something, not merely be in a hurry to get rid of him.

'Yes, I'm here. Are you both all right? Was it an easy birth?'

'No, it was bloody awful but thanks for asking.' There was a long pause. 'My part's done and you are welcome to your darling son. He does nothing but cry and if I have to spend a night in this hospital I'll join in with his caterwauling.'

'When was he born?'

'Five thirty this morning and not before time, I'd been in labour for almost twenty-four hours. Bloody excruciating. When can you collect him? The nurses say he's perfectly healthy and can be released early tomorrow morning. Does that suit you?' Joe made no comment about her choice of words. He wasn't disappointed, or altogether surprised, that seeing the baby hadn't made her change her mind. He had known she wasn't maternal and had never been under any illusion that there would be a long term relationship. If he was truthful he had to admit that there never had been what could be called a relationship, they had merely enjoyed a brief "fling" which had resulted in the pregnancy.

The day she had informed him that she was "preggers" and would be getting rid of it as soon as possible was the day that changed Joe's life. It wasn't that he disapproved of abortion per se but this was his child and he knew that he wanted it. A decade before he had got married, separated and divorced, all in a few uncomfortable months. He and Jenny had been in the same class at school, St. Cuthbert's High, and had married at eighteen, neither of them ever having gone out with anyone else. For many people this is a sound beginning to a wonderful, lifelong arrangement but not for them. Joe's parents had hoped that he would go to university but once married all he wanted to do was start earning

7

money. A week after the wedding he began to work with his parents in their caravan business. A year after the wedding the marriage was over.

'Thank goodness there were no babies, makes it easier and the lad's young, he'll find someone else,' was his mother's comment on hearing the news. Despite several affairs, of varying lengths and intensity, his mother's prediction never materialised and Joe remained alone and, on the whole, happy to be so.

It had been several months before Joe had felt able to tell his parents of his impending fatherhood. He waited until it was too late for a termination. Until that time he feared that the mother might still abort and it was after phoning her one evening when she was again adamant that he could *have it* and that he was *more than welcome to it* as she was not intending to have any contact at all once it arrived, that he plucked up the courage to inform his parents.

'You're what? When did this happen? What in the world are you thinking of? You can't look after a baby,' followed a stunned silence. His parents looked utterly shocked and sat, immobile, all too aware of the difficult future their son was creating for himself.

'The mother doesn't want it and when I heard that she was expecting I knew that the baby was all I wished for in the world.'

'And has this mother got a name?' his father asked, failing to keep the hurt out of his voice.

'Yes, but you don't know her and it was just a laugh, nothing serious, we were never going to be together long term.'

'The trouble is Joe that a baby is long term, and no laughing matter. You're an adult and we're still dealing with you,' she said, failing to lighten the tense atmosphere. 'A baby is forever and it will alter your life completely in ways that you just can't imagine.'

'Nothing you can say will change my mind. It's all agreed when the baby, a boy (he added proudly), is born I will bring him to Seahouses to live with me. I'm looking into child-minding. I know I've got to work but I also know I will love him and I hope you will both feel the same. You love your granddaughters and he will be your first grandson.'

'The difference is Faye and Angela have two parents to look after them and that's hard enough. You really have no idea what you're taking on.'

After Joe left, his parents sat in their first floor living room and looked out at the North Sea which was providing a dramatic backdrop to the day's events. Waves were crashing over the low sea wall opposite their house, high tide less than an hour away. Michael was a fit man, playing golf several times a week and still coping with the demands of the caravan park business which had expanded over the years thanks to untold hours of hard work. He had retained a head of thick hair and was often taken to be many years younger. His plan was to retire within two years and hand over the running of the firm to Joe.

Evie was five years younger and, after years spent supporting her husband in the business, now preferred her days to be filled with shopping, coffee mornings and looking after her granddaughters, though the latter only occasionally.

'Might as well tear up our retirement plans. No hours of leisure and foreign travel now,' Evie moaned, 'looks like we'll be baby-sitting.'

'Not full time, tell him, not full time, he can't expect that. We've done our bit bringing him and his sister up. We've got our lives to think about.'

'Yes, but...'

'No buts, he can't expect us to start again, we're not as young as we were and we've worked jolly hard over the years. This is our time now.'

'We'll help him out and he said he was looking into child care.'

'As long as the child care isn't us.' Michael was becoming agitated. 'He wants this child, goodness knows why, so he will have to take responsibility.'

'I'll phone him after and say we were just so surprised by his news that we maybe didn't say the right things.'

'Shocked more like. Our Joe a single father. What in the world is he thinking?'

'I suppose we should be proud of him wanting to do the right thing.'

'Trouble is Evie I'm not sure he is doing the right thing.' They sat talking for hours. Neither noticed the retreating tide or heard a word of the ten o'clock news that played in the background. Bedtime was late that night and neither slept well.

Chapter 3

Six weeks since the accident and no knock on the door, no bobby on the doorstep. It's macabre to feel so inordinately proud – but I do. I remain amazed that it was so easy and it gives me hope for the future. I keep telling myself five to go: two pairs and then the finale. Most fairy tales have a wicked stepmother but this story has an evil sister. Believe me what she did was malicious. I will have no qualms about dispatching her to Hades and may even put the apocryphal penny in her hand to pay the ferryman.

Unfortunately, because of her, six other people must die. One could argue that it is therefore entirely her fault. If only she had treated me with more humanity, met me somewhere in the middle, none of this would be necessary. But necessary it is.

The Northumbria police were no nearer to solving the hit-and-run "accident". As the weeks went by Detective Chief Inspector Rogers, in charge of the investigation from the beginning, was more convinced than ever that far from being an accident it had been an intentional act: in other words murder.

What looked like a young man, of average height and wearing the usual post-school uniform of dark trousers and a navy hoodie, had been caught on the

CCTV camera in the Bamburgh car park, both taking and returning the car. Unfortunately the footage was blurred and everyone agreed it would be of little help identifying the thief and as Clive Rogers added, 'The murderer.'

The Forensic Operations team had examined the car and had failed to find any helpful fingerprints or other evidence of the driver. Indeed the car had been deemed "remarkably clean". Every surface, inside and out, had been wiped and most had been cleaned with a spray polish.

The phone call, following a request for a second inspection of the car, was of little help. 'We did find one hair though not human. Our expert, Rich Walker, said it was the type used in top-of-the-range wigs. The owner of the car is adamant that no one in the family has ever worn one and they aren't aware of any passenger who might have been so attired.

'The criminals have been watching too many episodes of *Silent Witness* and are getting far too clever. They know not to leave anything incriminating behind and almost unfailingly wear gloves, but spray polish… that's a new one,' had been Clive Rogers rather bitter comment on the day he heard the forensic report. 'Not many men wear wigs and yet our witness was sure the driver was male.'

'And how many men think to clean the car with a spray polish?' This thought was spoken aloud to the empty room after he put down the phone. Too impatient to wait for the written version he had pestered the forensics team on an almost hourly basis and was frustrated by their meagre findings.

The autopsy had shown that both father and son had been hit twice and from different directions, indicating that the witness who said that the car had turned at the top of the cul-de-sac and driven back at high speed had been correct. There were no skid marks, no indication that the car had attempted to stop or even tried to avoid hitting the pair. Unfortunately the road was not covered by CCTV cameras. Despite Clive Roger's findings his superiors were not interested and continued to treat it as an accident, the driver being viewed by them as typical of the majority of hit-and-run drivers: either selfish or scared. Such incidents were seldom cold-blooded murder.

What no one seemed able to answer was why the father and son had been targeted. Joseph Nightingale was a popular man, his many friends speaking highly of him. He seemed to have been a model father: attending Parent's Evenings, school concerts and his son's sporting activities on a very regular basis. His parents said that he had worked in the family business for almost two decades and had done brilliantly, successfully establishing new parks both in England and abroad. Everyone agreed that his care for his son had been "exemplary".

'We never thought he'd cope as well as he has, oh dear me, did,' his mother sobbed, the past tense a painful reminder of what they had lost. 'He loved Peter, always maintained that he was the best thing that had ever happened to him and the lad was a credit to him. Not easy being a single parent, especially a single dad, but we were proud of the way he was bringing up the boy.'

Mr Summers, the head teacher at Peter's school, Chafferton Community College, spoke of Peter as a delightful young man. 'He was the kind of boy who makes our job easy: clever, hard-working, popular and full of good humour. He will be sorely missed.'

No one had a bad word to say about either of them.

Clive Rogers had been in the police force for almost three decades, a length of time he found hard to believe. It had flown past, rather like the RAF planes that regularly soared over the North East coast on one of their training exercises. He had always loved the job and enjoyed being an important part of the community where he had grown up. Having endured spells in Newcastle, where he had gained his promotion, he had been relieved to return to his beloved home town when an appropriate vacancy came up: a most welcome sideways move. With so many daily challenges he found his present role fulfilling and felt no inclination to seek further advancement. He believed that he held one of the most important positions in the police force: in charge of cases, enjoying a direct influence over other officers whilst still engaged in the hands-on day-to-day action. Of one thing he was sure...he had more than enough paper work.

He was fortunate to be that rare breed of policeman who was happily married, the only disappointment being a lack of children. They had tried for years and had undergone every test and procedure known to the medical profession, all to no avail. Mari, the girl he had met at a local Farmers' Harvest Supper twenty-three years ago, was less upset by this than he was. She had mentioned (on several occasions) the possibility of adopting but Clive had said no on the grounds that you didn't know what you were taking on and he would hate to think that they might be harbouring the kind of individual he dealt with on a daily basis.

'But he or she would have our input – nurture over nature,' Mari had argued. 'Yes and think of some of the monsters you teach. Are you sure they are all like that due to their upbringing or were they "born bad", full of dodgy genes?' And so it had remained the two of them, both finding endless fulfilment in their chosen professions.

As in most relationships a routine had been established early on which almost invariably included spending part of the evening discussing their days over a glass of wine. However, for weeks, ever since the hit-and-run, Clive had been unsettled and unwilling to say much. He was frustrated by the lack of progress and the incident was starting to dominate his thinking. Mari reminded him that there were bound to be times when it would prove impossible to find out what had happened but he hated any unsolved case and this one felt personal. He had often seen Joe and Peter at social events in the town and had admired the way Joe appeared to deal with being a single father.

'What I can't explain is why they were the victims. It just doesn't make sense.'

Mari was becoming tired of her husband's obsessive interest in the accident. She was about to tell him that his constant repetition of the same phrases was becoming boring but restrained herself and replied, 'Perhaps there was something in his past no one knows about. Have you found out any more about the child's mother? There must have been one in the beginning.'

'Of course we've looked into that. No birth certificate has been found and Joe's parents never knew anything about the woman, just that she didn't want the baby. She's a total mystery.'

'You should maybe get *Crime Watch* involved,' Mari added, only half joking, longing for this case to be solved. The rest of the evening was spent without conversation, both pretending an interest in the latest David Attenborough wildlife documentary.

Chapter 4

Looking at the newspaper cuttings and articles I have downloaded from the internet is so rewarding. I've even started a scrapbook. It was vaguely disappointing when the case went "dead" (pardon the pun) but at least it must mean that they have no idea what happened. What fun it is to realise that my outfit worked: denim trousers, teenage-style hoodie and a peaked cap. All purchased from different charity shops. Being of above average height helped and when I looked in the mirror even I thought the person standing there had changed sex.

This weekend I am treating myself. It was advertised as an "Extended Rally Driving Experience" at Brands Hatch with forty minutes of driving and lots of frenetic races to watch. I got the idea after Henry gave me a "Silverstone" weekend a few months ago which was fantastic. Done Silverstone, next stop Brands Hatch. How delightful to have my own Mini Cooper S, my eighteenth birthday gift from Henry and my pride and joy. It's ensconced in a local garage I hire whilst my everyday car, an ancient Honda Civic, stands on the drive. I leave my garage empty. One never knows when it will come in useful. Needless to say neither car was used to dispatch the Nightingales. It was necessary to "borrow" a car for that particular event.

My life without Henry, my amazing godfather, would have been so different: no excitement, no dangerous driving, for me or I suppose others!

Clara loved the North East: empty roads, ruined castles, rolling hills, fish and chips, the locals calling her "pet" and most of all the seemingly endless miles of amazing beaches. When she and her sister were little the family had gone there during most school holidays, staying in a selection of "Town and Country Cottages". They had visited at all times of the year but her favourite had always been the winter when the bulk of the holiday-makers had gone and the miles of sand were almost deserted, only a few dog-walkers battling valiantly against the winds and the infamous horizontal snow. She adored the hike from Seahouses to Bamburgh and never failed to be impressed by the castle that loomed over the beach at the end of the walk.

'If only we had the weather there'd be no need to go abroad. The beaches here must be as good as any-where in the world,' her father was fond of saying. Once family holidays stopped Clara continued to return to Northumbria as often as she could, which usually meant each school break. Working as a Teaching Assistant in a primary school had its advantages. How pleasantly surprised she had been on learning that Peter was going to be living in the area. She regarded it as an almost unbelievable coincidence and knew that it would make keeping up-to-date with the boy's progress so much easier. No need to get to know the place, she was as at home on the North East coast as she was in Sale where she had grown up and still lived. Strange to recall that until recently her interest in him had been altruistic: totally without malice. How things had changed.

The first time she had driven over, taking a beautifully scenic route via York where she stopped for a night, she was as nervous as a miscreant standing in the dock waiting to be sentenced. Why was she going? What if Joe saw her? He would want to know what she was doing. What was she doing? A good question to which at the time, she had no answer, just a gut feeling that she must track Peter's progress. She wasn't really interested in Joe but was certain that she would always want to know all about the boy.

The initial visit to Seahouses when Peter was a baby had been a nightmare. She had spent the entire time looking suspiciously at everyone, afraid they would know why she was there. It was a busy week in the height of summer and the town was packed. She knew that Joe's family owned the large caravan park overlooking the North Sea and she hoped it would be easy to find where the pair lived. Blackthorn Cottage, where she was staying, had a telephone directory and Nightingale wasn't a very common name. An hour after arriving she was standing on Smithfield Road looking at their house.

For that and every subsequent visit a different disguise had been necessary. She knew that Joe would recognise her and so she became an old lady, a punk-style teenager, a dowdy holidaymaker and a variety of males, both young and old. On each occasion she wore one of her many wigs. The day she had come face-to-face with Joe, in the middle of the high street, she had been dressed as a jogger with running gear, headband and dark shades. She had almost given the game away by her reaction.

'Sorry, not looking where I'm going,' Joe had said after she had nearly fallen into him. Clara had been afraid to speak so just mumbled, 'My fault,' and ran on, like a sinner with the hounds of hell after her. She was never so careless again and whilst in Northumbria was constantly alert, totally in charge of the situation.

From her numerous visits she knew that the two were doing well. Joe looked happy and Peter was obviously thriving. On several occasions she talked to the locals in a selection of pubs in the area and heard how well the Nightingales' business was doing.

'They're setting up in Spain this summer, nice place to work.'

'Bill, my mate who does some of their maintenance, says that they might go as far as Croatia next year.'

'They deserve their good fortune, they're hard workers the lot of them.'

Over the years she observed Peter grow from baby to toddler to schoolboy. She watched him play football for the local town under elevens and observed him taking his dog, a mutt of indeterminate breed, for walks on the sand.

It was many years before Clara knew that he would have to exit the scene, his father collateral damage.

Chapter 5

People die. They leave us. Some have no choice. Others choose it: cowards, unable to take life's vagaries. My mother was one of those: sleeping pills and alcohol were her modus operandi. Her disappearing act.

She knew I loved Tuesday, the one day when we had an after-hours hockey practice or monthly game against a local school. Hockey was the only sport at which I excelled.

People say that someone contemplating suicide doesn't think of others, that they don't mean to hurt the ones left behind. Indeed the psychiatrist (the incomprehensibly useless woman I saw every week in the months following mother's death and who wanted me to be on first name terms and call her Natalia) once said that the person believes that others will be better off without them. A ridiculous idea especially as my mother must have known that her daughter, aged thirteen, would be the one to discover her dead body. That must constitute a total lack of empathy and however "lost in the mire of insecurity" (another of Natalia's gems) it surely entered my mother's thinking that I might be traumatised by being the first one to arrive on the appalling scene. Ever since that afternoon I have thought that it meant she hated me. Who knows? She would now.

For many years the Bedfords were a happy family. The business was expanding and Mary and Robert Bedford enjoyed each other's company and that of their daughters. Over the years an array of pets kept them amused: hamsters, goldfish and a gerbil were superseded by a Recue dog, Brandy, who having been mistreated by his former owners was forever seeking reassurance that he was behaving appropriately. Sophie and Clara were allowed to take him for walks as long as they promised to stay together. Quite why their parents thought that they would be all right out in the open spaces of one of the town's parks with the softest, most cowardly mutt in the world remained a mystery. He would have run a marathon had anyone approached.

Home was a huge detached house on the outskirts of Sale, near Manchester, or as Mary Bedford insisted on saying Sale, Cheshire. Until she met Robert she had lived in a rented house in Moss Side and wanted everyone to know she had "gone up in the world". Despite her need for improvement she never lost her working-class roots and did all her own cleaning, made the curtains and many of her daughters' clothes. Each evening knitting needles provided a percussive accompaniment to the radio or television. Socks, jumpers, gloves and scarves were created, most in very bright colours. No food was ever wasted even when some sell-by dates had long gone. Until her final months when the unexpected and appalling depression engulfed her and her world became one endless dark night, she was a calm, positive woman and a reassuring part of the household.

As the twin's birth had been so difficult, no further children were ever contemplated. At the time Robert had been told to expect the worst: one or both girls might not survive. Arriving six weeks early their joint weight was less than a medium sized bag of potatoes.

'You were little fighters and determined to stay here,' was a phrase their grandmother loved to repeat. However, they were at times sickly infants and one or both endured spells in hospital, often with some ailment that to others would be minor but which for them quickly became serious. It was worse when it was only one of them who became ill as it meant days or weeks of separation.

'Look what I've brought you, a new doll,' Sophie screeched as she ran down the ward soon after their fifth birthday. Clara has the doll still but recently its looks have been ruined by the piercings it has endured. An entire set of sewing pins employed, each inserted for maximum damage. It is no longer a pretty sight, unlike Sophie, who improves with each passing year. No guilty conscience for her, no feelings of regret for the manner in which she treated her sibling. So far only the doll has suffered – if you discount Joe and Peter.

Until the age of thirteen they adored each other's company. At primary school the two were always together and tried to sit side by side whenever possible. The only way teachers could tell which twin was which was that Sophie had a tiny mole on her left cheek, a blemish that in later years she attempted, rather unsuccessfully, to hide with foundation.

In Year 3 Miss Golding suggested that they separate and sit on different tables and an attempt was made to persuade them to make their own friends. When that failed she made games lessons a penance.

'Clara you have Julie as your partner in P.E. today, I'm sure you'll work well together.' The entire lesson was spent with pinching and poking poor Julie who became so upset that the day was won and the twins were reunited. After Parents' Evening, that same month, Mary and Robert came home looking worried. Both girls were making good progress academically and always worked hard but Fiona Golding had voiced her concerns about them not relating to other pupils.

'Just because you are lucky to have each other doesn't mean you can't have other friends,' their mother suggested, adding, 'why don't you each choose someone to come to tea after school one day next week?'

The matter was decided when Mary issued the dreaded invitations herself. At least Julie wasn't involved this time. Rain soaked the four girls as they plodded reluctantly up the path the following Wednesday afternoon. It had been pouring all day, the entire school enduring wet breaks. Mrs Bedford had baked cakes and as Clara and Sophie stomped into the kitchen they saw that the large kitchen table had been set with a gingham tablecloth, always a sign there were guests. Sandwiches, jelly and a choice of home-made lemonade and orange squash were awaiting them.

Half an hour is a long time for young children to sit in silence. The afternoon tea was delicious but almost totally unappreciated. What should have been a treat became an endurance test. What Angela, Clara's new "friend", and Lucy, Sophie's, made of it is not recorded. The girls were not due to be picked up until six o'clock so once the meal was over Mary suggested that the visitors were taken upstairs to the playroom.

The upstairs room was enormous and was jam-packed with toys, jigsaws and books. An enormous doll's house, made by Uncle Colin, a lover of creating "things", as his long-suffering wife called them, resided centre stage, the mansion attracting the attention of anyone allowed into the twin's sanctum.

'Wow, what a room, it's bigger than my house,' Angela enthused. If they were jealous there was no sign of it but for the remainder of the time (centuries pass quicker) Angela and Lucy played together and Sophie and Clara sat and talked behind the curtains in the bay window.

'Angela and Lucy, your mums are here.' They had in fact been here for some time. The hostesses, somewhat of a misnomer, had seen them arrive, driving in convoy along the road. They had listened to the voices from downstairs and waited sullenly for the intruders to be gone. Whenever she thought about that afternoon Clara realised that their guests must have felt unforgivably unwelcome and were probably as keen to leave as the twins were to see them go. She knew it wasn't their guests' fault but at the time nothing was allowed to separate her from Sophie. Two was the perfect number.

'Thanks for having us,' they had piped in unison, winning the duet of the year award. Once their cars were out of sight Sophie and Clara complained so vehemently, insisting that the afternoon had been a disaster, that the episode was never repeated.

And so Sophie and Clara remained a very happy double act, taking turns to be the comic stooge. It was not until their mother's death that they drifted, then plummeted, apart. Neither of them was to find it easy to develop new friendships, though over the following years both were to revel in numerous affairs, of varying lengths and intensity.

Chapter 6

Far too late to alter my plans.
As I am responsible for two deaths I may as well continue.
No point stopping now.
None at all.

Arriving home that never to be forgotten Tuesday afternoon was a turning point in Clara's life. The shrinks she
saw, with increasingly frustrating frequency for all
concerned, said that she must move on, make a new life,
one even suggested that she should "rise above the
tragedy". Natalia Howard's efforts were eventually
discarded in favour of Drs Smith, Jenkins and Ellis, all
equally useless. Dr Smith urged the girl to "restart her
life" but he didn't have to live with the memories: the
fight with her father, on her mother's penultimate night,
broadcasting the appalling secret or the moment when
she walked into the kitchen yelling, 'I'm home, mum,
great hockey practice, I scored a hat-trick,' only to see
her mother sitting in the arm chair, body slumped at an
unusual angle and face devoid of life. The note, left in
the middle of the kitchen table, was addressed to
My Family, two words forever rendered obsolete. The
smell of the stew emanating from the huge pot on the
Aga has lived with her ever since and remains a meal
never countenanced.

How strange, and at the time almost inexplicable, that Mary had retained sufficient self-control, and perhaps the remnants of love for her family, to cook their favourite meal before swallowing the copious number of pills that killed her.

The small kitchen clock, sitting on the Welsh dresser, showed a minute short of five o'clock, the second hand halfway on its rhythmic perambulation to the hour. Clara stood transfixed by the hand's dog-leash jerks, finding them preferable to the sight of her mother. Later she was to wonder why the clock had continued to tick tock with an almost comical sound. Why had it kept recording each second, minute and hour? In the well-known song the Grandfather Clock understood that its duty was to stop at the moment of death: the one in the Bedford's kitchen was obviously a far less sensitive time-piece.

Over the years the sequence of events following the gruesome discovery became blurred. On entering the enormous kitchen-diner Clara knew there was no need to touch her mother. She was so obviously dead. Tablet containers and Vodka bottles sat empty on the small table beside her, the table that normally held her latest novel and reading glasses. Clara had no idea to which part of the house these had been relegated but they had not been allowed to witness her demise, an end that must have taken many minutes. Had there been a moment when her mother regretted her decision? Had it been too late to stop? Probably not. They over-heard the doctor saying that she had consumed a far greater quantity of tablets than was needed.

Robert was contacted and the paramedics and police arrived. Mary Bedford was pronounced dead.

How do other families cope in such dire circumstances? Normal, everyday life appears to be impossible but that is exactly what happens. Cooking (the stew was thrown away – no one able to face it), shopping, washing, ironing, work, school and homework all resumed within an astonishingly short time. Clara continued to play hockey, the season lasting, in the circumstances most fortuitously, far longer than normal due to the appalling winter and spring weather that had been endured in the North West which had led to the postponement of several matches. The following weekend she was appalled to realise that she cared about the result. The game was won by four goals to three, the team's centre forward scoring the vital goal early in the second half. Clara celebrated as enthusiastically as the rest of the team.

For weeks Sophie and Clara comforted each other but were of little help to Robert who, when not spending extra time at work, cocooned himself in his study with a bottle of whisky, staring into space.

'Go away girls, I want to be left alone,' was his constant refrain, a chorus from a Blues song. Clara dared not ask him if he realised that they were also suffering. Empathy had never been his forte.

Weeks became months and Mary's name was hardly mentioned. All knew she had been ill – the depression striking with the speed night falls on the Equator. Day after day had been spent in bed, the curtains drawn against the light. The rest of the world had become an unwanted entity. There were weeping sessions when she was beyond comfort and, even more disturbing, the long hours of stillness when there would be no response to any attempt at conversation.

These abominations had been the norm for many months. However, just before she died there had been some slight improvement and Robert and the girls had been hopeful that life was ascending once more, like the scales she loved to play on the piano in the front room. Unfortunately, both scales and their mother's mood had the capacity to descend.

A few weeks after it happened, Robert attempted a rare conversation with his daughter. He looked broken. His dark hair was inflected with white and his face covered in several days of unnoticed stubble. He reminded Clara of the elderly vagrant they passed occasionally in town. The smell of booze and body odour was overpowering and he must have seen her shrink away. If she hoped that, finally, he was trying to bring some comfort she was wrong.

'Clara, it must have been truly awful for you, finding your mum like that.' Clara sat on the edge of the bed and stared at him. 'You do know that she was ill and that there was nothing you, or any of us, could have done to help her. She was determined to end her life. Even if you had got home earlier it wouldn't have made any difference, the doctor said she'd been dead for a little time.'

Robert did not sound convincing. He reminded her of the amateurish actor the class had seen recently in an appalling version of *She Stoops to Conquer*. The man had delivered his lines without any feeling, merely regurgitating the words he had learnt, making each speech feel like a gargantuan effort. So that was it, Clara thought, her father was blaming her, thinking that if she hadn't gone to her hockey practice she might have prevented the tragedy.

Worse was to follow. Robert repeated, almost verbatim, the slanging match the two of them had engaged in, the one overheard by Mary the night before her death. The implication was clear: Clara was responsible for her mother's suicide.

Sophie, as always, had got off scot-free. She had been the dutiful daughter going into Manchester after school that fateful afternoon to help dad choose a present for their mother who would have been thirty-eight had she lived a few more days. It was the first time Clara realised Sophie was the favoured sister.

Dear goodness, if that was the beginning it was to escalate with unforeseen consequences.

School became a panacea. Soon after Mary's death, how much easier that word was to become, how painful at the time, the twins took their Options, both choosing Business Studies. Sophie added history and R.E. whilst Clara chose to pursue languages and geography. The decisions were indicative of the separation they were beginning to experience. Just a short time earlier both would have selected the same subjects, more than happy to sit together in every class and help each other with homework.

Several months after the funeral, which had been delayed due to the autopsy and inquest, they started in Year 10 and became engrossed in the work that would lead to the exams the teachers assured them were of such vital importance. The girls wanted to do well academically but it had always been assumed that one day they would take over the Bedford's ever-expanding firm.

The family had made its money with a chain of jewellery shops, Robert's parents establishing the first one on Deansgate, in the centre of Manchester, soon after the war. Within a year they had added two others in the city and before long new ones had been opened across the North West. By the time Robert Bedford took control of the business, following his parents' very early retirement, there were eighteen outlets. Others followed and *Bedford's Jewellers: Affordable Luxury* could soon be found in Newcastle, Birmingham and London.

The empire was just waiting for the girls.

Both maternal grandparents had died not long after the twins were born. 'At least they saw both of you and thought you were the most gorgeous creatures in the whole of creation,' Mary said, on one of the few occasions she spoke about them. Early family photos were cherished items. One had Mary with her parents standing outside their house, a small terraced, with Manchester City's old ground at Maine Road in the background; another was obviously taken in Blackpool with the Tower in the distance and candy floss in their grandpa's hand. Several others were of Mary on her own or with one of her many siblings, all of whom were some years her senior. Once she died almost all contact was lost with that side of the family, only Aunt Hannah keeping in contact.

In the year following mother's death, looking after the girls fell to Robert's parents, Mike and Sheila. A home-help was engaged to help run the house but one or other grandparent felt duty-bound to be there at the end of each school day. It must have been a burden for them but neither was ever heard to complain. They were a lively pair with activities most days ranging from bird-watching to ballroom dancing but Clara and Sophie became their main priority.

Vacations now took place during the school holidays though the grandparents had little idea what the two got up to when not sitting by the hotel pool. The local boys found them very good company: very good indeed.

Robert preferred to stay at home. He had always worked hard but since his wife's death had become a workaholic, a strategy he used to avoid the family, especially Clara. As the months, then years passed, it was as though he couldn't bear to be in the same room with her. That was absolutely fine. The feeling soon became mutual.

Many years on Clara's diary read, "How can there be no change after a mother has absconded, abandoned her duties? We were still children and needed her. Life would have turned out so differently had she been there. Dad would not have been allowed to do what he did. Sophie would definitely have been prohibited from such an act of pure malice. Had that been the case the hit-and-runs would not have been needed. No deaths. No murders."

Chapter 7

Inquest into the death of Mrs Mary Bedford: Coroner's Report

This is a tragic case. The death of a young woman is always a cause for sorrow. She should have had many years of life ahead of her.

The autopsy indicated that at the time of her death she was in good health physically. However, her medical records show that for many months prior to her demise she had been suffering a bout of severe and debilitating depression and this undoubtedly had a profound effect on her outlook on life. No cause for this state of mind has been established though her husband said that prior to the depression she had become very fearful of the future, imagining the worst case scenario at all times. Panic Attacks and extreme anxiety had been diagnosed and Mary had attended a course of counselling sessions.

The evidence would appear to be conclusive: the taking of a large number of pills, the excessive consumption of alcohol and the farewell note. I therefore have no alternative but to declare that Mary took her own life when the balance of her mind was disturbed.

Families are left with a sense of guilt when a loved one commits suicide but in her note Mary assured her husband, Robert, and her beloved daughters, Sophie

and Clara, that they could not have prevented her final act. She was finding life overwhelming and described it as feeling like Saint Sebastian with the arrows wedged in his skin. Her arrows were, and I quote from her moving final letter, "Barbs: they pierce my soul, immovable and unendurable. Their numbers grow on an hourly basis and life has become insupportable."

Mary then asked the family to forgive her. This is not easy but having read many suicide notes I believe this one was sincere and that she meant none of you any harm. For Mary, on that afternoon, there did not appear to be a viable alternative. My sincere condolences are extended to her family. I hope that good memories of happier times will aid you over the next, extremely difficult, months.

Driving lessons with her godfather became the focus of Clara's life and the first hobby she started without Sophie. Henry Wilfred Mellor had been Robert's boyhood friend and the best man at his wedding. He had always taken a close interest in the twins' lives and at one time hoped that one of them would be spouse material for his son, Sam, a boy they both enjoyed playing with as children.

Henry had inherited a large farm near Alderley Edge where flocks of sheep kept him busy. When Sophie and Clara were little they loved going to visit at lambing time, though the first sheep they saw miscarried rather dramatically leaving a trio of half formed lambs on the blood-splattered ground.

'That wasn't meant to happen but the mother very rarely delivers three youngsters, two at a time is about her limit.' The two stood wide-eyed and open-mouthed, too shocked to respond. They might never have gone again if normal service hadn't been resumed and four mothers gave birth to healthy offspring. The best part of the afternoon was being allowed to feed the lambs, those either orphaned at birth or who had been rejected by their exhausted mothers. The tiny creatures delighted the girls with the ferocity with which they attacked the fake teats, the bottles full of lamb milk replacer. Henry kept a good stock of it as it was needed every year.

'Is it as good as the real thing?' Clara asked, thinking nothing could be as suitable as the proper milk.

'Well, ideally the mother feeds her little ones but this has had vitamins and nutrients added so they seem to thrive on it and you always know how much they've drunk. The one you're feeding was a twin but its mum is young and a bit silly and can't cope with two. I remember when you two were that new the problems your mum had keeping you both satisfied.' This was too much information and the conversation moved on.

Long after Sophie had grown tired of the farm Clara continued to visit Henry. He was several bus rides away but the effort was worth it. He was, in many ways, the father she lost once her mother died: she felt like an orphan and Henry became her confidant, the one person with whom she could discuss her feelings. 'Part of me died that day, I wish I hadn't been the one to find her,' she said on one occasion, bursting into noisy tears. Even a year on the pain was still sharp, like the razors she had started to use on both arms. Immense relief was experienced when the gouging became deeper and the blood flowed. It had become a daily ritual, one of the few moments she enjoyed. The Cutting continued until the day Henry noticed her arms and was so shocked that it made her stop. He was the one person in the world she never wanted to disappoint.

'Part of you did disappear, but will come back given time.' He spoke so quietly she had to strain to hear him. 'To lose your mother when you are still so young leaves an enormous hole in your life. My dad died when I was in my twenties, so I was considered to be an adult, and that was hard enough. You miss the person who cared for you more than anyone else ever can and you long to talk to them again, as whatever you said, or told them you had done, you knew they would be on your side.' Robert never spoke to either of his daughters like that and during those awful adolescent years Clara sought more and more help from Henry. Sophie looked elsewhere for her consolation.

It was after a long afternoon, when Henry had done more to help than any official counsellor, that he suggested to his god-daughter that he would teach her to drive. Who can say how different the future would have been had that offer not been made. 'It's my land, private property, so I could give you lessons.' As Clara was only fifteen the idea of driving had never entered her head. 'It would give us both a new project and should be fun. By the time you're seventeen you'll be able to take the test on your birthday. I started to teach Sam at that age, though Amy didn't like the idea of her precious son behind the wheel of a car.'

Two old cars, both in working order, stood in a disused barn. Henry loved motors and spent hours restoring them or "tinkering" as his wife called it. The first lesson was terrifying, Henry encouraging her to drive fast, far faster than she had anticipated; she was hooked! From then on lessons were undertaken most weeks, a fact kept secret from the rest of the family as Henry wasn't sure they would approve.

'You're a natural, we'll have you rally driving next,' he announced as they sat in the kitchen one dark day deep into autumn. Clara had never heard of that style of driving but as Henry explained it knew she would adore it.

'Why not come with us next weekend? Sam's home from uni and we're going to a Rally in Ashton in Makerfield near Merseyside. It's a racing school for rally driving and would give you a taste of rallying on various terrains. It'll get your blood pumping and the old adrenalin flowing. Sam and I have entered various races and you could be our cheerleader. We could do with a "groupie" to make a fuss of us when we win. There's no feeling like it, nerves on edge and reactions tested to the hilt. It's a purpose-built course and a real, heart-pounding experience. There are hairpin turns, dips and inclines over gravel and wonderfully thick dirt. You'll love it.' And so six days later the love of her life, (no long-term man for her), began.

The day was everything Henry had promised. It augured well when the early mist lifted to give way to a day of blue skies, sunshine and unseasonal warmth. Sam drove to the event in the old Ford Escort he'd been seen working on in the barn. It was obviously well past its prime but according to Sam, 'Drove like a demon.' Henry and Clara travelled in the car she was familiar with and Henry was only half-joking when he suggested she could drive part of the way. The vehicle was almost certainly too powerful for a learner – a bright red Peugeot 205 which was soon to lose both its colour and its shine once the races started. Clara had never seen so much mud, even on the farm, but it only added to the experience.

Rallying is man and machine pitted against the conditions. The weather can play its part and the terrain is designed to make driving as challenging as possible. That day neither Henry nor Sam won any of their events but the thrill of watching them hurtle at breakneck speed was totally exhilarating, like a death-defying ride at Disneyland. The day sped by almost as fast as the cars and by the end of it she had only one thing on her mind: to get behind the wheel and enter a race.

'I can tell you enjoyed that,' Henry said as they returned home.

'It was the best day of my life,' she shouted, enthusiasm not allowing any semblance of self-control.

'They say it's one of the most exciting ways of driving and it's perfectly safe, as long as the driver is sensible.'

'Am I too young to have a go? I so want to try it,' she asked, dreading a negative response.

'Not at all. There's a Junior Supercar Rally next month in Anglesey and as long as you have an adult with you, anyone can enter from the age of twelve as long as they're over four feet ten inches. You're a bit of a midget but you are over twelve aren't you?' Digging him gently in the ribs she was overcome with glee. 'We'll have to top up your lessons beforehand to make sure you're ready. Better start using Sam's old banger. I'm sure he won't mind. My son is easily bribed and if I dangle the carrot that he can drive this beast next time he's sure to agree.'

Sophie and Robert never knew about any of the driving exploits. They remained a wonderful secret. Robert was happy to have his daughters out of the house and didn't worry or care about their activities. To be fair to him he assumed that Clara was being well treated at her godfather's house and that Sophie was with friends.

After the driving lessons Clara often stayed overnight at the farm. Amy, Henry's wife, was soft and gentle, the opposite of her husband who filled every silence with a mixture of talk, exuberant laughter and stomping through the many rooms in the eighteenth-century building. She was taller than him by a few inches and slim to his broad, fair to his dark. They were in most aspects a mismatched couple, both physically and emotionally, but they appeared to enjoy a happy marriage and liked each other's company. At times, Clara was so consumed by jealousy, realising what she was missing, that she turned a most unfortunate shade of green.

Amy never talked about Mary or her tragic end, though the two had been good friends. She knew that her husband was the one in whom Clara confided and she left the counselling to him. Henry once told her that Amy would be happy to talk to her and that a woman's point of view might help. The offer was never taken up.

Apart from her baking, Amy could not be described as the archetypal farmer's wife. But what baking: bread, tarts, buns, cakes and puddings of every description filled the larder, cake tins and freezer. Little wonder that her husband was slightly on the plump side. Meals at home were often utilitarian. Alice, the home-help, relied on a range of roasts and salads, all presented in an uncomfortable silence.

What of Sophie during those years? A few months after her mum died Sophie discovered the wonder of boys and, more to the point, sex. Mum would have talked to her daughters about the importance of safe sex and the need for love and respect in a relationship. Such conversations never entered their father's head and he had no idea what Sophie got up to but realised she was staying out far too late.

'In by ten Sophie, it's a school night,' was the order issued the one and only time there was an attempt to rein her in. Madam arrived home at midnight and as no further action was taken the pattern was established: out by six, in at whatever time she chose and often late up for school. Very soon she was staying out all night, claiming to be at a girlfriend's house. Robert loved her (and perhaps even felt some affection for Clara) but he was inadequate to the demands of his daughters' teenage years. In different ways he failed them both, though for Sophie that was not always to be the case.

Chapter 8

I have always liked Amy and she has invariably invited me to celebrate family occasions with them. Unfortunately her birthday party this weekend has been postponed, the entire family succumbing to a nasty bout of gastroenteritis. The plan had been for me to go on the Saturday morning, help with the party preparations, enjoy the festivities and stay until Sunday. Henry phoned late on the Thursday evening, sounding awful, and apologising that the weekend fun couldn't take place. 'We'll do it soon, let you know, hope you are OK,' and with an unusual abruptness he rang off, probably needing a quick dash to the bathroom.

I hate it when something I have been looking forward to is cancelled. To be truthful I don't have many engagements and my social diary is almost non-existent. My brain went into sloth mode wondering how to fill the now purposeless weekend. I sat for ages, just sat, can't claim many cogs were even moving, let alone turning. Then it came to me, one of those Eureka moments. I would do something I had been thinking about for some time. I would return to Northumberland; revisit Smithfield Road.

Setting off straight after a long day in the classroom was not the best game plan ever devised. I have my Special Needs Groups, one in each of the Key Stage Two classes on a Friday. Why teachers give their Teaching Assistants the hardest group to work with is beyond me. They're the ones who are trained. They have the expertise to know how to help the ones who require the most assistance – but that's another story.

The motorway was horrendous and a journey that was normally just over three hours turned into six. I seldom take the most direct route to the North-East, choosing instead a quick dash up the motorway and then along beside Hadrian's Wall, often stopping at one of the ancient Roman settlements. The M6 from Preston to Carlisle must be one of the most beautiful in England. Rolling hills appear soon after the Carnforth junction and further north there is the excitement of going over the elevated ground between Tebay and Shap where the north and south carriageways divide. By the time one reaches the summit of Shap Fell the sign informs drivers that they are 320 metres above sea level, one of the highest points on any motorway in England.

Two accidents had brought all three north-bound lanes to a standstill and at one point I only covered two miles in sixty long, frustrating minutes. Fortunately the hour had gone forward the previous weekend and at least half the journey had daylight to accompany it. Arriving at the hotel after nine I was too late for a meal but accepted the offer of sandwiches.

'Are you here for the bird-watching?' the barman enquired, obviously wanting to talk. The room was empty apart from us. 'It's supposed to be quite something this spring.'

'No, just a weekend off, walking and eating fish and chips,' I replied, thinking it was almost certainly better not to divulge the real reason for my visit.

'You'll see lots of twitters this time of year. Can't say it's my favourite pastime but some customers came back really excited today having spotted razorbills, guillemots and eider ducks and one couple went over to the Farne Islands yesterday and saw the first puffins of the season. They insisted on showing me all, and I mean all, their photos. Everything is happening early this year, must be the good weather.'

When my meagre meal arrived, an egg and cress sandwich the best they could offer so late at night, I went to sit at a table too far away for further conversation. Once I had eaten I went straight to my room, exhausted by the extended drive. I sat in bed and spent a few minutes contemplating the next day then fell into a deep, untroubled sleep.

'Please stop talking about that case.' Mari's voice sounded shrill even to her but she succeeded in making the men look at her. 'We're having a pleasant evening out and all you can do is talk shop. Barbara and I haven't spent hours making sure we look this good just to hear you two rabbiting on about police matters.'

Ellis looked apologetic but didn't help the situation when he replied, 'Sorry, but I know only too well how an unsolved case can get under your skin and gnaw away like a mite that's burrowed deep. The constant itch makes you want to keep scratching.'

'Well one doesn't usually scratch on an evening out whilst enjoying a meal with friends – whom we don't see very often,' then attempting to lighten the situation she added, 'and as far as I'm aware none of us has had nits since primary school.'

Clive and Mari had met Barbara and Ellis in The Riverside Restaurant, their favourite venue in Newcastle for a Saturday night get-together. Ellis Winterton was a detective in the town's CID and the two couples had known each other for a long time, ever since the men had started as raw recruits, walking the beat together and boasting how they were going to be a double act and solve every case in the North East. Ellis's comment had been sincere as he had often experienced the frustration his friend was feeling. He had gone for promotion at an early age and had never regretted it, but even in CID he had known numerous occasions when it had proved impossible to bring someone to justice or feel satisfied that a case was truly closed.

'We'd better leave it for now but if you want I could come up sometime next week and take a look over the case-notes and visit the scene with you. I'd have to clear it with my boss but a fresh pair of eyes might help.' Ellis was aware that Clive's wife was not happy with his offer of help so added, 'You never know, Mari, it might finally lay the case to rest and let Clive know it was merely a tragic accident and that the driver felt too scared to report it. That would get it out of his system.'

The matter was dropped and the rest of the evening passed with friendly discussion about up-coming holidays and gossip about mutual friends.

As Mari had not drunk any alcohol during the evening she was the one driving home. The atmosphere in the car would have given the Arctic a rosy glow. 'For god's sake you are becoming a bore about that case. When are you going to let it go? Really Clive, what were you thinking? Fancy you agreeing to Ellis wasting his time and coming to review this case. Honestly I don't know what's got into you.'

'What's got into me is that two people were murdered, in cold blood, and it doesn't get any colder than running over the bodies on the return journey.'

'Well in future keep work at work and don't bring it up when we are having a pleasant evening out. Goodness knows we don't exactly have that many of those.' Clive decided that any reply would only exacerbate the situation and the remainder of the journey passed in a glacial silence.

Chapter 9

Waking in Beadnell felt strange. I was only a few miles from the scene of the "incident". I never know how to describe it: hit and run, accident or murder - none seem appropriate - so it remains in my mind with that rather euphemistic designation.

Kippers, smoked in Craster, just down the coast, have been described as the best in the world, though as it was a Geordie who said it there may have been an element of bias. That morning they certainly tasted wonderful and as I looked out to see the glorious day I felt totally elated. Three mugs of strong tea and several slices of toast followed and I thought that would suffice until lunch time. Eating has always been one of my main pleasures and as I had a lot of walking, thinking and hopefully investigating to do I needed my sustenance.

'You look happy, better than you did last night.' It was the garrulous barman, reincarnated as the breakfast waiter. 'Did you sleep well?'

'Yes thanks, I was tired and the bed was so comfortable, just what I needed.' I didn't want to say any more as I had already broken my rule of remaining incognito. Barry (his name was written in huge cursive script on his lapel badge), would surely remember me, but then as far as he was concerned I was just another guest and

of little consequence. There was no reason he should be asked about me and I was here seven months after the incident – that word again – so any link to it was tenuous in the extreme.

'Are you going walking? I think that's what you said you were planning to do,' the man would not give up.

'Yes, a stroll along the beach to Seahouses. I might take a trip across to the Farne Islands after lunch but only if the water's calm. I'm a terrible sailor.' Stop, I thought, stop talking.

'Try to hold on to those fish and chips if you have them, rough seas have a way of letting you see them again.'

'That happened once, when I was a child, but I learnt my lesson, so the gentlest swell will stop me even thinking about a boat trip.'

There was no getting rid of him as he stood obviously enjoying our exchanges. 'So you've been here before, to this area?' Having opened my mouth only to place both feet firmly inside I had to acknowledge that I used to come for family holidays with my parents and sister.

'Bet you stayed in Nightingales' Caravans, most people with young children choose them.' I sat bereft of speech. The situation was flying out of control, a kite whose string has been torn from a child's hand allowing it to disappear beyond the horizon. It was the name Nightingale that left me sitting, a duck at the fairground waiting to be shot down. My lack of response didn't stop Barry who knew he had a captive audience and obviously wanted to gossip.

'Tragic accident here in the autumn,' my new friend's voice took on the eagerness common to those who enjoy imparting ghoulish news. 'Young Joe Nightingale, *lovely fella, and his son Peter were both killed on the street where they'd lived ever since he brought Peter home. No mum, poor little soul, but everyone said that his dad was doing a right good job. Hit-and-run, driver didn't stop. How callous is that? You can't tell me that a driver doesn't know if they've hit someone and this was two of them – you're bound to know you've done it. Drunk likely as not but even so do the decent thing and ring for an ambulance.' There was no stopping him and I sat mesmerised unable to react, a child relegated to the naughty step with no hope of speedy salvation.*

'The police have no leads though my elderly aunt, Rose Helliwell, told me she'd been interviewed by a policeman and she'd been able to give him valuable information, the words she told me had been used by the officer. She'd seen a lad take a car from the car park in Bamburgh. The car she saw matched the description of the one the police believed had been used in the incident (my heart almost shuddered to a halt at that word). She knew it wasn't the young man's because the car's rightful owner arrived soon afterwards. She's not the best witness in the world as her eye sight isn't what it was but she's adamant that it was a young man. Rose told me that she had noticed the lad because he was wearing sunglasses and she thought that was strange as the day was very cloudy. He also had on a pair of gloves, though it was warm. My aunt made the policeman laugh when she said that only the oldies needed gloves in that kind of weather.'

By the time Barry had stopped talking I felt sick. I mumbled something vaguely appropriate and added that it was time I was going.

Ellis had arranged to drive up and meet Clive in Seahouses one Saturday when Newcastle United was playing away at Southampton. He had been part of "The Toon Army" ever since his dad had taken him to St. James' Park as a five year old. He was a long-standing season-ticket holder and as well as attending all home matches he tried to get to as many away games as possible, but the journey to the south coast was too far even for him – or so his wife had told him.

Before going to the station to look at the notes that Clive had compiled on the case Ellis had asked to be taken to Smithfield Road.

Clara arrived at the top of the cul-de-sac at the exact moment as the two policemen. Life is full of inexplicable coincidences. There, within metres of each other, stood Clara and two men dressed in weekend civvies. Having looked at Clive's newspaper picture every day for the past six months she felt herself recoiling as she recognised him: the person in charge of her case. From the way they were studying the location of the hit-and-run she assumed that his companion was also in the police.

They merely glanced at the young woman, dressed in hiking boots, waterproof jacket and carrying a walking stick and continued their all-engrossing conversation.

Strolling at an easy pace into Seahouses had been most pleasant. The whole weekend stretched in front of her and Clara felt the kind of excitement she had invariably experienced at the beginning of each holiday in the area. Most had been innocent affairs, and until recently, totally devoid of anything sinister. From the hotel Clara had taken the footpath across a field, its long grass being enjoyed by several sheep which took no notice of her as they continued their uninterrupted grazing. Her route had then continued by the sea. On one side of the almost deserted pavement (she passed one hiker) was a jumble of old cottages interspersed with more modern houses, mostly now advertising themselves as holiday rentals.

Despite the sunshine the day was fresh with a strong breeze blowing from the north and once on the beach she was glad she had put on extra layers. The tide was coming in and white horses cantered across the water which looked uninvitingly cold. She knew that no one, apart from the most hardy, would be swimming or even daring to put a toe in the water: this was the North Sea in the spring! Once she left the village Clara climbed the stile to the sand-dunes and ran up to the top, standing for several minutes admiring the view. She remembered as a child sliding down the dunes onto the beach but without the aid of a large black plastic bag, the essential piece of equipment and cheaper than a toboggan, she decided to be more circumspect and walked gingerly down the narrow path.

'Good morning and what a lovely one,' was the refrain, like the chorus of a communal song, that emanated from the numerous dog-walkers sharing the final three miles of beach. She was glad to see that, with one exception, they were responsible owners, picking up their dog's dirt and carrying it with them. These days that would put me off having a dog Clara thought, though what fun it was to watch the animals racing, like things possessed, in and out of the sea. The cold water was obviously not a deterrent. She felt extremely annoyed with the one lazy individual who had walked away from his poodle's mess. It didn't enter her head that she was guilty of a far more serious crime.

Accessibility to the beach ended just south of the town and the path moved inland beside the popular golf course. Clara stopped for a few minutes to watch a pair finishing their round. The man dressed all in black was obviously the better player and she was impressed by his final shot. The older man, accustomed to defeat, yelled, 'Looks like I'm the one buying the first round: no change there then!'

'Just not your day, Nigel, though you did rather well at the twelfth.' Oh dear, thought Clara, only one good hole out of eighteen – that used to be me at crazy golf and Sophie was even worse and used to get in a strop. No wonder Mum and Dad ended up avoiding that particular activity.

Shoulders back, smile in place, Clara moved on. No time to dwell on the past, only the next few hours mattered. She had a schedule for the day: revisit the road that she knew so well and which had provided such a unique (at least for the moment) memory; buy a local paper; then go in a pub and listen to any relevant gossip.

The first, though easily accomplished, made Clara wonder if she was being foolish returning to the area. Was it idiotic to walk up Smithfield Road? What if someone recognised her: height, demeanour, the shape of her head? Yes, the male outfit had fooled any eyewitnesses but what if, those two words that cause such universal disquiet, someone looked at her and thought they could identify her. Paranoia almost made her retrace her steps.

It is often fortuitous that others cannot hear our internal voices, the ones that engage us in endless conversations. On seeing the two detectives Clara's grew louder and more agitated until she was sure they must hear them. *"You're a fool, you'll be caught'"; "No one knows you and you look totally different to that day,"; "Give up now and go home,"; "You've come all this way, might as well find out what the latest thinking is."*

She stood, unable to move, unable to think. The men continued to ignore her, too engrossed in discussing the case to notice her reaction.

'This is the exact spot?' the man she didn't recognise said, in a voice loud enough to carry.

'It is...eighty metres from the top of the cul-de-sac. Joe and Peter lived in the penultimate house, the one over there on the right with the blue door.' Clara was near enough to half-hear his reply. Her initial instinct had been to flee. However, once normal service had been resumed and she had regained some semblance of control, she thought that doing so might look even more suspicious than walking past. As she came level with them she stooped down to retie her boot laces.

'You're absolutely sure they were hit twice?' Ellis asked. He knew Clive had already said so but had warned his friend that he would ask every question relevant to a case review.

'The autopsy showed that they were both hit from two different directions. The old man who lives at the top of the road is certain that the car turned and drove at high speed at the pair a second time. Whoever did it was using the vehicle as a weapon. It was premeditated murder. He fully intended to kill.'

'We both know that in any case we deal with, the first twenty-four hours are vital and in events like this it's the first minutes. Sorry to sound negative as I know we're a long way past those time scales.'

Clive stared at his friend before retorting, 'Yes, and there are over sixteen thousand hit-and-runs each year that result in serious injury or death and only a fraction are ever brought to court.'

'The main problem is that in the majority of cases the driver and the victim have no connection so it's impossible to find a motive: if there is one.'

'All I keep hearing is Mr Bolton repeating that the car ploughed into them a second time. If the driver didn't know them, why would he do that?'

Ellis had always believed that eyewitnesses were notoriously unreliable. Several people all claiming to have seen the same incident very often gave totally different accounts. 'Did he actually see the car hit them either time?'

Clive knew this was the weakest part of his investigation: no one had actually seen anything. 'No, all he saw was the car do a quick turn at the top of the road and drive off at "the speed of a fly escaping the squatter's hand" to quote him.'

Playing devil's advocate Ellis proposed a possible scenario. 'Maybe the driver knew he'd hit them and as it's a dead end wanted to turn and get away as fast as possible and he was in such a state ran them over again.' Ellis paused looking for some reaction. Clive's face suggested that Medusa had been playing her old tricks. 'Might have been a young driver, someone uninsured and facing the consequence of what he'd done was just too much for him.'

Clara had not been able to catch every word but had heard enough to know that they were still looking for a male driver. Realising she couldn't extend the time she had taken to deal with her laces she started to walk down the road.

'Going far?' Ellis asked as the men passed her, 'not a bad day for a walk.'

'I'm going on to Bamburgh.' How amazing that her voice sounded normal but she thought it prudent to keep her answer to the minimum.

'Enjoy it, take care.' If only her brand of Inspector Morse knew to whom he was speaking. The idea amused her for the rest of the day.

Ellis returned to the station with Clive to have a look at the relevant paperwork. Reading it carefully Ellis had to agree with his friend that there were grounds for suspicion. It certainly looked more than a straightforward hit-and-run where the driver panics and flees the scene. The pair went for a pub lunch at the Seaman's Rest and Clive continued their morning discussion. Ad nauseam.

'Sorry Clive but I have a feeling that this is just one of those cases: it won't be solved. You and I both know that on certain, extremely annoying occasions, despite our very best efforts, we never find out what happened. Probably best if you can let it rest.' Looking at Clive he knew he was wasting his breath.

Chapter 10

What a weekend! I'm still tingling. Following my "encounter" with Chief Inspector Rogers and his side-kick (rather dishy, wonder where he came from) I had a fantastic walk to Bamburgh... And back. I had so much nervous energy following the eavesdropping on Smithfield Road that it felt like an easy and utterly enjoyable stroll. Fish and chips in my favourite chippy half way up the main street in Seahouses then the final lap back to the hotel where I slept for hours before dinner. Yes, I even ate another meal and relished every morsel: nothing like sea air and euphoria to develop an appetite.

I slept better than any baby. Why does one compare a good night's sleep with an infant's? Don't they wake up every couple of hours? I woke to early morning fog, the infamous fret, the mist that develops at sea and drifts inland. I was served breakfast by a young wait-ress, probably a schoolgirl on the minimum wage, and very little was said apart from me asking for my food and her, 'Here you are then,' each time she brought something. The management should probably give her some inter-personal skills training.

By the time I'd eaten, packed and paid my bill the fret was even thicker so I decided to head for home. I knew from past experience that the mist is more often than not confined to the coast and by the time I'd gone five miles the road was clear, no fret encroaching inland, but the day remained dull and overcast. There were times when I wondered if I was safe to drive. My heart was pounding and I might as well have been in charge of a large Boeing as all my manoeuveres were being performed on auto-pilot. The excitement of the previous day left me shaky and unable to concentrate.

By the time I reached Hadrian's Wall I knew I had to stop. I had already driven many miles, thankfully without incident, but the last thing I wanted was to have an accident and for the police to become involved. The first Roman site at that end of the Wall is Chesters, for me one of the most impressive of the Roman remains. I had stopped there many times before but walking where Romans trod two thousand years ago never ceases to impress me. The fort was built to house a garrison of soldiers whose job it was to guard the nearby bridge across the River Tyne. The weather had worsened and I imagined the soldiers, so far from home, living in such inhospitable conditions. How they must have longed for some Italian sunshine.

Ambling around the remains calmed me and when I drove on I was back in control. On arriving home I added some observations to my journal.

Six months on they still think it was a male driver. No more eye-witnesses have come forward and the old bloke's testimony would be useless if, heaven forbid, the case ever came to court. The police are no nearer to solving the event. I'm pleased I've used a different word to incident.

An unforgettable weekend.

By the start of Year Twelve Sophie and Clara had gone their separate ways and the only time they spent together was in the Business Studies Centre where both were studying the subject for A Level. Extracurricular activities abounded: two choirs, debating society and the thrice-weekly hockey practices plus weekend games made the year special for Clara. Academically she continued to be the more able of the two and found much of the work straightforward. Success and impressive grades were delivered without too much effort.

Sophie struggled, her social life winning every time, 'Another assignment late?' Clara's comment was loud enough for all to hear. 'Less time with the latest boyfriend might help.' Clara was amazed that Sophie managed to complete any work at all as her sister continued to absent herself from home on a regular basis. The general appearance of the string of paramours who collected her sister from the house made Clara doubt that any were capable of helping her with her academic studies. Their talents were obviously of the more physical variety.

For Clara the highlight of her final years at school was being picked to play hockey, initially for Cheshire and then on two glorious occasions for the England Schoolgirls' first team. Running out at Wembley the week after the nation's football team, the male variety which had beaten Holland three-nil, was a moment she would never forget. Her father had made the effort to attend and sat with Henry and Amy.

'This has been one of the proudest moments of my life. To watch my goddaughter play for England – that's something special.' It wasn't her best game and the English team lost five-four, the goalie, a Londoner with the voice of a loud-haler and the build of a sumo wrestler, letting in the opposition winner a minute from time.

A month later, Clara was back on a windy, rain-soaked afternoon when England was pitted against France. Rather frustratingly no one came to watch her as she played well that day, though England continued its losing run. Sophie declined both invitations to watch the games and only enquired about the results when prompted by their father.

The twins had morphed into a redundant couple, the sort who had once loved each other enough to get married but then, a few years down the line, decided that they hated each other and wanted a divorce. Unfortunately one can't divorce one's sibling.

'Which universities are you two thinking of putting on your UCAS Forms?' Henry asked one Sunday evening when he and Amy had been invited to tea.

'Whichever she's not putting down,' Sophie spat, saliva dribbling down her chin.

'Feeling's mutual, only she won't get into the ones I've chosen, they need high grades.' Clara was the only one pleased with this response.

'Good God, what in the world is wrong with the pair of you?' Dad muttered, 'Why can't you just be civil? I've just about had enough of the two of you.'

'You won't have to put up with us much longer; we'll both be off your hands after the summer.' Clara knew that for once she was speaking for both of them.

'Yes, but think how upset your mum would be to know that you don't get on any more.' This was Robert's trump card but his daughters had heard it on many previous occasions and were now impervious.

By the end of their time at school Clara had been accepted at Exeter University and Sophie was bound for Wolverhampton. Both had chosen to read Business Studies, Clara adding French, thinking that one day the business might expand abroad.

Sophie wanted a year out, not travelling and not exactly a gap-year but staying in Reading with her aunt, her mother's only remaining sister. 'I'll find work and be self-sufficient then maybe travel next summer before starting to study again. I need the break and Aunt Hannah is keen to have me, says I'll be company.'

Only Clara knew the real reason for the euphemistically designated "Year Out." She rather suspected that Sophie would never get to uni: fun triumphing over work every time.

Chapter 11

North East Guardian

Police Question Man About Hit-and-Run Tragedy.

A man is being held in custody following an accident in Seahouses last Friday when Lynda Hull and her daughter Rachel were knocked down. The driver of the black Fiat abandoned the car at the scene and ran off. He was later arrested.

Mrs Hull (aged 38) was pronounced dead at the scene. Her daughter (aged 7) was air-lifted to The Royal Victoria Infirmary in Newcastle where she remains in a critical condition. Police are keen to hear from any eye-witnesses to the accident.

No, not me this time though how delightful it would be if the police thought that it was the same "man". As I don't have regular access to a copy of the North East Guardian I have to rely on the internet as my source of information and check it every day. I bet my friend Clive thinks the two accidents are linked.

When I first read the latest hit-and-run report I danced in the kitchen. Literally danced for joy. My kitchen is not exactly the Tower Ballroom at

Blackpool but it's big enough for me to cavort to ear-splitting Elvis.

What fun. What a wonderful development. How amusing. Just when it had all gone quiet.

Clive Rogers and his team were finding it neither fun nor amusing. The young man, Kyle Tinton, an eighteen year old from Tyneside, wearing the ubiquitous teenage outfit of low slung jeans and a black hoody, was being questioned and was giving frustratingly monosyllabic answers. He wasn't the brightest individual Clive had ever interviewed and had declined the offer of a lawyer. He was well known to the police in his home town who faxed through his extensive, and for one so young, rather impressive list of previous misdemeanours, several involving the taking of cars and driving without a licence or insurance.

'Yes,' he was the driver.

'No,' it wasn't intentional (a word that had to be explained to him).

'Yes,' he had left the scene.

'Yes,' he had panicked.

'No,' he hadn't been driving carelessly.

'Yes,' he was probably going too fast.

'Yes,' he lost control.

'No,' he wasn't in Seahouses last October.

'No,' he hadn't hit Joe and Peter.

'Yes,' he had an alibi for October 15th.

Clive terminated the interview and left the room. He was sorry when the man's alibi corroborated his story for October: the one that claimed that he had been out celebrating a friend's birthday on a day-long pub crawl in Tyneside. If needed at last six others could substantiate Kyle's whereabouts on the relevant day.

Although this accident had borne few of the hall-marks of the previous one, Clive had hoped that it would finally solve the case that he couldn't lay to rest. Six months, and counting, was a long time to live with the daily reminder that he was no nearer to solving the mystery. It had become like the recurrent nightmare where one is trying to reach a destination only to be thwarted by an inability to move at the necessary speed. There had been no progress since the day it happened. He had, in the past, become obsessive over cases that he didn't solve. Whilst he acknowledged that others were involved he took failures to heart and felt they were personal.

The Nightingales felt different. So different. Two upstanding citizens deliberately killed on the street where they lived. Two people he had known and liked. Two people whose lives had been terminated far too early – years of life denied them.

'Sorry I'm so late love, but the interview with the young hit-and-run driver took forever.' From long experience Mari knew not to ask any questions. Her husband would tell her in his own time. When he came in stressed, an increasingly frequent phenomenon, he would be lost in his own thoughts until after dinner, which these days usually included at least two large glasses of wine. Only then would he feel able to discuss the day with her. Over the past year she had said less and less about her days: lessons that had gone well or, despite careful planning, had not worked; children falling out in the playground; meetings with awkward parents; the endless paper work; and the wonderful moments that made the job so rewarding when a child suddenly understood a concept or one of her seven year olds said something that made her laugh. Maybe compared to Clive's days her stories were routine, devoid of originality or interest.

The ten o'clock news meant that the meal was not eaten in silence.

'Thanks, that was delicious,' he said, having not tasted a mouthful, 'sorry I was so late. I've said you should eat at the normal time and mine can be microwaved when I get in. I know how tired you get and it's your class's assembly tomorrow.' Mari tried to hide her amazement that he had remembered. Clive took a whisky through to the living room whilst Mari washed up. She took her time, allowing Clive to spend a few minutes alone. Strains of The Temperance Seven soon floated through and Mari thought how appropriate it was that the first track was *You're Driving Me Crazy*. Hopefully his favourite jazz would help him to relax, though he was so wound up that she doubted that would happen for several hours. Most nights when he was bothered by a case she was tucked up and asleep before he came to bed.

'I was so sure that we had the man. How often do we get hit-and-runs in Seahouses?'

'So, it's definitely not him?' Mari listened as Clive rumbled on. If only that irritating case could be solved. She was becoming worried that it was affecting his health. Her suggestion of a holiday at Easter had been rejected. Maybe Whit. Maybe not. She would go to stay with her old school friend in Bournemouth if no joint plans could be organised. He wasn't the only one with a stressful job.

North East Guardian

Court Review

Kyle Tinton, aged eighteen, appeared before Newcastle Magistrates charged with Causing Death by Dangerous Driving and was remanded to appear at Newcastle Crown Court in July. Lynda Hull was killed in the incident and her daughter is in a stable condition in hospital. Mr Tinton was also charged with leaving the scene of an accident and driving without insurance.

Chapter 12

I have the letters that Sophie wrote during the year she spent living with our aunt. Aunt Hannah had never married or had children but enjoyed her career with Marks and Spencer where she was Section Manager of the fashion department at the large store in Reading. She has since moved to Paris where she has a similar role and sends us regular updates on her life in the city she loves and the shop she claims to be "the most exciting this side of heaven" though it hardly seems likely that there will be a celestial version of M and S. Would the otherworldly slogan read: Not just Paradise, but M and S Paradise?

She was kind to Sophie that year and just what was needed. They both loved the same activities: meals in expensive restaurants; nights at the theatre; and Sundays spent doing nothing more strenuous than reading the latest fiction best seller. I think they both, in different ways, got a lot out of the year and have spoken of it with an unfailing enthusiasm. As much as Sophie is capable of loving someone I think she loves Hannah and they continue to meet up regularly in England or France.

Strange to think that my sister and I became reconciled during that period and for several years were once again quite good friends. Meeting her in Reading the first time was almost surreal: we were both happy! I was enjoying my first year at Exeter Uni and she was more relaxed – a year without any academic, or fatherly, pressure. To say she blossomed that year would be an understatement. She revelled in it. Thank goodness for Aunt Hannah.

Three years later Clara graduated with a First Class degree. Robert had promised her a position in the family business, but to her surprise he expected her to begin as a sales assistant in the shop on Deansgate in the centre of Manchester.

'You need to learn the job from the bottom up. Two years from now I might consider promoting you, if you do well on the lowest rung. No one can prosper when they are elevated to the top of the ladder straight away.' Robert was adamant and he remained deaf to his daughter's protestations that the post he was proposing would be a total waste of her outstanding degree.

'As you won't be paid much, in fact the same as all the other shop assistants, I'll give you the down payment on a house and help with your mortgage. You choose it and let me know.' He stated the maximum he was willing to advance and added that he would make the same generous offer of a job and a house to Sophie.

'That's really not fair,' Clara heard herself say. 'Sophie can't be compared to me. She never made it to university. I'm the one with a First Class degree in Business Studies. I must be better value than her.' Robert gave his daughter a look that told her, louder than any brass band, that the subject wasn't open for discussion.

Determined to utilise every penny her father had offered, Clara chose Sale, where she had grown up and which she had always liked, as the neighbourhood to start looking for her new home. Weeks were spent searching the area and worrying a legion of estate agents. Finally she viewed the one she wanted. It was on a quiet road away from the busy street linking Sale with Sale Moor. The open fields that had once lined the main road to the south were now built on. Another green-belt had disappeared: an irredeemable loss to the town, but the newly erected three and four bedroom detached houses were well within her budget.

The house she chose had a large garage, a prerequisite as her love of cars meant that at some point in the future she was planning to buy an old banger and restore it. There were small gardens to the front and rear, their size essential as she had no desire to spend hours growing plants only for them to be swamped by weeds. A large kitchen was fitted with all the equipment she could ever want and the two downstairs reception rooms were soon decorated in a style she could live with. Three bedrooms, one en-suite, and a state of the art bathroom completed the picture. In her more positive moments Clara realised that she was fortunate to be able to live in such comfort. Most of her peers would have to wait decades to own such a property. She would make an impression at the jewellers and hopefully gain quick promotion.

Clara wondered how would Sophie cope with the same offer of a job in the family business. Over the past four years she had flitted from relationship to relationship and hadn't held onto any occupation for more than a few months. Clara had been amazed when she heard that her sister was moving back into the family home and commuting to her new post in Bolton. No doubt she had pocketed the proffered money and, if she stuck to form, would move out quite regularly to live with her latest conquest.

Six weeks after starting work on Deansgate, Clara knew she wasn't prepared to spend two years as a shop assistant. At university she had enjoyed weekends and several holidays working with disadvantaged children on a variety of Play Schemes and Outward Bound ventures. Surmising that working with children was preferable to listening to the inane conversations of the other assistants and dealing with awkward, demanding customers she applied for a job she saw advertised in the *Sale Gazette*. Bedford Jewellers would be hers one day but until then she wanted nothing to do with it.

'I'm ringing to enquire about the post you advertised in the local paper. It says you are looking for a Teaching Assistant to work with groups of children, mostly in Key Stage 2.' By the start of the following term she was Miss Bedford, TA.

'Are you out of your mind? Have you totally lost the plot? I explained, very carefully, that everyone needs to start at the bottom, to learn the trade!' Robert Bedford was incandescent with rage. 'You've always been Miss High and Bloody Mighty! At least your sister sees sense and is getting to know the business.'

'If she has the staying power, something she's lacked so far: a few weeks waitressing; not many more cleaning and the last time I heard she was gainfully employed stacking supermarket shelves. It's hardly an impressive CV.'

'I believe she'll surprise you and when the time comes she'll be the one with the relevant experience to run the business.'

'When that day comes I rather think my degree will come into its own. Slamming down the phone Clara punched the air knowing she had managed to rile her father.

Part 2: Stewart and Paul

Chapter 1

Bliss: working with children. They can be exasperating, lazy, cheeky, and leave you feeling as though you've got a particularly debilitating bout of flu, but I love every minute, well almost every one, I spend in the classroom. No two days are the same as every lesson is different and every child unique. There are times it would be easier if they had fewer idiosyncrasies, but it all adds to the entertainment.

I'm in Katie's Year 4 class most of the time. She's a brilliant teacher and reminds me of my best teacher, the inspirational Mrs Meadows. I bet she's still going – we always joked that she'd have to move to a downstairs classroom when she started using a Zimmer frame. I can't believe I am enjoying the work to such an extent. It won't be for ever, but great while it lasts.

Clive Rogers and his wife were having a weekend at home, catching up on jobs. He was fixing a leaky tap and oiling the hinges on the kitchen door, the ones that had been squeaking for days, well weeks if he was truthful. Doing such mundane tasks helped him to relax, the only distraction was Della, his black and white cat and one of the pair he had brought home the day they had been left outside the police station obviously abandoned.

'At least someone cared enough to want them found. The note with them said, "Please find us a good home". They are adorable and we had been talking about a pet.'

Mari hadn't been so sure. They had talked about getting a cat but she had been reluctant as they were both out so much and she thought it might be lonely. 'I hadn't realised you meant two cats, but I suppose it's not the worst idea in the world as they will be company for each other. Do you think they're related?'

The tiny kittens were stumbling sideways across the kitchen floor like two drunks who had been asked to walk in straight lines. The larger of the two had begun a plaintiff meowing and Clive picked it up very gently. 'I expect they're related; better take them to the vet's later, get them looked over and ask him whether they're male or female, though that one has got to be called Fluffy whatever its gender.' That had been months ago and Della and Fluffy were now well established members of the household.

Mari spent the day gardening, putting the borders to bed for the winter. The duvet of autumn leaves filled three bags and when she finished she looked forward to the winter-weight coverlet her garden would receive if the Met Office had got it right and the hard winter they had forecast materialised. It was a few years since there had been an appreciable fall of snow but this winter all the indicators were there. She loved the snow, though it made the children at school overexcited and all they wanted to do was be outside making snowmen. The last time there had been an appreciable downfall she and a colleague had organised a competition to see which group of Key Stage 2 children could build the best one in twenty minutes. The photos were still on the school website.

Their garden looked straight out to sea, and it had been the deciding factor when they bought the house ten years ago. It had taken a long time to save enough money for a property on the sea front. So many homes were being bought by weekenders or by people who wanted them as business investments, letting them out as holiday lets at exorbitant weekly rents, that all house prices in the area had soared during the years when Clive and Mari were trying to save. At one time they had wondered whether they would ever be able to afford one. The situation remained the same, but it was now to their advantage and Clive was pleased that the property was both a wonderful place to live and a long term investment.

After her exertions Mari decided to take the easy option and drive into town for a Chinese takeaway. Traffic was heavy and the Golden Flower Chinese, the best in the area, was packed. It had only been opened for a few weeks but its reputation had grown at a surprising rate and she had never been the only customer.

Arriving home with a *Dinner for Two Special,* plus extra fried rice, she was greeted at the door by Clive. He was almost incoherent with excitement and was acting like an over stimulated child who has been told he can stay up late. Grabbing her arm he pulled her into the study and yelled, 'You've got to look at this. It's the same...absolutely the bloody same...the bloody same...I can't believe it.' Clive abhorred swear words and seldom employed them, saying that he dealt with people every day whose entire vocabulary consisted of expletives and he wasn't going to stoop to their level. For him to use one twice in a sentence was totally out of character, though there had been moments when "that case", as she thought of it, was getting to him to such an extent that obscenities had invaded his speech like a triumphant foe.

Clive's voice had risen to such a pitch that Della, who had been catnapping for many hours, shot off the chair that she had appropriated as her own. She had been disturbed and wanted to let everyone know. For the next minute she did a good impression of an Olympic athlete: sprinting up and down the curtains; hurdling over the footstool; and running, Usain Bolt style, along the carpet. Uncharacteristically Clive picked her up and put her out of the room, shutting the door behind her.

'No distractions. Look at this, you won't believe it!'

'Do we have to look now or can we have dinner first? I, for one, am famished.'

'No, no time to eat, you must look. You know I went to London on that two-day course last week.'

'Yes I did notice you weren't here.' Mari's sarcasm fell on stonier ground than the Sower's first terrain in the New Testament parable.

Clive carried on as though she hadn't spoken. 'It was on International Crime: people trafficking, drug smuggling, pornography, terrorism etc. Well, one of the speakers, definitely one of the more interesting and relevant ones, gave us some website addresses and said we might be interested in looking at them to view the different ways police across the world solve crimes. This site jumped out at me.' Mari stood looking at the computer screen that Clive had recovered. The title in bright red letters read *Hit-and-Run Accidents: A Modern Day Epidemic*.

As Clive continued to speak, talking mostly to himself, his fingers battered the keyboard, the sound like the hail that was hitting their conservatory roof.

'Yes, here it is, just read this and tell me I'm right. It's an exact copy, a replica of ours.'

The screen was now filled with a file from America.

October 15th: 2013. Report by Deputy Sheriff Dwayne Vanstory.

At three-thirty p.m. on Tuesday 15th October I was called to a motoring occurrence in school grounds out on Wilksboro Highway, eleven miles out of Statesville. I duly arrived at the same time as the Emergency Medical Service and the Volunteer Rescue Squad. Two bodies could be seen lying in the school's parking lot and the first responders were preparing to give acute medical care.

We later ascertained that the two victims were Stewart Wilson and his son, Paul. Both were declared dead at the scene. Mr Wilson was a single father and his son (aged 10) was a pupil at Martin Luther King Elementary where his father had been a teacher for several years. The accident occurred just outside the school building.

Mrs Misty Teague, an eyewitness and a Grade Four teacher at the school, said that the father and son had left the school field after the softball practice and were walking across the parking lot to their vehicle when they were knocked down by a car which she said was a dark blue Nissan Pathfinder 4 by 4 (her father-in-law has a similar car). This account was verified by a mom, Mrs Ashley Barnette. Both witnesses added that it appeared that the pair were run over deliberately, the driver then seen leaving the scene.

A report verified that a car of a similar description was taken from the Wells Fargo parking lot in Wilksboro on the afternoon of the accident and returned later that day.

Both Mrs Teague and Mrs Barnette say the car was driven by a man, probably in his late teens or early twenties. The description they gave described him wearing an Appalachian State Mountaineers baseball cap, dark glasses and possibly a blue checked shirt.

The case remains open.

Mari read the report twice, amidst constant interruptions from Clive. 'Don't you see they're exactly the same – exactly the same?' Mari sat staring at the screen, not wanting to respond. 'Well, say something, don't you think this has all the hallmarks of the one here two years ago?'

'There are similarities, but over the course of two years there must be hundreds if not thousands of similar accidents across the world.'

'But not involving single fathers and their sons and not usually so deliberate and so malicious.' He started to sound like the teacher in the family, 'As I've told you a million times most hit-and-runs are accidents and the driver just panics and flees the scene. This one feels different and more like mine.'

Mari was finding it hard to stay calm but knew that any display of emotion would only exacerbate the situation. She decided to change tack. 'Statesville is obviously in America. Do you know exactly where it is? It's definitely not a name you could make up!' Mari's attempt at alleviating the situation made little impact and Clive stood rocking from foot to foot, something he was unaware he did when excited.

'I looked it up when you were out.' Mari laughed and said she would have expected nothing less. Clive's voice hardened. There had been no need for the interruption. Mari wasn't taking this seriously. Once again Clive was in teacher mode, 'It's a small town in North Carolina, a state on the East coast which is the start of the Deep South. It's nearer the Blue Ridge Mountains than the sea and its population is almost twenty-five thousand. Looks like small-town America...so why should they have a pre-planned hit-and-run, a carbon copy of ours? What's the link?'

'Do you know Clive, I think you're making too much of this. In all probability there is no link and it's a merely a very strange coincidence. Why should anyone fly thousands of miles to commit such an act? If you think about it logically it doesn't make sense.'

'Unfortunately many crimes only make sense to the perpetrator. It's one of the reasons my job is so difficult. Often there is no logic.'

Like anyone with an obsession Clive found it hard to accept that his wife didn't share his interest in the unsolved case. Where this case was concerned Clive had mutated into a Duracell bunny with a battery that never needed recharging. 'My gut feeling is that the two cases are linked and I'm going to contact this Dwayne Vanstory. The States are five hours behind us so it's only three in the afternoon there.'

'At least come and eat before you do, I put the meals in the oven to stay hot.'

Clive made sure he had the final word, 'I might take some leave and fly over; probably best to talk face-to-face. I'll see if I can arrange that with him. I am one hundred per cent certain that his case and mine were carried out by the same young man and I intend to prove it.'

Chapter 2

Another October: another twosome removed from the equation. Stewart and Paul proved far trickier than Joe and co. It was such a long way to travel and extremely expensive, though I must say I rather liked North Carolina and managed to enjoy my three visits.

The main problem was how to organise the accident. Americans, and Stewart had his Green Card so was almost a Yank, don't walk apart from round parks and one can hardly run someone over on a leafy path through the woods. Directly outside school seemed to be the best option, it was either there or in a parking lot. (Car park doesn't sound right when talking about Statesville.) All our friends across the pond seem to spend most of their spare time shopping so the parking lots are always jam-packed therefore not the ideal location – far too many witnesses.

An elementary school is not the most appropriate location to run over a father and son. Traumatised children everywhere and the famous yellow buses packed at the end of the day. Too many eyewitnesses: moms collecting their kids and teachers watching their classes leave…all too problematic. I had to choose my time and venue very carefully.

Same date.

Different location.

Both incidents followed a sport's practice.

Rather a shame there's only one pair to go. I could get used to this.

Having reread that final statement I realise that others might worry about my state of mind. I am not a bad person and none of this would have been necessary if I had been treated fairly. But I wasn't!

Stewart and Paul had lived in America for just over four years and both felt settled, neither experiencing any desire to return to Manchester. In his mid-twenties Stewart had spent two years on a professional exchange programme, teaching in Statesville at the Martin Luther King Elementary School, where he would have remained if the system had been more accommodating. As a teacher he was allowed to work tax-free for twenty-four months but if he had stayed any longer all the accrued tax would have had to be paid back during the third year. Once home he knew that as long as he didn't return to the States for at least twelve months he could start again and it had always been his intention to do so, making sure that the next time he took sufficient funds to stay there until he had his American citizenship. Cody Sloan, the school's principal, had said there would always be a post for him and the two had kept in touch during the intervening decade.

The ideal time arrived. Paul was the right age to join the American kindergarten class and had the added benefit of having spent twelve months in an English Reception class. Stewart was ready for a fresh start. The move had proved to be every bit as successful as he had hoped. However, leaving had provided some tricky moments.

'Hi Mum, it's me. How are you?'

'Fine thanks Stewart, though your dad's got his arthritis back, could hardly move this morning, seems to improve as the day goes on. Anyway, how are you?'

Stewart knew that the news he was about to impart wasn't what his parents wanted to hear. Standing, gripping the phone tightly, he made small talk for several minutes before diving, without the skill of an international swimmer, into the real reason for the call. 'I've got the job in America, starting in July. I know you and Dad were keen for us to stay here but as you know I really feel this is for the best, especially for Paul.' There was a prolonged silence which he was determined not to break.

'Oh dear, sorry I mean, oh dear, we were hoping you wouldn't go but you must do what's right for you and Paul,' Stewart could tell that his mother was trying not to break down.

'Remember how you loved coming for holidays last time I was there. No reason it shouldn't be the same now. You'll be more than welcome whenever you want to come over. We can all go travelling and see parts of the U.S. that none of us has been to, though I expect we'll manage the odd trip to the beach. We loved the Outer Banks and the beaches in South Carolina are near enough.'

'I'll get your dad,' (her answer to all of life's problems). Stewart wondered how she'd cope if, or increasingly when, his father was no longer there.

'Hello son, your mum's told me your news. She's somewhat upset, she'll really miss Paul.' It was surprising to hear how weary his dad sounded and Stewart was finding the conversation even harder than expected. His parents had been so supportive since he'd found himself on his own with Paul and he knew he'd feel guilty taking their only grandson so far away.

In the early days, after Paul's mother had walked away, they had lived with his parents, Dan and Holly, who had taken over most of the baby's care. Paul was just six months old and a demanding baby who cried most nights, waking at three hourly intervals something that stopped, to everyone's relief, just after his first birthday. Holly had done the night shifts, with Dan on duty during the day. Stewart was teaching full time at a school near the centre of Manchester and, especially in the early days, wondered how he would have coped without them.

He knew they had given up a lot to care for Paul. Their retirement plan of travelling the world had been put on hold but they always said that Paul gave them more joy than the Taj Mahal or three weeks in New Zealand would have done. Even so, Stewart knew they had made huge sacrifices and he would be eternally grateful to them. But, and it felt like a huge but, he felt certain that America was the future for him and his son. It wouldn't matter to her, the absentee mother, as she never bothered with Paul. She had kept her word. No cards, either birthday or Christmas, and not even the occasional phone call to see how he was getting on. Holly often put what he was feeling into words, 'How can a mother just leave her baby? Doesn't she wonder how he's getting on? Fancy missing his first word, first birthday, first day at school, I just don't understand the girl. She should be ashamed of herself.'

Paul had been a planned baby, the couple keen to start a family after two years together. She had sailed through pregnancy, calm waters the entire nine months. To begin with all was well. She took maternity leave and didn't appear to miss her high-powered job, apparently being content to meet up with other new mums for lunch or coffee mornings. Stewart had just gained promotion becoming a deputy head at a nearby school and everything appeared to be going smoothly.

There was no warning. Absolutely none.

'I'm leaving. Motherhood is not for me.'

'What on earth do you mean? Leaving? You can't just leave. What the bloody hell do you mean?' She stood and stared, no emotion on her pretty face, every strand of her blond hair in place and with a face recently layered with make-up, her prelude to any outing. He still didn't think this one was going to be permanent.

'I mean what I said, I'm leaving. My bags are packed and I'm off.'

'Is there someone else?' Stewart asked, not really thinking that was the case but knowing it was the obvious question.

'No, nobody else. As I said I'm just not cut out to be a mother. I've tried but Paul will be better off without me.'

'Good of you to mention our son. I wondered when he'd be considered.' His sarcasm was ignored.

'I have considered him and I know that in the long run I'm not good for him.'

'Not good for him? How bad is it for a baby to lose his mother?'

'He's got you and lots of infants lose their mothers, some women die you know.'

Stewart sat down, his legs giving way, as he realised that she meant it, that this was the end of their time together, time that he had imagined would go on forever. She was the only woman he had ever loved and had assumed that the feeling was mutual. Had he missed the signs? Had she been unhappy? Was there anything he could have done? Was there anything he could say now to make her change her mind? The questions swished around in his head, a maelstrom of convoluted feelings, and his body began to quiver with abject fear as he slowly and painfully assimilated the news.

'Can we talk about this? Surely we can talk. You don't have to make your mind up at this exact moment.'

'I've made up my mind. Being a mother is not for me. No debate, it's all organised.'

'You can't leave us like this: no warning, no planning, nothing.'

'My plans are in place and I'm sure Holly and Dan will help you.' Throughout the exchange she had been as cold and unfeeling as Hans Christian Anderson's Ice Maiden.

'Have you got a new address? I'll want to bring Paul to see you,' Stewart asked thinking that everything would be all right once she'd been given some time to think.

'No, this is it. No contact, no meetings, no phone calls, nothing. A clean break.' Stewart stood up unsteadily, tears drenching his face.

'Goodbye Stewart, I wish you both well.' That was the last time he saw her.

Chapter 3

"Hell's teeth and damnation," one of Henry's favourite expletives. The two incidents have been linked. Who managed that? Perhaps I underestimated old Clive. Must be him. Can't imagine the Americans being interested enough to link the events. Clive's article in the North East Guardian made engrossing reading. He's been to Statesville!

Two weeks after reading about the hit-and-run in Statesville Clive was on a transatlantic flight to the U.S. The first part of the journey was without incident, eight hours of watching the latest films and drinking too many cups of insipid coffee. There was the expected three hour lay-over in New York before his onward flight to Charlotte where Dwayne was meeting him.

'Delays to all flights heading south due to severe storms and high winds.'

The intercom announcement sounded almost cheerful. 'Please see your carrier for details.'

By the time Clive reached the American Airways desk the queue was doubled back on itself.

'Gee, this always happens to me. I take this flight every goddam month and I can't recall the last occasion it was on time.' A business man of American proportions was regaling anyone within earshot. Clive was bored so engaged the man ('Hi my name's Elijah, guess my parents were religious') in conversation.

'Are the delays always due to bad weather?' he asked, Elijah responding by bursting into stomach-shaking mirth.

'Guess y'all not from these parts…English?'

'Yes and hoping to get to Statesville sometime today.'

'Well good luck with that. These delays can be fearsome. When the weather takes control no power on earth can stop it. We get some beauties down the east coast and today it's just short of hurricane status. Are you here on business or for a vacation?'

Admitting to a work related trip Clive managed to avoid furnishing further details.

Arriving six hours late he was relieved to see a large man in full deputy sheriff's uniform waiting at the Arrivals gate holding a sign bearing his name. Dwayne was a mountain of a man, an escapee rock from Monument Valley. He was well over six feet tall and broad without being overweight. A mass of curly black hair complemented the most enormous moustache Clive had ever seen. Dwayne's voice matched his size and the entire terminal must have heard his greeting, the southern drawl in sharp contrast to most of the accents he'd heard in New York. 'Well y'all finally arrived. Welcome to North Carolina, the finest State in the old U.S of A!'

Almost too exhausted to talk, only good manners forced a response. 'Sorry you've had such a wait for me. A prolonged delay in New York then once we boarded we sat on the runway for two more as the pilot informed us that the storm had resumed and no planes were being allowed to land in Charlotte. He also apologised that the flight would be slower than it was normally as the head winds were still ferocious.'

'Ferocious, I sure am going to enjoy talking to y'all I don't never hear words like that. We're plain country folk in Statesville.' Dwayne was remarkably cheerful for the early hours of the morning.

Clive spent two days in Statesville: visiting the scene of the accident; talking at length about his own case at home; and reviewing the almost non-existent information from the latest forensic report.

'No spray-polish this time though it says that the car was returned in pristine condition.' After explaining the polish reference the men continued their discussion.

Disappointed and surprised to learn that there was no CCTV coverage of the school, the parents having boycotted any surveillance of their children, Clive asked about coverage of the Wells Fargo car park. 'Don't rightly think the cameras were operational. The company told us it costs too much and they never expected anything significant to happen. We don't get many car thefts in this back of beyond part of NC.'

Attempting to move the conversation on, hoping to gain some positive input, Clive reminded Dwayne that the thing that had first alerted him to the accident in Statesville was the date.

Dwayne seemed to think with his mouth and repeated most of Clive's last sentence. 'Y'all know I just can't get my head around the fact that the two accidents happened on the exact same calendar date, October 15th. Yes a couple of years apart but the same date. That's got to be more than just a coincidence. The only difference is that your accident was on the street where father and son lived, mine was outside a school, albeit the school where they were teacher and pupil. The cases are similar but there is that one discrepancy. Boy I sure do love that word.'

Clive interrupted, 'There's one more difference. My pair was hit twice, from two directions, yours only once.'

'But y'all remember the witness, Shelly Nantz, the mom walking out from the gymnasium with her son Tommy, who said that she saw the car do a wheel turn and approach the stricken pair a second time. When the driver saw her running to see if she could help the driver swerved and then drove off at a sedate speed. That sure as hell surprised her. There was no speedy escape. Just a steady left out of the main school drive and onto the Wilksboro Highway.' Clive was annoyed with himself for not reading her eye witness statement carefully enough.

Having believed that Clive was the smarter of the two Dwayne was pleased that he had added a vital detail that his English counterpart had overlooked. For the next few minutes he looked like a little boy who has just achieved top marks in the latest test.

The deputy sheriff continued. 'Here's the thing...let's just chew over the similarities: both carried out in broad daylight; both after a sport's practice; both by a young man driving a stolen car; both killing a single dad and his son; both apparently deliberate.'

Yes, that word, the word that Clive had longed to hear, like the gods answering a prayer. 'And that's where the real issue lies. If they're deliberate, and it looks more and more likely that they both are, then why? And why two years apart? It's a long time to wait to commit exactly the same crime. And that's the thing that's stopping my people in Northumbria taking the accident seriously. My superiors won't accept that mine is anything other than a straight forward hit-and-run.'

Standing up to stride round the room, Clive hoped that some movement might increase his thinking powers. 'Anything new turned up on the car that was used in your accident?'

'A Mr Koplinski contacted us on the evening of the occurrence to say that his car had been "tampered with". He leaves it in the Wells Fargo car park in Wilksboro each day and then walks two blocks down the street to his office. His wife often uses the car during the day but returns it to the car park for him to drive home at the end of the day. They're kind of strange as they only have one car and she uses it to go to the malls and take her purchases home. She then returns it to the parking lot and walks the mile or so home. Unusual for anyone to walk that far but he says she likes the exercise. Addalyn Koplinski isn't your usual southern belle as she likes to walk everywhere but needs the car for the big food shops or when she's venturing a distance to a clothes mall.'

After pausing to think, realising that the next part of his account was important, Dwayne continued, 'Anyways, here's the thing, she didn't want it that day as her friend was picking her up for a girls' lunch.' Clive sat as patiently as he could, not wanting all the extra detail that Dwayne was imparting. Desperate for his new colleague to get to the main point he asked when the owner realised his car had been "tampered with".

'Just imagine how Chase Koplinski felt when he arrived to collect his vehicle at just after six o'clock and saw several dints and bashes on it. At first he thought another car had pranged it but on looking at it more closely he noticed what looked like something dark red on the paintwork. Forensics later identified that as blood and matched it to the Wilsons' blood group.

'So whoever took the car was bold enough to return it. It was exactly the same in Northumberland.'

'We've got one cool dude on our hands. Ten out of ten for self-confidence. We can rest assured that this is no wilting dogwood!'

'Hopefully the person is overconfident and has made a mistake, though I can't see it at the moment.'

'There's one thing that I find strange,' Dwayne drawled, each word taking twice as long as any of Clive's, 'and that's why there just don't appear to be a mom on the family scene. Not a single soul we've interviewed knew anything about her. Stewart Wilson's friends and colleagues at school said that he never spoke of her. Don't know if she died or if they were divorced or separated. Certainly she never arrived with them when he and Paul came to live here. Over the years Stewart did date a couple of his colleagues and had a longer term relationship with a waitress at the IHOP in town so I'm thinking he was a single man.' Clive didn't believe that this was always the case but kept quiet. It didn't seem to have anything to do with the murders, the word he now felt entitled to use in connection with both cases.

'Were there no relatives to contact in England?'

'We believe from the principal's report that Stewart's parents came over to live with their son and grandson soon after the pair moved to North Carolina. The old couple are inconsolable. There doesn't appear to be any other family.'

Clive sat, deep in thought, in the corner of the Deputy Sheriff's office, a huge space filled with rows of filing cabinets, two computers, a photocopier, a state of the art fax machine and a coffee making facility that would serve his entire force at home. One wall comprised floor to ceiling windows which looked out over the main street and had an uninterrupted view of the town centre's four-way stop, the alternative to an English roundabout but which to Clive appeared to have far more room for error. Dwayne referred to it as the "Driver's IQ Test" as no one had right of way, each driver having to stop and wait his turn to proceed.

'They operate in a clockwise direction, the one the furthest to the right having priority. If two or more arrive at about the same time the rule is first there first move. It's kinda fun to watch. I enjoy hours of almost innocent amusement observing the drivers trying to decide who goes next.'

Dwayne's explanation lasted a further ten minutes; the only point Clive deemed to be pertinent was that pedestrians had right of way, 'but sure as hell not many of those.' He laughed at his own joke knowing that the good people of North Carolina seldom went anywhere without their cars. His visitor thought it was probably just as well that few walkers approached the road junction as it was without the traditional "Walk" and "Don't Walk" signs. The system employed seemed to be fraught with difficulties, drivers, anywhere in the world, not known for their magnanimity.

Clive returned to the issue of the absent mother. 'That's a very good point. There has never been any sign of a mother for Peter, Joe Nightingale's son. No birth certificate was found and we know nothing about her. Peter's grandparents only knew of his existence just before Joe took him home when he was a day old. They never met or spoke to the mother of their grandchild. Most peculiar.'

Their discussion continued that evening over dinner: cheese scones followed by the biggest steak Clive had ever seen. Sweet potato and corn bread accompanied the meat and he wondered how often Dwayne ate any green vegetables. The waitress –'I'm Sydney, I'm your server for the evening, great to have you here, anything you need just holler,' – persuaded Dwayne to order double brownies with ice cream.

'There is one more thing the dads had in common: they were both well respected, no one has had a bad word to say about either of them,' Dwayne muttered through a mouthful of pudding, 'and the boys were good kids: neither seems to have been in any sort of trouble.'

Spending time in North Carolina searching for any similar events proved fruitless. Most of the second day was occupied with the pair going over and over the two cases which, they had to admit, were separated by several thousand miles A not insignificant fact.

'I feel as though we're stuck in the Hampton Court Maze with no sign of the escape,' Clive said, sounding despondent for the first time since arriving.

'Guess that must be some sort of strange English ritual,' Dwayne laughed, attempting to lift his new friend's mood. During the short explanation that followed Dwayne shook his head in disbelief. 'So people get lost deliberately? And that's a pastime?' Clive found it hard to see the funny side. The atmosphere improved when Dwayne was shown the website where Clive had first discovered the incident in North Carolina and both men promised to check its contents regularly and keep in close contact. Any developments would be shared.

'Let's hope there are no more, three would be more than a coincidence,' Dwayne commented.

'But at least if that happened the powers that be might start to take it all seriously,' Clive replied, realising how awful it was to hope for more killings: far better to solve the ones they had. His journey had been worthwhile. From today there were two minds at work and someone to talk to: someone who believed his theory.

On the way to the airport on a bright sunny morning, the blue sky and warm temperatures making it feel more like June than mid-November, Clive was able to enjoy some of the lovely countryside and he promised to return for a holiday, bringing Mari with him.

'Y'all more than welcome any time. As you know Cathy's been away looking after her sister but she'd love to meet you and your wife and as you've seen we've got plenty of room. We raised six kids in that house and it seems awful large when it's just the two of us.'

'I'm sure we'll be over some time, hopefully for a vacation. In the meantime if there are any developments maybe you could come to England. I'd love to show you my beautiful part of the world. Thanks for everything. I'll email when I get back.'

The return journey was uneventful, Clive even managing a few hours of deep sleep on the "red-eye" from New York to Newcastle.

Whilst he had been away autumn had converted into winter. The first frost had been the prelude (definitely in a minor key) to a day of sleet which obscured his view of the North Sea. Was this the start of a long hard winter? Driving through the inclement conditions he felt as low as the ever-thickening weather. It was not Clive's favourite season but he reasoned that time spent indoors would help him with the two cases. He wanted them solved before the spring.

Arriving home he had the house to himself. It was a school day and Mari had left a note saying she hoped the trip had been successful. Clive looked at that final word for several minutes. Had it been a success? Yes, but only if he acted on what he had discovered. An article in the local – and hopefully a national newspaper – was needed.

North East Guardian

Readers may remember the tragic event in Seahouses in October 2011 when a father and son, Joe and Peter Nightingale, were killed by a driver who left the scene. DCI Clive Rogers has recently returned from a visit to Statesville, a small town in the American State of North Carolina, where a similar event occurred on the same date this year. In both cases a single father and his son died. DCI Rogers said that he is convinced that the two cases are linked as they bare amazing similarities.

The police are keen to hear from anyone with further information regarding the local hit-and-run in Seahouses or anyone who is aware of similar accidents – either locally or world-wide.

'What exactly did you think you were doing putting an article in the local rag without passing it by our press gurus? It's been picked up by three of the national dailies and today we're famous, or bloody infamous, as it's on the front page of the *Mail*. We're a laughing stock. You're making us look stupid, linking an event in Seahouses with one in Statesville. Even that name sounds totally invented, just like your obsession.'

Clive's superior, a little man with an inflated opinion of himself, was bawling, the entire department privy to the reprimand. The few remaining hairs on his head, normally trained over the bald summit in the style perfected by Bobby Charlton in the 1960's, were standing up like an array of machine guns all trained on the hapless Clive. 'We have procedures and they are there for a purpose. You can't go off half-cock on a whim.' Clive wondered about the use of two adages so close together but decided this wasn't the time to highlight them. 'I've had the Chief Super on the phone asking what the bloody hell is going on. He thought I might be behind it.'

He stared at Clive as if this was the most ridiculous idea since God expected Eve not to tempt Adam. 'I assured him that it was entirely down to you. You've always been a one-man band and this case has really got to you. I told him you had a bee in your bonnet.' By this stage it was difficult not to laugh. The man wasn't known for his command of the English language and was notorious for relying on clichés when agitated.

Many had suspected that Superintendent Toby Mullins had been promoted beyond his ability, to the level where he became incompetent. Someone had once muttered that he was Peter's notorious principle personified. He relied on the excellence of the men in his department and it appeared, with increasing regularity, that his sole purpose was to complete as much paperwork as possible and leave the real policing to the lower ranks. He stood glaring at Clive, his face becoming redder by the second, the veins in his neck throbbing dangerously. He had suffered a small heart attack earlier in the year but had declined the offer of early retirement on health grounds, much to the disappointment of many in the station.

'Well, what have you got to say for yourself? This is a disciplinary matter.'

'With all due respect sir, I felt it was the best way forward. It seemed the ideal way to bring the matter to the public's attention. Someone might have some information that could help solve both cases.'

'Both cases, both cases...do you know how ridiculous you sound. There is no question of "both cases". Two accidents, divided by the Atlantic for heaven's sake, cannot and I mean cannot, be linked no matter how hard you or anyone else tries to make a connection. Any link is tenuous at best and I am ordering you to drop this whole thing. Get on with some real detective work.'

'If I can just show you what I found in America I'm sure you'll change your mind...'

Clive was interrupted, mid flow, by the Superintendent stepping close enough for Clive to know that, contrary to his superior's assertions, he remained a prolific smoker. 'Chief Inspector Rogers I am issuing you with an order. Drop this case and any thought of the transatlantic one. There will be no disciplinary proceedings this time but if you disobey this instruction, and I can hardly be more direct, you will find yourself in very deep water: very deep water indeed.'

Stepping back into the main office Clive was greeted with comments that his colleagues enjoyed more than him.

'Deep water...deep, deep water, better remember your water wings.'

'Half-cock...oh what a pity, poor Mari,' were just two of the asides that stopped abruptly as the Superintendent left his room.

Having come this far Clive was not going to let the matter drop but it was obvious that any future investigation would have to be undertaken covertly.

The investigation would continue.

Chapter 4

The Daily Mail! People are tweeting and facebooking (is there such a word?) about me. I almost wish I could make an announcement. Such a shame to be the cause of anonymous publicity: one does so want one's nine hundred seconds of fame.

Perhaps it will, at some point in the future, prove fortuitous that none of my visits to Statesville can be traced back to me. I wasn't there, not me M'lud.

Despite the ultimate reason for the weeks spent in Statesville I was always glad to see how settled and happy Stewart and Paul looked. Once again it was a pity that such innocents had to die. Unfortunately, it was inevitable.

Stewart and his son had arrived in America on July 28th in the middle of a heat wave. Every year the summers in the Deep South were appallingly hot but this one broke several records. At the end of August the Weather Channel, twenty-four hours a day of climate updates, announced that the daytime temperature in North Carolina hadn't fallen below ninety for over eight weeks and the humidity had been registering almost a hundred per cent. The air-conditioning in their house was on constantly, drying the atmosphere and causing Paul's asthma to flare up. The doctor they saw suggested turning it off at night but neither of them could sleep in the resulting sauna, sheets saturated within minutes.

'Is it always this hot Dad? We can't do anything when it's like this. I hate it.'

'Don't panic son, once October comes it'll cool down and then you'll love it. Until then its air con car to the air con mall, air con car to air con school, air con car to air con home...' all delivered in a mock Southern drawl.

'Yes, I just wish we could do the things we did at home – get a dog and take it walks, play in the park.'

'It's all new here Paul, but you'll get to love it. How about we ask Jody and Rick for a sleep over at the weekend?'

Paul was a confident boy and had made friends easily at his new school. He had inherited his mother's good looks and had her blond hair and blue eyes. He was a bright youngster and his year in the Reception class in England meant he was very well prepared for the Kindergarten class he entered within a week of reaching North Carolina. It helped that his dad was teaching Grade 5 not too far down the hall and he could see him each lunch time. The two classes had very different breaks but Stewart's daily non-contact time coincided with the Kindergarten's period in the canteen so father and son ate lunch together most days. It was common practice for moms and dads, grandparents and older siblings to come into the dining hall and eat with their children during lunch recess.

Martin Luther King Elementary had been rehoused in a purpose-built school five years previously and was a delightfully airy construction with huge classrooms and wide halls. Stewart remembered its forerunner, the cockroach-ridden building he had taught in during his first stay in NC. He often told the story of going into his stock room to get his car keys at the end of a school day to be met by a legion of the creatures scurrying for cover: an army in retreat. In truth he was far more scared of them, not only for their ugly appearance which made him shudder, but also their notoriety as disease carriers: gastroenteritis, dysentery, asthma and the ability to exacerbate allergies all attributed to them. He had been warned never to take his school bag home as the roaches might have laid their eggs inside and his apartment would become inundated. On the way home he had stopped at the mall and bought Borax powder from the laundry aisle. Leah, his buddy teacher, had suggested it as the most efficient way to get rid of the invaders.

Within a few months both father and son had settled into their new routines and once the intense heat moderated long periods were spent outdoors: softball, the junior version of baseball, became Paul's obsession. He was like a religious convert, almost forgetting all about his former passions, football and rugby. However, only a few weeks later he was to join the school soccer team and attended every practice. Softball continued to be "awesome", the word he used unrelentingly much to everyone's amusement until his vowels elongated and he learnt to extend this and every other word.

'Are we off to look at houses again?' Paul asked, knowing that as this was Saturday the answer would be yes. Stewart wanted them to be in their own home as soon as possible but it took many weekends to find the ideal house. Six weeks after arriving there it was. A detached white clapperboard two-storey building set in acres of garden (he had yet to call it a yard) with a wooden veranda encircling all four walls. Rocking chairs and loungers were positioned on each side ready to catch the sun at all times of the day. Part of the garden was an orchard with trees drooping with apples, plums and pears many past their best, the present owners admitting that looking after the garden had got beyond them. They were down-sizing and going to live in a Retirement Village in Maryland where they would be near their daughter.

'It's a swell property, ideal for a family, but just too darned big for Jesse and me,' Walter said. He had lived his entire life in Statesville and added that he would be sorry to leave. 'The winters can be cruel up there, twenty feet of snow last year. My daughter had to dig herself out several times. I expect you know that we do get some cold snaps here, it's not always this warm.' Stewart explained that he had spent two years in Statesville and remembered the snow and the ice storm.

The two men spent the next quarter of an hour reminiscing about the infamous ice storm, which at the time was worldwide news. 'December 5th, my birthday,' Walter boasted, 'what a day. Bright sunshine first thing, then a few clouds, snow by lunchtime...'

'Yes, my school was closed by one o'clock after all the kids had been collected. The yellow buses had been organised to arrive straight after an early lunch and moms picked up the others, desperate to drive their children home. I lived fourteen miles away on the other side of town and only just made it through the snow which by early afternoon had become a blizzard. Total whiteout. I slipped and slithered on several occasions. Thought my last hours might be on the horizon.'

Walter was getting excited, remembering the end of that day. 'It snowed and snowed hour after bleached hour. Jesse and I retire about ten and I had a last look out and goodness gracious if it wasn't snowing ice, great shards of the stuff descending from the heavens, like the eleventh plague. I sure as hell wouldn't have wanted to be standing under it.'

As he drew breath Stewart managed to continue the story, 'Do you remember how beautiful it was the following morning? Perfect blue sky as though nothing had happened, like a god forgiving the skies their past misdemeanours. But what a sight, truly awesome.'

'Awesome, awesome,' Paul chuckled, hearing his dad use the word he regarded as his own.

'Everything covered in a layer of ice: trees, roof tops, cars, I had to cut the ice off my Chevy and it came away in great sheets,' Walter continued, 'and I don't know about you but we had a power outage for forty-eight hours.'

'Yes, same at my place and all the traffic lights and cables came down across the whole area.'

'The fire fighters and volunteers did a great job restoring the electricity so swiftly. I heard they were working twenty-hour days,' Walter stood more upright, proud of his countrymen. Jesse chose that moment to interrupt the conversation as she appeared with a jug of lemonade and a plate of home-made chocolate chip cookies which Paul devoured like a lone locust. They all sat on a shady part of the veranda and Stewart knew he had found their house. This place would soon become home and their new start could move up a gear.

Chapter 5

It seems so long ago. My first trip across the pond! I thought it circumspect to "borrow" my sister's passport and driving licence to enter the States (hopefully she wouldn't be involved in anything that would necessitate the latter's production). I knew I would be fingerprinted and photographed but as long as I always used her identification, the passport, fingerprints and photo would match.

I knew that Sophie was very unlikely to venture that far as she hates the idea of a long-haul flight. Her holidays consist of two weeks by a pool somewhere. Last year she went to Crete and spent the entire time in the hotel grounds. No visiting world-famous historic sites for her: far too intellectual and requiring a modicum of effort. Not her style. In case of some unforeseen eventuality Sophie and I had keys to each other's houses, so I popped along one day and appropriated the documents. A shame that I had to return them but she's usually got some break planned. I just had to hope it wasn't when I was away.

It had been easy to keep an eye on the Wilsons whilst they were living in Manchester especially when they moved in with Stewart's parents as this wasn't too far from my place. Imagine the shock I got when I saw a "For Sale" sign on his car one cloudy day in late June as I wandered past on one of my regular sorties. The vehicle was sitting, gleaming on the pavement. I took a note of the number to ring and when I contacted him later that day I asked the usual questions about mileage, MOT and the vehicle's most recent service and then enquired why he was selling it. He went into a long, rather rambling, explanation about moving abroad, telling me in great detail all about Statesville and the new life he wanted in North Carolina. What must he have thought when I put down the phone without another word. As I was calling from a phone-box there was no way he could trace me, though only my paranoia imagined he might have wanted to do so.

That day he was probably imagining his future as a straight road bathed in southern sunshine, with perhaps some minor diversions and re-routings. Only I knew that it would come to a dead end far sooner than expected.

Ever since I was a little girl planning has been one of my fortes and I knew I couldn't hurry this particular schedule. The first anniversary had, rather disappointingly, come and gone, the Wilsons gaining an extra twelve months. I wasn't able to go to America until my half term break late in October. I knew that the travelling twosome would survive my first foray to the bizarrely named town in the middle of nowhere. Looking at it on the internet I was disappointed that it really was an incognito type of place, but I reasoned that might prove advantageous as no major police force could possibly operate there. I surmised that they probably all rode horses which wasn't far from the truth.

Travelling to Statesville wasn't easy. The nearest airport is situated miles away and necessitates long drives down various interstates.

First impressions can be vital and I wanted time to look at the town, find out where they were living and form the embryo of a plan. I had not been on holiday since the previous summer, my wages as a teaching assistant almost all accounted for paying the part of my rather large mortgage that father didn't cover. My rally driving hobby is also rather expensive but a girl has to have some fun when not murdering people! So I wanted to think of my initial time in a new part of the world as a holiday though I should probably say vacation.

Upgraded to Business Class, Clara enjoyed the flight. Landing on a continent for the first time proved exciting. Putting her watch back five hours allowed sufficient time to hire a car (sister's driving licence put to dubious use), drive well within the speed limit along the pot-holed interstate (the last thing she needed was to attract the attention of the highway police), and find suitable accommodation (somewhere that didn't ask for too much ID).

'Y'all not from round here,' the young receptionist of the Holiday Rest motel said as Clara arrived late in the afternoon. He was obviously extending his auditory powers to their full capacity.

Thankfully she had her story ready. 'I read that your town was named "The All American City" in 1997 and 2009 and I was interested to see how it gained such a wonderful accolade – and was so impressed when I read that it received it twice!'

Bradley Reavis looked inordinately proud and seemed to gain six inches, 'Well ma'am it sure is a great place to live. Folks round here would do anything for anybody. We invented the phrase good neighbours. If you want any help with anything you just have to ask.'

Deciding to play the game she asked, with as much enthusiasm as possible, 'Where's the best place to start sightseeing?'

'I guess that would be Fort Dobbs ma'am, the final frontier in the old days. It was built by the British settlers in the eighteenth century for protection against the Cherokee, Catawba, Shawnee, Delaware and French raids on North Carolina. A reconstruction of the log-walled cabin is still there but y'all have to use your imagination for the palisade and moat. Tomorrow is your lucky day as Friday is the only day it's open to the public.'

After ascertaining the whereabouts of this piece of local history Clara went to her room. It was, without doubt, at the lower end of the accommodation available but suited her purposes. No forms to fill in or request to see her passport. Despite the mixed emotions of excitement and trepidation she slept until morning.

Having undertaken hours of research before leaving the U.K. Clara had all the information she needed: the Wilsons' address and its location, local phone numbers and several Google maps of the area. Once in Statesville the material, all neatly labelled and carefully organised in see-through pockets, felt like a lifesaver. What a shame it was to have the opposite effect on Stewart and Paul!

Leaving Statesville that first morning she passed fields of cotton and several defunct tobacco farms which now grew wheat and rye. The fall colours were amazing: a conflagration of yellows, oranges and blood-red leaves gave the countryside the appearance of a raging inferno.

Fortunately there was no need to go back on the interstates, with their unbelievably potholed surfaces which had reminded Clara of the latest pictures to be sent back from Mars, and driving proved to be a pleasure on the empty country roads. Every half mile there was yet another Baptist church, all gleaming impressively in the morning sunshine. They were white clapperboard structures of generous proportions to accommodate the huge congregations which were expected in that part of the world. Outside each church there was an enormous sign, advertising the services and with slogans warning of the hell and damnation that would be the result of deviating from the word of God. Clara allowed herself a tiny smile and wondered what God was making of her actions and plans. A small corner of the fiery furnace probably had a "Reserved for Clara Bedford" notice already in place.

Finding the house she wanted was almost too easy. Several miles out of town she passed the school with its sign "Martin Luther King Elementary: The Stars of Tomorrow". Salvation Road was the turning immediately after it. Stewart and Paul lived three houses down on the right. Each residence was set in acres of ground, their nearest neighbour hidden by trees and vast swathes of bushes. Driving past very slowly Clara saw that access to the Wilsons' house was via a long gravel drive with lines of trees forming a guard of honour on each side.

Two enormous dogs were patrolling the yard, a totally inappropriate Americanism for such a wonderful garden. They were bearded Schnauzers, each adorned with the most impressive facial hair and Clara was unsure whether they were pets or guard dogs, though as there was no gate safety didn't appear to be a high priority. Not daring to stop and stare she continued to the end of the road where the houses stopped and open countryside began. She drove on until she was away from any habitation and stopped the car to think. This was going to prove more difficult than she had expected, rather like the instructions on a "build it yourself" piece of furniture from IKEA. Disappointed that their road was inappropriate for the incident, too short a distance from the main road to gain sufficient momentum, she knew she would have to find a better location.

In order to have a topic of conversation with Bradley Reavis, should she be unfortunate enough to bump into him at the motel, she spent the afternoon at Fort Dobbs learning all about the vital role the Fort played in protecting the early settlers from enemy attack. She thought it was strange to think of Statesville as a frontier settlement, the Atlantic being about three hundred miles away. It had long since mutated into middle-America, the archetypal small town conurbation and an ideal location to live and raise a family. Clara learnt that centuries ago it was the perfect site for the various native Indian groups. At the time they were friends with the French who helped them challenge the newly arrived people. She didn't like to point out that the various Indian groups had been in the country for far longer than the immigrants, many of whom had recently arrived on the continent.

The guide was well informed and delighted to furnish some of the gorier details of the battles that took place in the eighteenth century, including a graphic account of an Englishman being scalped by the Indians. Despite her earlier misgivings Clara managed to enjoy the tour. 'Great to meet you ma'am, we don't get many English visitors. You never know one of your distant ancestors might have been here.' Ezekiel, the young guide, was full of the overwhelming enthusiasm she noticed in almost every American she met: an eagerness that must have been imbibed with their mother's milk. 'Make sure y'all visit the art gallery before y'all leave.'

Fortunately the small gallery contained some interesting Native American art work. Clara was particularly taken with the basket weaving, learning that the woven reeds and cornhusks that were used to create the intricate baskets traditionally had two purposes: to transport fruit and vegetables and as beautiful objects to be admired. The ones on display were dyed with intricate tribal patterns and she was tempted to buy one of the many modern-day copies on sale in the gift shop. Instead she treated herself to a brightly coloured rainbow-patterned woven blanket, a facsimile of the ones the women would have spent many hours creating by weaving threads together. She was tempted to buy one of the pendants, all created as homage to a variety of animals: bears, eagles, walruses and whales, though she doubted whether the last two would have been prevalent in Statesville.

Outside the gallery a minute café faced the fort. Coffee and chocolate brownies in front of her, Clara thought about her interesting visit and couldn't help surmising that a hit-and-run annihilation was far preferable to being scalped.

Spending the remainder of the day walking round the tree-lined avenues of the small town, with their hugely impressive colonial style houses, Clara could see why it had been recommended as a place to "live the American dream", a phrase highlighted in one of the pamphlets she had picked up in the hotel lobby. Strolling down street after street of enormous detached properties each set in their own grounds, with wrap-around verandas littered with wicker settees, life looked very easy.

Downtown Statesville was far more plebian: two roads of shops that had all seen better days. As she walked round a corner she found a library, two banks and a café that kept strange opening hours. New malls on the outskirts had obviously decimated the town centre.

The sun was shining and the sky was the kind of blue she recognised from the American films she enjoyed watching so Clara continued her stroll.

As she approached Mitchell College, the most impressive building so far with its vast façade, cream paintwork and grand columns, she knew this was a place she could live and work. The notice board near the main entrance encouraged its readers to enroll for the extensive list of courses on offer. Fearing that she was becoming conspicuous (few others were on foot) she returned to her car.

Three days of the trip remained and there was a lot of work to do: routes to revisit; school times to confirm; hobbies her prey enjoyed to discover; and day-to-day routines noted, though she realised that these might well change over the next twelve months.

October 15th was the best part of a year away, plenty of time for a penultimate visit between now and then. Every aspect of the final act must be organised, the prey remaining in total ignorance and the predator fully prepared. It felt like a game of cat and mouse, but far more serious.

She was only too aware that she was a stranger here and could easily draw attention to herself. The town did not receive many "out-of-towners". This time her disguise had been sufficient: a medium length red wig, a thick covering of dark make-up, bright clothes and the ubiquitous sunglasses. Next time she would go blond. (She was blond already but would choose a style, shade and length of hair very different from her own.)

Next time she would book a room some distance from Statesville, maybe in Wilksboro, the best part of forty miles down the highway of the same name. She would feel more comfortable staying some distance away. The small town was on the appropriate side of Statesville, the school situated on the Wilksboro Highway, making it easy to drive to the school and, of even greater importance, make her get away. During the final visit next October she planned to revert to a male outfit, the kind she'd used in Seahouses. The hardest thing was going to be retaining sufficient patience between now and then.

Chapter 6

On the day I returned home my next flight was booked. It would have to be during my six week summer holiday, perhaps August, near enough to the vital date that hopefully Stewart and Paul would have a routine that would then remain reasonably consistent. Their school year started at the beginning of August and there was no break until Thanksgiving in November. Hopefully by that stage I would be the only one giving thanks.

Then, in October, the final hop across the pond. A short period to refine my plans: "borrow" a suitable car; enjoy the hit-and-run; remove myself from the scene and mission accomplished. Going in the middle of October would prove difficult as my school's half term is always at the end of the month and I would have to think of a reason for some extra days off. An ill relative, a sudden bereavement or a much needed operation: that last one rumbled too easily. Once again I wouldn't be using my own passport so there would be no record of my entering America.

What had this first time in Statesville achieved? Notebooks filled with minute details of places, people, busy times and street layouts were enough for me to feel confident that I would be able to devise a deadly plan. But why, oh why, on my final day there, had I driven a second time down Salvation Road?

Clara wanted a final look at the house, the rather nauseatingly named, "Little England". She was keen to ascertain its distance from the main road and was disappointed to find that it was less than point one of a mile. Once outside she stopped the engine and sat staring into the yard. Out of all the billions of seconds in the average person's life a few become trapped in the mind, held more securely than any lifer serving time at Her Majesty's pleasure and with as little hope of escape or release, even with good behaviour. This was such a moment.

Watching as Stewart and Paul drove down the path towards her she became immobile, unable to move or catch her breath. By the time she realised what was happening she was eyeball to eyeball with Stewart. He smiled as he turned left towards the main road and gave a small wave but there was no sign of recognition. Exactly what she would have said had he known it was her was beyond logical thought. It would have been impossible to make up some story about why she was there. It was interesting to see how Paul was growing up and becoming more like his father: same oval face, large forehead and unruly hair. He looked a pleasant young man and had grown a lot since leaving England.

As they turned onto Wilksboro Highway she realised that the raucous gasps were emanating from her. Loud sobs followed as she succumbed to a bout of jagged crying, giving way to unaccustomed emotion. Seeing them in the flesh again made them real and no longer merely names, or people on the old photos she kept in an album labelled Stewart and Paul: no random packets of snaps for her.

Did they deserve to die? Should she stop her planning? Would it be better to return home and carry on with her life? Did what was done to her justify more deaths?

No.

Probably.

Impossible.

Yes.

Continuing to live with the wrongs done to her was intolerable, but in order to have justice the Wilsons would have to die. A shame, but there it was.

Badly shaken by how near she had been to discovery, Clara vowed to be more circumspect. Maybe, just maybe, the incident would prove advantageous in the long run. She would be far more careful in the future.

Eight months after Stewart and Paul arrived in America they had been joined by Holly and Dan. After serious thought they knew that being with their son and grandson overrode any misgivings they had about leaving their friends and comfortable life in England.

'We're not getting any younger and we're bound to need some medical assistance soon and it's hellish expensive over there,' was the only concern that Dan raised prior to the pair's decision to move.

'I know, but we've got savings and being near our boys will keep us young and healthy,' was Holly's mantra each time her husband raised the obvious dilemma. 'Any money from the sale of this house can be set aside for medical bills. Stewart is very keen for us to share their place. As we know it's got more than enough room for all of us and he's been able to afford it without a mortgage, so as long as we pay our way it'll be fine.'

They had been out to NC to stay that first September and again at Christmas, falling in love with the seemingly endless sunshine and more easy-going lifestyle. They were pleased to see how well Stewart and Paul had settled but Holly had been distraught each time they went back to England. 'I hate goodbyes and saying it when we are leaving them so far away is unbearable,' she had sobbed, the tears invariably flowing for several days. 'I wish we were closer again. I miss them both so much.'

And so they arrived, allegedly to stay forever, unaware of what lay ahead. The future – despite wormholes or the hypothetical Einstein-Rosen Bridge – remaining inaccessible. At least the time they had in America allowed them some good years with their boys.

The four soon established the routine necessary when people share a house. Fitting into other people's lives can be difficult but it had worked before when Paul was a baby. The "retirees", as Paul loved to call them, quickly created their own schedule which ran on parallel tracks to the "kids", almost as smoothly as the Amtrak trains on which the quartet sometimes travelled. Paul and Stewart both adored their school with its many extracurricular activities and Holly and Dan became regular worshippers at the nearest church, the Providence Baptist, which claimed to be the oldest in Statesville and one of the few that joined forces with an all-black church on the other side of town. Holly joined the choir and Dan signed up to transport those older than him to services and the many social activities organised by the various committees.

'Spring vacation is coming up next month. Any thoughts?' Stewart asked after losing another game of chess. Paul had only recently discovered the game but was able to beat his father every time. They were sitting on the veranda, drinking cold tea and enjoying the perfect weather, sunny and very warm, ideal conditions until the oven-like summer temperatures arrived. The yard looked wonderful though Stewart hated gardening, an almost never-ending task that he left to his parents.

Dan's job was to keep the extensive lawns under control. A large Briggs and Stratton ride-on mower had been purchased as soon as he arrived. 'With that much grass I need a proper machine or I'll spend every waking hour cutting it,' was how he had justified the rather exorbitant cost of the 13.5 HP machine. Holly had been determined to create English style borders near the house which she stocked with a selection of flowers to remind them of home. Snowdrops appeared in January quickly followed by crocuses and later on her favourites: a profusion of hyacinths, tulips and daffodils.

'You know spring is here when the garden comes alive with so many colours. I can't believe how well they all grow here.' The dogwoods and azaleas were long established and added to the show.

Stewart repeated his question about their holiday. He worked hard at school and loved to get away during vacations. 'Beach, beach, beach,' Paul yelled, waking the sleeping dogs who, thinking they were missing something, raced around in a frenzy of excitement. Myrtle Beach in South Carolina had become their favourite venue, only five hours drive, nothing by American standards.

'What do you think Holly? Are you happy to go there again?'

'I think the decision is made,' she laughed, 'and it's fine by me.'

Two weeks later the quartet was on the sands below the crowded boardwalk with its many shopping options. They were acting like any family: building sand-castles, swimming in the warm ocean, sunbathing and eating vast quantities of ice cream. Stewart thought that his parents would appreciate some time to themselves so suggested that they played golf the following day and pointed out that on their last visit they had only tried a couple of the hundred Championship courses the area boasted.

'Can we go back to the aquarium?' Paul pleaded, 'we only saw a bit of it last time and I want to stroke the sting rays again.'

'That sounds rather dangerous,' Dan said attempting and failing to sound serious.

'No, everyone does it, you stroke them as they swim past in the open tank; it's awesome.' Father and son spent the next day at Ripley's Aquarium, going round and round the three hundred and thirty feet of moving path situated below the "Dangerous Reef", the main exhibition, with its thousands of fish of every shape and size. 'It feels as though we're in the ocean with them. I love it. I want to stay here for ever and ever. Awesome.'

'Spectacular is the word I'd use, though I don't care if I never see a Green Moray Eel again, rather repulsive.' Stewart was determined to use words that might extend his son's somewhat limited and increasingly American vocabulary.

By evening, all four were back at the beach house they had rented for the week. This was their third stay at the appropriately named Ocean View. In the past they had stayed in a hotel but much preferred having sole occupancy of the house which was twice the size of theirs in Statesville.

'Five bedrooms and four bathrooms should be sufficient for our needs,' Holly had joked the first time they arrived.

'A fifty inch plasma TV and two pools,' Paul exclaimed, thinking he'd never seen anything as posh in his life. He loved using that adjective as his American friends thought it was cool. A great attraction of the condo was that the dogs could accompany them and as the front door led directly onto the beach the two bounded across the sand at every opportunity. The ocean views were stunning and every evening was spent sitting and gazing at magnificent sunsets.

As they sat eating Sloppy Joes they discussed their day's activities. Kayaking and shopping were on tomorrow's itinerary, age deciding the option each would choose.

How fortunate that as they sat and spoke of Myrtle Beach becoming their regular holiday destination they had no idea that the next vacation would be their last.

Chapter 7

Off again next week. Where have the past nine months gone? I spent many of them mourning Henry. No one could have had a better, more caring, godfather. He meant far more than my own father and did infinitely more for me. He wasn't old, mid-sixties, so cruel not to achieve the Biblical three score and ten years. I felt cheated on his behalf. He would have said that it's not longevity that's important but what you do with the years you're given. At least he didn't suffer or have the ignominy of his loved ones watching an irreversible and possibly undignified deterioration.

I feel better knowing that there are positives to my duos' demises. They don't suffer. They have no inkling of their abrupt end, no "intimations of their imminent mortality" (to misquote). They live life to the full up to the moment...

Amy rang Clara a few days after Christmas. Henry had complained of feeling "funny", as though he might be sick, and had gone to bed early the night before. At two in the morning he had woken his wife to say he had a dreadful pain in his chest and upper arm. His pyjamas were soaked with sweat and his breathing was, 'Like an old man's, he could hardly draw the next one.' Amy had given him some brandy and dialled for an ambulance. By the time the ambulance arrived, laden with medical paraphernalia, hope, and futile dreams of recovery, Henry was in agony and unable to speak. The paramedics dealt calmly with the situation, maintaining a reassuring commentary during the journey to the hospital which seemed to last another lifetime.

'I was so scared, Clara, I knew what was happening but felt totally helpless, it was like attempting to protect a loved one from the eye of an unforgiving hurricane. All I could do was sit and wait outside the Emergency room whilst the doctors worked on him. He was so kind, the doctor who came to tell me. I don't know how he managed to be as extraordinarily thoughtful. I learnt afterwards he'd been on duty for fifteen hours. He certainly went the proverbial extra mile and I've written to the hospital to thank him.' Amy broke down, the long speech having taken her last attempt at self-control.

Driving to the farm, where she had spent some of her best days, Clara wondered what words she would find to say. None seemed appropriate in the circumstances and any she thought of sounded either banal or maudlin. Amy would not appreciate any sentimentality. She would be lost without her husband who had been her soulmate and best friend. Forty-five years of marriage had ended without warning, no Cassandra available to prophesy the tragedy. Gravel shouted her arrival and Clara was surprised to see Amy standing confidently at the door, smiling and greeting her as though this was a normal visit.

'Come in, come in, it's an awful day, come in and get warm. I've just popped the kettle on.' Totally nonplussed Clara stood and burst into tears. Being in the house minus Henry was unbearable and she fell into Amy's arms.

'Sorry, sorry, I shouldn't be the one crying,' Clara sobbed.

'Oh, my dear girl, I've done so much weeping that the local reservoir is full to bursting. This rain isn't needed: not needed at all.'

Afternoon slouched into evening then night, the light absenting itself shortly after four. The two women sat and talked, agreeing that Henry would not have wanted them to be unhappy. He had enjoyed a good life: one full of people, laughter and hard work. They reminisced, drinking copious quantities of tea, both surviving spells of weeping which were counter-balanced by moments of side-splitting laughter. 'Do you remember when he was teaching you to drive and you almost went into the slurry pit?'

'Yes, and the time we had to get the tractor to pull the marooned car out of the field. The car survived which is more than can be said for the gate. I'm surprised he didn't give up on me, I was far too confident and made stupid mistakes, but he was always patient and told me I was a competent driver.'

'I wouldn't want to see an incompetent one!'

'I was an unhappy teenager and the driving was just what I needed – capable or not. Henry was my life-line and I will be forever in his debt.'

Clara had been invited to stay. The funeral was still three days away but both were in need of the company. Despite her misgivings Clara slept well, unlike Amy who looked drawn in the morning light. After breakfast, which neither felt like eating, they went for a walk. The rain had cleared leaving a cold, bright morning, snow flurries attempting, unsuccessfully, to cover the ground.

'Dear Clara, I was so busy talking about Henry and my feelings that I never asked what was happening in your life. How was Christmas with your new fella?'

'Nigel's lovely, but I'm not ready to get too involved. The Christmas break with his family was a bit of an endurance test, worse than a spotlit interrogation. I'm sure his mum used to work for the KGB. I felt as though I was being constantly assessed. She kept asking me all sorts of questions which I found hard to answer.'

'Maybe she was interviewing you as a prospective daughter-in-law.'

'It certainly felt like that. He's coming on Thursday. I hope that's all right. You'll meet him then.' Short sentences were becoming the order of the day.

'Can't wait. Give me plenty of warning when the time is approaching to buy the hat!'

'Ha, ha, that is a long time off: if at all.'

In truth Clara hadn't meant to start, let alone pursue, any relationship, but for the first time in her life she thought she might be falling in love. Over the years there had been plenty of other men with some fairly long-lasting and, at the time, serious relationships. She had lived with two of them but on both occasions the arrangement had ended with unpleasant recriminations on both sides. Were the circumstances different, with no annihilations to gloat over or plan, she would be happy to take the affair with Nigel more seriously and do as he had asked just before Christmas and move in with him, but then she would not be able travel to North Carolina without giving an explanation… and he could hardly be invited to accompany her.

Sam, now a banker in the City, arrived later that evening. 'I'll leave you two to talk,' Clara said, knowing that Amy would want to have time alone with her son.

She was rather disappointed, on Amy's behalf, that he hadn't made the effort to arrive earlier though she knew they had been in contact several times since Henry's death.

'He's not very good at showing emotions and hates any fuss,' Amy had said, a mother forever making excuses for her offspring's tardy behaviour. How different from his father Clara thought, but stopped herself from saying.

On the morning of the funeral icy roads created difficult conditions for the hearse and the family cars that followed. The single-track lane leading from the farm to the village church was even narrower than usual with banks of snow packed at the sides. 'I've heard of dead slow being appropriate but we'll all be joining him if this journey takes much longer,' Amy whispered, knowing that Clara would appreciate the black humour.

As the coffin was lifted from the hearse one of the bearers almost lost his footing on the slippery path which had an unfortunately steep incline. As his left leg decided to go its own way, Clara and Amy avoided eye contact, afraid of descending into helpless giggles, both thinking that Henry would have appreciated such a moment. The churchyard was obscured by the thick snow which had fallen overnight. The ancient tombstones, many leaning at a dangerous angle, looked as though an impressionist painter had created them. Bright sunshine added to the almost surreal scene.

Following the bier into the sixteenth century church, a building that must have witnessed so many goodbyes, Clara was delighted to see how impressive the interior looked. Amy had organised an almost overwhelming array of winter flowers and numerous candles lit the aisles. The flowers both looked and smelt wonderful and the candles provided an unearthly glow. No cathedral could have provided a better send-off.

The church was full. Although family members only occupied the first few pews Henry had been a popular figure and most of the village had attended to pay their respects. It was a moving service with the beauty of the traditional words complemented by several heartfelt eulogies. Amy spoke of her "rock", the man who was "utterly dependable" and who had been her support and soulmate for over four decades. Henry was described as a father who was "always there" though the congregation laughed when told that he had not been afraid to wield the "big stick, metaphorically of course!"

Knowing she would be unable to speak during the service Clara had written several paragraphs about her godfather, which the vicar, a young man new to the parish, managed to summarise in a brilliant fashion. His direct quote of, "He saved me from myself and made me into the woman I am today," brought tears to her eyes and made her wonder what he would have thought of her recent escapades. Would he have remained proud of the person she had become?

The local hostelry, where Henry had enjoyed many evenings, provided an excellent venue for the buffet lunch which followed the interment. Unfortunately it meant that Clara had to endure contact with her sister.

Over recent years the two had avoided each other, both thinking that catching the plague would be a preferable experience. These days they had little in common. Sophie was flourishing: Clara wasn't. Wealth and life experiences separated them like the proverbial chaff from the wheat.

'How are you?' Sophie enquired, displaying no interest in the answer.

'Fine I think…And you?'

'Yes, very well thanks,' was more than enough conversation.

It was fortunate that Nigel had been unable to come, his excuse a bout of debilitating flu. The situation was already unbearable without the added pressure of introducing her new boyfriend whom Sophie would inevitably deem inferior. She could just imagine Sophie's snide comments about Nigel being the best Clara could find.

To compound the situation her sister had arrived at the church with a man whom none of the family had met. Sophie looked well and had all the trappings of success: clothes that shrieked "designer", Jimmy Choo shoes (totally inappropriate in the inclement conditions) and a Chloe handbag. Her latest beau was merely another accessory with his suave looks and impeccable manners. He was "something in the City" and as Amy said later, 'Looked as rich as Croesus.'

'Did you see his car? A top of the range Porsche. Not something you or I could afford.' Amy wasn't the jealous type but felt for Clara. Sophie's life was so much more prosperous and successful than Clara's, the twin who had missed out. Life wasn't fair: Clara was the better, more caring person, but when did that ever help one make progress?

'One day the tables won't just be turned but will look like Whirling Dervishes,' Clara responded, 'and I'll buy a Jaguar, no foreign rubbish for me.'

'It's amazing you two still look exactly the same. I remember when you were little and dressed identically. I do believe, if you chose to do so today, no one would be able to tell you apart,' this from Janine, Henry's younger sister, totally unaware that whilst it was not what one sister wanted to hear the other was delighted. Utterly delighted.

Chapter 8

Ditched Nigel. He was far too interested in my trip to America and couldn't understand why I wanted to go alone. Understandable I suppose as he had continued to drop hints about us getting together on a more permanent basis. Feel sorry in a way as he is a good bloke and excellent company. Keep telling myself he was proving to be a distraction and a danger. I don't need to be thinking about anyone else at the moment or risk anyone knowing what I'm doing. And I definitely won't miss his mother!

North Carolina in August: unbelievable heat, unbearable humidity, unreal moments. Meeting the family in Love Valley was one of the most terrifying moments of my life. I had intended to be so careful. Surely the previous encounter had given me sufficient warning. The inappropriately named hamlet lies a few miles from Statesville and is like something out of a Wild West film. It's definitely stuck in a time warp: everyone travelling on horseback (including the sheriff), boardwalks taking the place of pavements and people dressed in cowboy outfits.

The sign in the only "shop" said, "Wife and horse needed, please send a picture of the horse". The sad thing is I don't think it was a joke.

When I came face to face with Paul and his family I certainly didn't feel like laughing. For a few seconds I really thought that my planning would be in vain. As I wasn't wearing a cowgirl outfit I didn't exactly blend in with the crowd. No one had remembered to let me in on the little secret that everyone dresses up when visiting Love Valley and outsiders are not made welcome. In the guide book it had said that going there was "a journey back to a long forgotten era, a place where Americans lived like their forefathers, enjoying a simple life, one that existed before the advent of cars or modern day amenities". There was no mention of weirdos who imagined they were John Wayne waiting for the cavalry to arrive.

Thankfully I was attired in that year's disguise of a long, curly blond wig, flowery blouse (the sort my grandmother favoured and which I would never normally have in my wardrobe), white cut-off trousers and American size sneakers. Dark shades and a baseball cap, this time advertising the Carolina Panthers, a local football team, the American variety of the game which bears no resemblance to the Premier League, completed the outfit. I felt confident that even my own family wouldn't have recognised me but in that situation I knew I couldn't be too careful. They seemed to be taken in by my drawled 'Excuse me,' as I sidestepped off the boardwalk onto the dirt track which in Love Valley passed as the one main road. I wanted to see them, just not up close.

As I was in the area I wondered whether I should finish them off that week. It was all planned. It would save another air fare and hotel costs and had the added bonus of saving me months of worrying that something might go wrong. But the thought of October 15th

stopped me. So infinitely more appropriate. The date wouldn't mean anything to them but it did to me. And I was the one in charge.

Clara was bored. So much was in place that there wasn't much she needed to think about before her October vacation. Everything was ready. The summer trip to NC had been a success and she knew exactly how she would perform the drama: yes, she thought it was a performance, just a shame that any audience would fail to appreciate it.

Asking for unpaid leave she told the head that an elderly aunt, who lived alone in Kent, was recovering from an operation and needed her help. There was absolutely no mention of going abroad.

Her flight was booked for early October, allowing plenty of time to refine any details and have a few mock runs. That idea appealed. She would use her hire car and would be there at the end of several school days, just another mom collecting their offspring after a softball, soccer or basketball practice. Her exact spot was halfway up the school driveway, the position allowing sufficient pathway for enough speed to be gained in order to collide with Stewart and Paul as they exited the building. Sitting, waiting and anticipating the moment of contact would ameliorate her position beside the ridiculous Kindergarten's post box, the one with a squirrel collecting letters instead of nuts.

Once sure that Stewart and Paul kept to their routine Clara would be ready to pounce. Not many predators were as well prepared as she intended to be. If anything changed she would have several days to alter her plans. So many moms collected their kids, both at the end of the day and then later following the variety of games' practices, organised by the parents, that she felt confident one more vehicle would go unnoticed.

Patience had never been her forte. How she envied Penelope, the forbearing wife of the Greek hero Odysseus. Having read all the Greek myths Clara had been most impressed by Penelope who had the virtues of faithfulness and patience. She had waited 20 years for her husband to return: how hard could six weeks be?

Chapter 9

Tomorrow. I'm off tomorrow. How I agree with old William that the petty pace can indeed creep in. The day-to-day has been almost unendurable. Only two months since August but oh how slowly the time has passed. I long to share my plans with someone, but that would be suicidal. No one will ever be persuaded that what I am doing is right. Or that it is really necessary. Come on girl, no guilt, no doubts, no backing out. Too much has been planned. An early night and then Manchester airport.

'A final call for all passengers booked on the British Airways flight to Raleigh. Please now go to gate twenty where final boarding is under way.' Extra leg room made the eight and a quarter hour journey slightly more comfortable and the latest films helped pass the time as did her most recent game: thinking up various euphemisms for the next happening. Upset, bump, calamity, smash and the phrases employed for American car accidents: "fender-bender" and "car-wreck".

As the plane descended Clara was amused to hear that the pilot was trying to sound as southern as possible. She had obviously missed any earlier announcements. 'I sure would like to thank the crew for a great flight. Good job fellas. Hope y'all enjoyed the trip and sorry about the turbulence mid-ocean. Y'all have a great stay in the little old US of A.'

On her initial trip she had surmised that it would be inadvisable to stay too near the planned misfortune and opted to keep to her plan and book into a motel in Wilkesboro about thirty-eight miles from Statesville.

Not having visited the town before she hoped she would blend in as yet another tourist interested in the infamous Tom Dooley story. From the tale told, in graphic detail on the internet, she learnt that the song *Hang Down your Head Tom Dooley,* a hit for The Kingston Trio in the fifties, was based on the trial and execution of the young man Thomas Dula, pronounced Dooley, accused of knifing his sweetheart, Laura Foster, in a vicious attack. His time in custody was spent in the jail in Wilkesboro. Many people thought him innocent as, during his trial in Statesville, he had refused to speak and it was assumed that he was protecting a jealous ex-girlfriend. The nineteenth century courthouse on the outskirts of Wilkesboro was now a museum and the town's main claim to fame.

After a night in the Easy Way Inn and suffering from a slight queasiness, probably a mild form of jetlag, Clara found herself outside the old Courthouse a few blocks from her motel. She needed some time to acclimatise before going into Statesville and decided to act the part of a tourist. How surprised the other visitors, listening to the guide giving the background to the gruesome case, would have been had they known that they had a modern day murderer in their midst. The tour was interesting but added little to what Clara had ascertained from her Google search. The rest of the town held little appeal though she was informed that she was fortunate to be in town for the *Bushy Mountain Apple Festival.*

'It's kinda fun – entry free but any money made on the stalls goes to the local community.' Brandon, the effusive young man in the Tourist Information Centre was enthusiasm personified. 'Hundreds of events: Bluegrass bands, line dancing competitions, Gospel choirs, oh y'all don't want to miss it. It's all day Saturday in the Wells Fargo parking lot.' Ye gods and little fishes thought Clara, using a saying that Henry had loved, a car park named after the Gold Rush's pony-drawn stages and railway. Her motel overlooked the parking lot so she had no excuse for not attending the event. As she walked round the town she saw a bank with the same name and realised that the Wells Fargo legend was still very much alive.

The next day was Saturday: no school, no dummy runs planned and definitely no final deed. There was plenty of time to think about the vital date. October had arrived but not the 15th. That weekend the weather was glorious with perfect blue skies, warm sunshine and a light breeze. Having arrived from a wet and windy England, Clara thought how good it would be to enjoy such lovely autumn weather each year. It must shorten the winter.

The Festival was as expected with grown-up Americans acting and sounding like over excited children. How did they maintain such an overwhelming exuberance and be so enthusiastic about such banal activities? Everyone had dressed like extras in a B movie: checked shirts, coloured shorts, baseball caps, sneakers and white socks. How old were they? Determined not to stand out, Clara was similarly attired. She hadn't dared take a final look in the mirror before leaving her room or she would in all likelihood have remained there.

Few of the entertainments interested Clara and the day passed slowly. By midafternoon she was about to return to her motel when a man asked if she liked line dancing.

'I've never tried it,' was her curt reply, hoping to make him realise she was not seeking company.

'Well ma'am now's the time to break that old habit and join a line.' Without waiting for a reply he grabbed her arm and dragged her onto the stage where the next dance was about to start. Dozens of people formed lines facing the band, no partners needed. 'Next dance is the *Cowboy Boogie,*' the woman announced to rapturous applause. She was wearing an outfit of fringed shirt, Levis, cowboy boots and a hat that had Clara recalling the Wild West films an elderly uncle had adored.

'Wow, great way to start line dancing,' her new friend yelled, his voice blending with the general cacophony, 'this all's one of my favourites. Just follow the calls – or me – whichever all is easier.'

'Vine behind, side hitch' meant absolutely nothing to Clara who tried valiantly and unsuccessfully to follow the movements. The next directions of 'forward, hitch, boogie with the hips, quarter turn and…vine behind…' made her a personification of the phrase "odd one out". The dance went on for what felt like an eternity and by the end of it Clara felt sure that a new species must have evolved somewhere on the planet.

'You're doing just great; next time around y'all will have it.'

'Sorry, got to go, but thanks, it was fun.' The last thing she needed was to be remembered. One dance would hardly form a lasting impression, though she had performed so atrociously that perhaps her new buddy would talk about her and laugh at her ineptness.

Better to depart before any further recollections could be established.

'Well y'all enjoy the rest of the day. Hog roast supper at seven, everyone'll be there.' Not me though, Clara thought. After thanking her partner she walked slowly back to her room.

Fog, dense, I-need-a-guide-dog style fog, enveloped the town the following morning. Religion had never played a part in her life but Clara decided to visit the oldest church in Wilskboro: The Greater Providence Baptist Church. Fortunately she had passed it the previous day and knew it was within walking distance, only a few blocks from her motel. Arriving early she was greeted by an elderly black man, dressed from head to foot in white: suit, tie, shirt, hat, gloves and shoes.

'Thank y'all for coming to worship with us today. You are so welcome. We are all God's children. No strangers here, just friends we haven't yet had the pleasure of being acquainted with.' Although he was elderly, maybe even in his late eighties, his voice was that of a much younger man. He stood erect and shook Clara's hand until it ached. 'Service starts in twenty minutes and you'd best find a seat as we'll be full to overflowing, praise the Lord. Welcome, welcome, you are so welcome.'

Thanking him and taking the proffered hymn book, Clara retreated to a back pew. If she had hoped to blend in she soon found that she was mistaken. Apart from two other people the entire congregation was black. Hundreds filled the interior, all wearing white. The ladies had the most wonderful hats she had ever seen and the children were decked out like imitation adults with their tiny white suits, shoes and gloves.

Feeling decidedly uncomfortable and thinking she had made a grave mistake she wondered how to extricate herself. If she left before the service started that would look unacceptably rude and would definitely make people notice her. There was nothing to do but stay.

Pastor Jeremiah Maddox leapt, gazelle-like, to the front of the church to address his congregation. It was hard to gauge how old he was but Clara had overheard someone saying that in a few months he would be celebrating forty years at the church. She thought he must have been little more than a child when he started. Maybe religion should be advertised as an alternative to anti-wrinkle creams.

'On an unforgettable summer morning in August of 1967 the Good Lord, glory to his name, convinced me of my sin and my need for Him through a Gospel presentation at my daddy's church in Charlotte. I was a child and from that moment became a child of God. Since that day I have known I was saved. I am assured of my salvation. Are you? Are you? Are you?' As he repeated these words he danced around the church, Nureyev in a cassock, pointing at various members of his flock.

Shouts of, 'Yes, glory to God, I am saved,' echoed, filling the air which appeared to have come alive. At one point Clara wondered if she was the only one not entering the realms of the saved. Once he started there was to be no stopping the Pastor and his voice rose with each new pronouncement.

'Like many preachers' kids, I desired to be my own man and anything other than a pastor, but God's call grew louder. So I stand here before you today, certain in my earthly faith and eternal home with God.' His flock were obviously inspired to respond.

'Glory to God. Hallelujah.'

'The Lord is good.'

'Praise be to our eternal Father.'

Clara sat bemused. Only once before had she experienced such undiluted passion and that had been when a former boyfriend had taken her to a pop concert in Manchester. An eruption of sound, an ear-splitting racket, had greeted a local band as they walked confidently on to the stage. Utter fanaticism was to become ever more frantic throughout the thirty appalling minutes the group had been allocated. It was dedication to a cause that was now being replicated.

The Gospel choir that she had seen at the Apple Festival stood to sing. Wearing purple gowns they could have been escapees from a re-make of Queen Latifah's *Joyful Noise*, a film she had watched on her first flight to North Carolina. Their enthusiasm was infectious and the congregation were now on their feet, hands raised to the heavens, literally dancing in the aisles.

After what must qualify as one of the longest songs ever composed the choir resumed their seats to rapturous applause and it was the Pastor's turn again.

'Can you hear me now?' This was greeted by a roar of laughter and Clara recognised the catchphrase used by a cell phone company. The adverts for the latest mobile were on the television at least three times an hour, each one employing that phrase to show what outstanding connections the phone gave.

'Can you hear me now? That is what God is saying to each and every one of us all the time. Sometimes we don't hear Him. Sometimes we hear and forget. Sometimes we hear and take notice. He sent His only son, our Lord Jesus Christ, to talk to us and still we don't always hear.' His voice was an operatic crescendo. Puccini would definitely have hired him.

As the pastor shouted his finale, going into great detail about Jesus hanging on the Cross and asking God to forgive His persecutors, he produced a dramatic pause then repeated the title of his address, 'God is saying, "Can you hear me now?"' The entire congregation rose and the building reverberated to the sound of the exuberant worshippers.

Clara sat; her mind a maelstrom of emotions. Was some deity, some ultimate being trying to talk to her? Had he led her here today?

At the front of the building, behind the choir who sat engrossed by every word their leader uttered, the Ten Commandments were highlighted in all their law-giving glory. Clara knew the one that was universally acknowledged to be the supreme one. The one she had broken. Should she abort her plans? No more killings. No gentler word substituted today. If she went to see Pastor Jeremiah after the service, confessed everything, begged for forgiveness, would her deeds be erased by a divine rubber?

The service continued: more contributions from the choir, more rhetoric from Jeremiah, more adherents voicing their devotion to God. Towards the end of the morning members of the congregation were encouraged to go forward, confess their sins and pledge themselves to follow Jesus and listen to God's word. Many did.

At the end of the service the final words added to Clara's disquiet. 'I know that deep inside every heart is the awareness that he or she is a sinner. We do not enjoy admitting it. "Sin" is not a popular word. In fact it's offensive to many – but I still believe we all instinctively know that Romans 3:23 is as pertinent today as when it was written. It applies to each and every one of us when it declares that *"ALL have sinned and fallen short of the glory of God"*. We are fallen and falling sinners who sin in thought, word and deed. Listen to God. He is talking to you. Follow the teachings of his Son. He spoke to us all.'

Chapter 10

To think I almost chickened out! Unbelievable (pardon the pun) that I was influenced by such speechifying. He had me going for a while, almost made me a believer. What arrant nonsense. Tub-thumping pomposity: there's no old man in the sky keeping an account of my misdemeanours.

Group dynamics played their part and it would have been so simple to go with the herd. However, I retained my station in life as a goat rather than a sheep (yes, Matthew Chapter 25, another passage I learnt in my Church of England primary school).

Almost as soon as I stepped outside into the normal world all my worries and doubts evaporated and I had my self-confidence back. It was like regaining control of the steering wheel after skidding on a patch of ice. I had come too far to back out now. It was still two down five to go.

Following the two hour service, a hundred and twenty minutes aimed at making one feel bad, Clara resumed her role as a tourist, a pleasant pastime and one that made her think she might return one day and make visits to some of the other attractions available in the Carolinas. But there was work to do.

For several days she sat and watched as Stewart and Paul left school. She was delighted to see that they were still heavily involved in their various sporting activities and didn't go home until almost five o' clock on Tuesdays, Thursdays and Fridays. October 15th was a Thursday. So sad they wouldn't be attending the Friday practice.

As hoped, she appeared to draw no attention to herself. So many cars arrived to collect the children that one more passed unnoticed. Her hire car was a wine coloured Chevrolet Aveo. It was, as almost all American cars are, automatic and a lovely model to drive. For the big day though a new vehicle would be required, one "appropriated" for the afternoon.

The Wells Fargo car park was always full during the day. Office workers used it as did shoppers visiting the town. The main attraction appeared to be the book shop situated in the middle of the town's one shopping street, the amusingly named Downtown Boulevard. As far as she could tell there was no uptown. Clara had been to the "Wilksboro Wonderland of Words" to enjoy its coffee and cake temptations. Sitting on a large chair, hidden behind a book, she hoped she had remained incognito. Little else would attract visitors to the town: two banks, a café that boasted "The Best Home Cooking in North Carolina" and an outdated dress shop were the sum total of the rest of the street.

Clara didn't want to take the new car too soon in case the owner returned early and reported it missing. She had seen the one she wanted. A silver Kia Rio parked each morning at eight and collected at six. With luck she could take it, use it and return it before the owner had even noticed it was gone. This was the chosen car. She had seen the well-dressed driver leave the keys under the sunvisor, making it easy for his wife to use the car at lunchtimes. It was invariably returned to the same parking spot by early afternoon.

October 15th. Despite a disturbed night Clara woke to a feeling of excitement rather than fear. Planning was all and although the most careful arrangements could go wrong she felt confident that nothing would. As she opened her curtains her one worry was that the state's notorious autumnal fog had arrived.

'We sure do get some murkiness at this time of year: none in any month but October. Don't rightly know why but they are beauties when they come,' Shelley, the server that morning, sounded inappropriately proud of her town's weather.

'Will it last long?' Clara asked trying to sound unconcerned.

'Don't rightly know, can come down and stay for days.' Shelley was still happy to spread gloom as thick as the weather.

'Usually it's over by noon when the sun burns it off,' the old lady on the next table entered the conversation. 'I come here every year about this time to visit my husband's grave and it's the same-old, same-old: fog till midday then back to good old North Carolina sunshine.'

'Same-old, same-old?' Clara asked, having not heard that particular Americanism before.

'Guess it's not great English,' chuckled the elderly lady, 'but it sure sums up a situation that doesn't believe in changing.'

The elderly guest's prediction was accurate and by one o'clock normal service was resumed. By now a tsunami of nerves had inundated her, making the long wait for the fog to clear almost unendurable. An accident in the mist outside the school might look like a misfortune but driving there would have been tricky.

It was a country road full of twists and turns with steep banks at the sides. Animals roamed freely and crossed the road without warning. Only that week the local paper had reported a serious accident involving a huge deer and a four by four which had been forced off the road, injuring both passengers.

Sitting in her room, mesmerised by the car park, Clara knew this was not the way most tourists would choose to pass the time, even in such adverse weather. Her chosen weapon had arrived as usual on the dot of eight o'clock. Big Ben would have been impressed by such meticulous timekeeping. That day the woman didn't appear to take and return the car. Perhaps she had been too upset by the fog. As the landscape escaped from its confusion the edge of the car park came into view. All would be well, the roads could be seen.

Fortunately the car was unlocked and the key in its usual place. Setting off, in the glorious afternoon sunshine predicted at breakfast, Clara was jittery, a feeling she had not anticipated. Last time it had gone smoothly, like an airbrushed photo: no blemishes. Reassurance was needed but only the voice in her head, normally so reassuring, could provide it and for a time it remained mute. "What ifs" rock-and-rolled making her brain ache; she had not suffered such doubts in Seahouses. Why should this afternoon be any different? Should something go wrong there was always tomorrow but that would mean the 16th so, although not impossible, it would be extremely disappointing – it had to be the 15th.

On approaching the school Clara realised she was earlier than anticipated. Was the plan starting to unravel, a thread that once pulled undoes an entire hem? Turning down a road on the right she got out for a short walk. Calming down, she knew she was too near to her next triumph to stop now.

Chapter 11

Great to be home. Good journey though I am not sure what time of day it is. Boring jetlag: though it's a small price to pay for such total success.

I am becoming an expert: plan which car to take; wear a disguise (young male); drive to the destination; wait patiently (without doubt the hardest part) and then goodbye father and son.

Unfortunately there were more witnesses than I wanted. Usually my duo was amongst the last to leave the school, the pathway and car park almost deserted. However, on the 15th they appeared much earlier and were in the middle of a large group of sweaty youngsters. For a moment I thought it would be impossible to strike them without hitting others and I had no inclination to hurt anyone else. But then, joy of joys, they separated from the melee and walked towards their car.

Accelerate. Aim. Hit. They went down like the last two skittles left standing at the end of the bowling lane. Unfortunately there was no chance of a second hit. I was almost sure that one had sufficed but twice would have made absolutely certain.

As I drove away I could hear people screaming and was aware of several parents running towards the stricken pair. Not slowing down I was soon back on the highway where I resumed a more reasonable speed.

No point attracting the attention of the local sheriff though the only police car I saw was more interested in getting to the school than in anyone exceeding the speed limit.

Car returned, albeit with unfortunate dents and some areas of blood and goodness knows what else splattered on the front.

Yes, that was identified as the vehicle involved in the accident.

Yes, the accident was reported as deliberate.

Yes, the witnesses said that the driver left the scene without stopping.

Yes, it was on the local channel that night and made the headlines in the paper the following day.

However, all is well. I am back in England without anyone suspecting me, the English tourist. Like everyone staying in the motel I was asked, in a very brief and apologetic interview ("Don't want to spoil your vacation, ma'am") if I had seen the relevant car being taken or returned. I assured them that I had seen nothing and after recording my answer they moved on to the next guest.

Her last days in North Carolina had proved entertaining. 'Did y'all see the tragedy at the Martin Luther King School yesterday? A dad and his kid knocked over and killed outside the building. He was a teacher at the school and his son was in the top class. Folks are saying it was deliberate, the driver drove straight at them and didn't stop.' This morning's server, an earnest young man called Harvey, was even more garrulous than Shelley and there was to be no stopping him. 'Sheriff Cody told my mom that the car was taken from the car park right by us, you know the one we can see from the bedrooms, and returned with guts and entrails all over the front. Everyone's talking about it but nobody rightly knows why someone would kill a father and son. Maybe they were targeted by some hoodlums. Guess the FBI will soon be here.'

Thinking that last statement was highly unlikely Clara made some appropriate noises, thanked Harvey and left the breakfast room. The papers had arrived and all three had the previous day's event as their headline. Taking them up to her room she was able to enjoy their speculations. Fortunately all the eyewitnesses agreed that the car was driven by a male.

'He was either late teens or early twenties. Drove like a maniac and seemed to go directly at Stewart and Paul. They didn't stand a chance.'

'We couldn't believe what we were seeing. No one could stop him. Oh, it was awful.'

'A young man, maybe mid-twenties was driving the car. He was totally out of control. Poor Stewart – he was a lovely man and a great teacher.'

'Everyone loved Paul, a polite, caring youngster. He was my son's best friend.'

The head teacher spoke of the school's loss. 'We are today without one of the best, most professional teachers it has been my privilege to work with. He cared deeply about education and will be sorely missed. His son, Paul, was a fine young man with a love of learning and sport and his whole life ahead of him. Our thoughts and sympathies go to Stewart's parents who came from England to live with their son and grandson.'

Reading the next paragraph Clara felt an overwhelming exhilaration. A second police officer, a deputy sheriff, had been called in from Statesville. They were obviously taking it seriously. He was most concerned that the accident appeared to have been deliberate. Really? When he spoke to the press he stated that hit-and-runs, whilst not unknown, were thankfully extremely rare in Iredell County, one of the areas with the lowest crime rate in the Carolinas. Oh well, Clara thought, at least she had raised their profile and given them something to do.

'If it was deliberate no one has yet come up with any reason to target such a well-respected family. Naturally the school and community are shocked. Our thoughts go to the relatives at this unhappy time.' Anyone with any information was asked to contact the Sheriff's office in Statesville.

The absence of a mother wasn't mentioned. Not yet.

All three newspapers were packed at the bottom of her suitcase. Had she been asked she would have said she wanted them for their coverage of the Apple Festival, that her friends back home would be interested to see how she had spent her time in North Carolina.

'Hope you had a good time staying with us and that everything was to your satisfaction,' the earnest young man drawled as Clara paid her hotel bill in cash.

'Yes, it's all been just as expected,' Clara replied, not wanting to say anything memorable.

Basking in a job well done, she was keen to enjoy the final two days of her holiday. Wanting to avoid the locals, who seemed to have only one topic of conversation, she drove up to the Blue Ridge Mountains, a drive of a little over two hours through glorious scenery and on almost deserted roads. The mountains were aptly named as they appeared to be iced with a dusting of pale blue. Having purchased the latest edition of the prosaically named *Walking and Driving the Blue Ridge* she set off. The trail she had chosen was very clearly marked and Clara found herself skipping for joy, kicking at fallen leaves and whooping loudly – a child again, one whose longed-for birthday gift has just been unwrapped. As she set off she tried to ignore the notices giving advice on what to do if one met a bear. Run like hell she thought.

Having loved the day, Clara booked herself into the Blue Ridge Number One Motel for the night. No point spending too much time back in Wilksboro, of giving anyone the opportunity to recognise her. On her last day she decided to drive part of the Blue Ridge Parkway described in her guide book as "America's most visited National Park and world-renowned as America's favourite drive." She knew she would manage only a few of its four hundred and sixty miles but looked forward to the promised "stunning views of the Blue Ridge mountains, forests, and pastoral landscapes". She was not disappointed and the fall colours were stunning. She vowed to return to this beautiful part of America. Next time merely on holiday!

Part 3: Matthew and Natasha

Chapter 1

Hubris. Am I too confident? Am I over estimating my ability? At school they sing a hymn called "Don't Build Your House on the Sandy Land" and I wonder if my deeds are like that: without secure foundations.

Two weeks after returning home Clara visited her sister, the pretext being to see her new house. The visit proved useful as it reassured Clara that being a murderer remained essential. Things (the usual) were discussed and, as on every other occasion, Sophie was unwilling to budge, to meet her sister anywhere near any halfway line. No team work for her, just a self-absorbed solo effort aimed at snubbing Clara at every juncture.

That day she might as well have signed her own death warrant. It was definitely four down, three to go.

Sophie's house was superb: huge, tastefully decorated and in an elite area of Cheshire, the locality chosen by many of the multi-millionaire footballers who played for the Manchester clubs. It had been purchased recently following yet another failed relationship.

If Sophie was surprised to see Clara she showed few signs, just the raising of immaculately plucked eyebrows and a curt, 'Well, well, the prodigal sister.'

'Yes, good to see you too,' Clara responded, 'thought we ought to keep in touch, we are the only family we've got.'

'Family? You've never exactly been one to want to be part of a family. I seem to remember it was you that walked off, Clint Eastwood style, disappearing into the sunset as soon as dad died.'

'And we both know why that was,' Clara spat, unable to hide her loathing for the sister whom she believed had ruined her life.

Determined to continue the uncomfortable conversation she murmured, 'How's business? Any new stores ready to open?' Asking such questions was to gouge deeply into Clara's wounds, far worse than the self-inflicted cuts of her teenage years. However, she knew it was the way to get Sophie talking. After half an hour of listening to how brilliantly the Bedford stores were doing Clara said she needed to go to the bathroom. It took ten seconds to return the objects she had borrowed. She must ask for spare keys to the new mansion: access essential.

Chapter 2

I hate her. I loathe her with every cell in my body. A repulsive, selfish, self-centred, greedy…it's really fine to feel such venom as it allows me to continue with the next "drive-through". That is my latest classification and one that particularly amuses me. I'm reading a wonderful biography of Queen Elizabeth the First by Roger Smith, an author new to me. Maybe I should start writing Sophie's. I know the ending!

Two more to dispatch before I consider exactly what to do with her: Matthew and Natasha. Thankfully back to English soil, no more transatlantic trips.

Matthew Lloyd had always found fulfilment in his job, but had never felt comfortable with this aspect of it. Emily Witherspoon had been his patient for twelve years and over time they had developed a mutual respect. She had taken the news with her usual stoicism.

She was, as always, smartly dressed. Today's outfit of a navy suit and pale lemon blouse was one that Matthew hadn't seen before. He knew she loved clothes and she had once said that updating her wardrobe would continue for as long as possible. White hair framed a face now ravaged by illness and she looked every one of her eighty-nine years.

Totally in character, she was now attempting to comfort him and he knew that she would face her final moments with the same fortitude with which she had endured the previous twenty-four months.

'Doctor Lloyd, we both knew this moment would arrive. You have done everything possible to help me fight this awful illness. I have had more years than either of us expected and for that I thank you. We both know I have just failed my final MOT!'

Feeling his eyes moisten he began the speech he used on such occasions, the one he never got used to delivering. The Hippocratic Oath where he promised to "use treatments for the benefits of the ill" no longer seemed to apply and in Emily's case he felt a deep sadness. At such times he invariably felt a sense of failure as he had to admit that the situation was beyond his control.

'Palliative care is excellent these days…' He got no further as Emily interrupted him.

'I know you will continue to do your very best for me but I am ready to go. Don't let's pretend we can delay the inevitable. I no longer have the desire to prolong my time here. I am an old lady and have had a good life. Let's face it I'm well past my sell-by date.' This last remark was made with her usual dry humour and Matthew decided to change the direction of the conversation, though only he was finding it uncomfortable.

'Tell me Emily,' always her Christian name whilst she insisted on using his professional one, being of the generation where such niceties remained important, 'do you believe in an afterlife?'

'No. Not at all. I have never been religious and see no need to change my mind now. I have no hope of eternal life nor do I fear a Day of Judgement. I have enjoyed a long, perhaps too long, existence and have, for the most part, been able to appreciate my time on earth. Although I never married or had children, my working life brought great happiness and was sufficiently well remunerated to allow me to indulge my passion for travel. I go with few regrets and many wonderful memories. My one lifelong regret is that I never really knew my mother. She died very suddenly, a totally unexpected heart attack, when I was five. My father was a strong character and brought me up without any help as there wasn't much available in those days. At the end of his life I was able to tell him how grateful I was for all that he had done for me.'

This was the first time that Emily had spoken of her childhood and Matthew was touched by such a personal detail. 'How good to hear you say that. I hope that one day my daughter will feel the same way. I have a lot of help but it's still not easy being a single father.'

'My dear Doctor Lloyd, she will be grateful. I know she will appreciate you. Any daughter, brought up by a father on his own, will as an adult realise all that has been done for her.'

Following a short silence she continued, 'Once again I thank you for all you have done for me. I know you have, both professionally and personally, done more than would normally be expected.'

After spending time organising palliative care at home, 'No hospital or hospice, thank you,' Emily left, maintaining the fortitude she had displayed throughout her extended and cruel illness. There was no doubt that Matthew was the more upset of the two.

Alone in his room Matthew considered Emily's remark about his daughter. Natasha was four and he had had sole custody of her for over two years. Others had suggested that he look for a new mother for her but he knew he would never be able to trust another woman. If he was truthful he didn't want anyone else and still thought he was a bit in love with her: the absentee mum.

Meeting Natasha's mother had been one of life's ultimate moments – the kind that occur so infrequently as to be almost non-existent. Had he known at the start how it would end would he have contacted her, rung the number on the business card she had thrust into his hand that first day? Probably. Yes, very probably, as the time they had together had been like no other and he had Natasha, the most important part of his life.

With an almost physical pain he recalled seeing Natasha's mother on Market Street a few weeks ago. His daughter had been with him. They were on their way to a matinee of *The Wizard of Oz* at the Palace Theatre and after laughing at one of his daughters silly jokes he had glanced up to see her mother approaching. She merely nodded to indicate she had seen him but didn't lower her eyes to look at Natasha. Matthew was aware that she had remained in the area but this was the only time their paths had crossed since she had left them.

Was it fate, the impersonal variety, or serendipity, sometimes so unspeakably cruel that prompted their first meeting? Perhaps the gods were playing one of their games, the sort they enjoy but which exhibit no sign of caring about the human consequences. The venue had been prosaic: an escalator in Lewis's department store on Deansgate – a stumble – a steadying hand.

'How gallant. May I repay you with a cup of coffee?'

Matthew was smitten. Had the gods indeed inaugurated the meeting how amusing they must have found it.

He admitted that he was tempted but said that he was already on the last minute for his afternoon surgery. Totally flustered he became garrulous, words spilling from his mouth and without the guidance of a thesaurus he was losing his way.

'I'm normally on time, indeed punctuality is very important to me, and I always feel it is disrespectful to keep patients waiting, but I have been to order my Morning Suit. I'm getting married next month and thought I'd better set the ball rolling.' Matthew never used idioms, deeming them lazy, but words were spilling out of control from his mouth, like small stones dispatched from a child's catapult.

The woman smiled, handed him her card and asked him to call. She added that she would be very happy to take him and his fiancée out to dinner, 'It's the least I can do to thank you for preventing a broken arm.' Two days later he made the call. Gillian, his fiancé, was already history.

Chapter 3

Planning stalled. Far harder than anticipated. Major problem – all too close to home. Travelling further afield has regained some of its appeal. Still, there's plenty of time. Next October is almost ten months off.

'Good afternoon,' the southern drawl woke Clive who had been dozing on the settee, his entire day off wasted. Heavy rain and gale-force winds had made him change his mind about a walk. Lacking the motivation to do anything else, the day had slipped by with little to show for it. Mari was out at a practice with the *Seahouse Singers* who were in the final throes of their latest production: *Grease*, the more mature members of the cast finding the dance scenes challenging. Clive was tired but knew he had been idle; there were plenty of jobs around the house that needed to be finished. One of the few things that caused regular arguments was Clive's habit of beginning a project and not seeing it through. The bathroom was half tiled and the units in the study were waiting for their top coat of paint.

'Good job you're not like this at work or the crimes would remain undetected,' was an oft-repeated phrase and one he had to acknowledge was true. The trouble was that DIY bored him and police work didn't.

The phone call was definitely the latter and demanded his full attention. 'Hi Dwayne, it's a bit later than afternoon here but great to hear from you.' For the next few minutes pleasantries were exchanged, both ascertaining that families were well and work as stressful as ever.

'Well here's the thing, my main reason for calling. We've had a development at our end. A new eyewitness has come forward. The lady says she saw the whole thing.' Each sentence was separated by a dramatic pause.

Clive felt the almost overwhelming feeling of excitement that hit him, like a boxer's right hook, each time there was a break-through in a case. He leapt to his feet, almost knocking over the vase of flowers that sat on the coffee table and paced the room, the mobile held so close to his ear that it hurt.

'A new eyewitness,' he yelled, merely repeating his friend's announcement, 'why so long after the event?'

'That's a good question and there doesn't seem to be a satisfactory answer apart from the definite fact that she's a bit of an oddball, a herky-jerky, a few chocolate drops short of a cookie.' Clive laughed at Dwayne's description then stayed silent as his friend added, 'Says she was there but was too scared to come forward as she had no legit reason to be outside a school watching the kids come out.'

'A paedophile? Interested in children?'

'Hell, no, nothing like that. She goes after work and on her days off because she likes to watch the kids but I'd put my life on there being nothing suspicious. She says she sits in her car and imagines that one of them might be her son. A sad individual – but I guess there's no harm in her.'

'Interesting, but no record of interfering?'

'Absolutely not and if you met her I think you'd agree she's one of life's innocents. Works at the Bi-Lo store, the one in the mall on the edge of town, mostly fills shelves or helps out on the tills when they're busy.'

'Think I've got the picture. What did she have to add to the equation?'

'If you're asking what she said…listen up. She is adamant, bet you're thinking I had to look that word up in the dictionary, that the driver was a woman and that she'd been there at least twice before, sitting on the school drive and watching as the kids came out. The first few times the car she was in was red but on the day of the accident the woman was driving a silver model, which matches the car identified at the time…'

Feeling this was the breakthrough they needed, Clive interrupted, 'She is definite that the driver was a woman?'

'Hold onto those reins, I'm getting there.'

'Sorry Dwayne but this just feels so important.'

'Sure thing, but if you'll just listen up her info makes it a slam-dunk. This was no accident. I know we've always suspected as much but this makes it certain. It was premeditated cold-blooded murder. The car was in exactly the same place on at least three previous occasions, parked by the mailbox on the school drive in a perfect position to watch the kids exit the building. Gloria, our loopy eyewitness, says she thought it strange that the lady didn't collect a kid at the end of the school day. Instead she remained there for an hour and watched the ones who had been to an after-school activity.'

'Doesn't she look a bit odd herself, sitting and watching?'

'No, she says her routine is to park her car a little away from the building and use the walking track in the school grounds. It's open to the public once school is out and is always busy. From it you get a good view of the front of the school, the path where the cars park and the main exit.'

'All the other witnesses have spoken of a male driver. Why is she so sure the driver was female?'

'She says that she saw the driver get out of her car to stretch her legs on the day before the accident, just for a minute but long enough to observe her. Above average height and slim – and yes she agreed that could describe a lot of men – but she said it was the mannerisms and walking style that were definitely feminine. She's a God-fearing woman and assured me she would swear on the Bible that the driver was a lady.'

'This changes everything; both cases need to be re-examined.' Clive was eager to discuss the new information but let Dwayne continue.

'Gloria is the only one who saw the whole thing. Her story is rather gruesome but it's all relevant and should be helpful. She said that on the day of the accident as the first of the children who'd been at the softball practice started to leave, the driver of the silver car switched on her engine.' Dwayne paused dramatically, 'Then when Stewart and Paul appeared and walked towards their car she accelerated and aimed straight at them. No doubt at all she meant to hit them. Having succeeded she turned round then drove out of the grounds and back onto the highway heading in the direction of Wilksboro.'

Almost too excited to speak Clive stood clutching the phone, his lifeline to the truth. As he paced the room Dwayne had to confirm that he was still there.

Forcing himself to take deep breaths Clive calmed down and responded. 'This feels as though it changes everything. Would your lady agree to be interviewed by me? You say she's a bit unusual but I'm used to vulnerable witnesses and if I brought my list of questions we could go over them together before I spoke to her.'

'Think it's necessary to come? If you send me the inventory I could re-interview her, though I don't rightly know what more she might add.'

'Agreed, but you and I both know that witnesses can remember the most helpful details when given the right encouragement. Believe me, I know that you are more than capable of conducting the follow-up questioning but I would like to meet her and get an idea for myself of how important this is: whether this really is the breakthrough we've been waiting for.'

'This time we'd have to go to her home, she gets kind of fidgety in the police station but I know she's keen to cooperate and I can set up a meeting if you let me know a date.'

Thanks Dwayne. Would she be spooked if it was the two of us asking her what she remembers?'

'I can ask her. Two heads are better than one: even if one's English!'

Due time off Clive didn't see a problem with another trip to North Carolina. He would request a week's leave without giving any reason for his sudden, and unusual, desire for a break. His main problem was Mari. Could he sell it to her if he asked her to accompany him? It was the school's Christmas holiday soon and he could wait until then if she agreed to travel with him. They could have some time in Statesville (sunny most days even at this time of the year) followed by a trip some-where in the States that his wife wanted to visit. He might entice her and so far they had no plans for Christmas. Mari was often too exhausted at the end of the long term to want to do much. However, a couple of weeks doing something entirely different might appeal.

Chapter 4

Overexcited children, stressed staff, a site supervisor who complains about the minutest speck of glitter on the carpet despite the fact I spent half an hour vacuuming after we made the Christmas cards this afternoon. This is not my favourite time of the school year. I don't "do" the festive season and am always relieved when January arrives. I am now working almost full time with Katie Furness. How does she maintain her enthusiasm? We make a fantastic team in Year 5 and I do things in the classroom before being asked. She says I can read her mind. Thank goodness she can't read mine!

Mrs Lamont, the Head, in her infinite wisdom – she truly believes that only those in charge have the unlimited variety – has decreed that the entire school is to take part in a Christmas production entitled "Jesus Christ Superbabe". Yes, like the famous West End show but concentrating on the events of the Nativity: angels, shepherds, stable, an innkeeper, kings, a donkey – an inspired piece of casting to give that part to Ethel, the girl hardly has to act – and of course Mary, Joseph and the baby.

In its entirety the school consists of two hundred and ninety-one children. It was two hundred and ninety-two until Alfie left. He was a cute and extremely likeable Year One but had the unfortunate penchant of leaving highly prominent teeth marks on the other children. His mother decided that he needed a fresh start, stating that he was so sensitive that he was getting bad vibes in the classroom. We all agreed that she was the one suffering from adverse comments and slanderous gossip in the playground. She must have been aware of the looks and discussions that certain parents revel in at the beginning and end of each day. However, Julie's mum did have a point as no parent likes to see an entire set of nasher marks on the left ear of their offspring when they arrive to collect them at quarter past three.

As per usual in these situations children make up faster than the speed of light and by the start of the afternoon Alfie and Julie had been sitting side by side quite happily on the carpet during the Literacy introduction. Honestly the kids cope but the mothers... well, I digress.

I am really looking forward to the hols. I will have uninterrupted time to begin thinking about the next event. Have rather let it all slide. The trouble with working in a school is that it tends to occupy one's every waking thought and being with young people during the day isn't conducive to planning a child's murder in the evening, though Bobby wound me up so much yesterday that I could cheerfully have strangled him by the Rivers and Mountains display! I know he's got problems but he certainly knows which of my buttons to push.

Six days to the extravaganza. If I survive that, the Carol Concert and the raucous parties I will make myself do some organising. A visit to the next duo's part of Manchester should be my starting point.

Clive travelled to North Carolina alone, Mari letting him know, in great, and at times extremely loud detail, why a last minute excursion across the Atlantic in December was not her idea of a good way to spend the Christmas vacation: bad weather for travelling; expensive last minute flights; what she would do whilst he was "dealing with that dratted case"; and not being here to spend time with her family.

'Mum and Dad, my sister and family will expect to see us at some point. I know we sometimes spend Christmas Day at home but my parents aren't getting any younger and we really ought to make the effort to go to see them. Dave and Chloe have invited us to their New Year's Eve party and I would like to go to that.' Promising to be home as soon as possible Clive left without his wife's approval.

Dwayne was ready. Reports of the incident littered his desk, witness statements were to hand and most importantly the new evidence was set out in duplicate.

'Gloria says we can see her this afternoon, she gets off work at three.'

'Better compile our list of questions so we're fully prepared. We don't want to leave room for error or miss anything and we've only got this one chance as I'm not here for many days.' Clive was determined to concentrate but was feeling the effects of the long flight which had indeed, as Mari had forecast, been delayed: due to fog in Newcastle and then unexpected snow in Greensboro, the only airport with tickets available at such short notice. The two men sat and discussed the best way to proceed.

'As I said she is a bit of a fruit cake so we'll have to keep the questions simple. Probably best if I do most of the talking and you can chip in as and when. Just hope she understands your British accent.'

'You can translate where needed,' Clive muttered, thinking that this was going to more difficult than anticipated. Interviewing a nutter – and one who didn't even know what he was asking.

Gwyneth Gloria Dolman lived in a ground floor apartment in the centre of Statesville. Three cats and a large hound of indeterminate breed filled the small flat, which was overheated and stuffy. When she answered the door Clive did a double take. The young woman standing in front of him was far more attractive than he had anticipated. Dwayne had not done her justice. He knew she was in her mid-twenties but she looked years younger and far more normal than he had expected. She was tall and slim and her long blonde hair shrieked "straighteners".

'Thanks for agreeing to see us, Gloria, we'll try not to take too much of your time.' Dwayne was at his most charming, Rhett Butler reincarnated. 'Shall we introduce ourselves?'

The men gave their names, ranks and the reason for their visit. Gloria, looking slightly uncomfortable, launched in, speaking so quickly (no Southern drawl for her) that Clive had to concentrate to understand what she was saying. 'My name is Gwyneth Gloria Dolman. I used to be known as Gwyneth until that actress made such a fool of herself at the Oscars that I got a lot of teasing and decided to use my middle name which I've always preferred. People say that I look like her, that other Gwyneth.' Staring straight ahead she continued, her speed of delivery not aiding Clive. 'Which name do you two think is better: Gloria or Gwyneth?'

Giving tactful answers the duo hoped that they could begin to discuss the purpose of their visit.

'Gloria, do you remember coming to the police department to tell me what you saw the day the father and son were knocked down outside Martin Luther King Elementary?'

Looking frightened, their witness said that she hadn't liked going to the police department because the room where she gave her statement was too bleak and it had made her think of all the bad people who had sat there before her. 'I feel happier at home.'

Clive nodded and agreed that police stations were uncomfortable for a lot of people, especially those who had done nothing wrong.

Jumping to her feet Gloria asked, 'Do you want to see my baby's room?' Knowing that she wasn't ready to answer their questions the men agreed that they would love to see whatever she wanted to show them.

A large cot, covered in a beautiful pale blue quilt, dominated the small nursery. Several mobiles hung from the ceiling and clothes, for every age of child, from baby to toddler to school age, hung from the fancy cornice that enhanced all four walls. In one corner of the room there were several containers overflowing with toys, again for every age of child.

'This is his room. I've always had everything he needs. He'll use it one day soon. It's all ready, just waiting for him.' Her voice had slowed down and each sentence represented a chapter of her story, one that almost certainly had no "happy ever after" ending. Clive thought it was one of the most heart-wrenching situations that he had ever witnessed.

Dwayne had filled him in on the background to the fantasy: Gloria's pregnancy aged fifteen and her parents taking control of the unacceptable situation. They were God-fearing Baptists for whom a baby out of wedlock was a sin and the baby had been given up for adoption. Gloria had then slumped into an illusory world resulting in periods spent in a mental institution. Fortunately things had improved and her recent attempts to live independently and work in the community appeared to be reasonably successful.

'I go to the school to watch the kids. I'm sure one of them is him. I just have to work out which one then ask him to come home.'

'And that's why you were there on October 15th isn't it?' Dwayne's voice had taken on an empathy that surprised his colleague. 'And you saw the whole incident, didn't you?'

During the next hour Gloria went over the days leading up to the hit-and-run: how she walked the track every day to keep herself fit for when she became his mother; watched as the children left school; and spotted the new car. She arrived finally at the event itself. 'She, I know it was she, was sitting in her car for at least three days before the afternoon she drove at them. I noticed it because it was a car I hadn't seen before and I know all the others as they're there every day.'

Losing patience, and desperate to get to the heart of the interview, Clive interrupted. 'Two things Gloria: first I think you told Dwayne that it was a woman in the car. Can you tell me what makes you think that? And what makes you so certain that the accident was in fact deliberate?' Realising he had been rather abrupt he added, 'Take your time, this is really important and we can't tell you how much we appreciate your help.'

Gloria had been upset by Clive's questioning which had been clumsy and off-putting and for several minutes the room resonated with emptiness – a vacuum which made further progress appear impossible. Neither policeman wanted to break the silence. They waited: one patiently, one fidgeting, desperate for their witness to speak.

After allowing time for Gloria to regain some composure, Dwayne was the one who broke the silence, 'It's alright Gloria, nothing you say will get you into trouble, we would just like you to repeat what you told me last time about the driver.'

The black and white cat jumped onto her knee and as she started to stroke it her voice became calm and a quiet monologue began which the men had to strain to hear.

'I watched the car for two days. I could see it easily when I passed it at the end of the walking track. Then on the third day she got out. I was surprised, really surprised, to realise that it was a woman as I had thought the driver was a dad. Some dads do come to collect their kids. She was dressed like a man but wasn't a man's size. The thing was...she took off her cap...it was a warm day... and her wig moved... then fell off... and I could see she had short blonde hair. The woman ran her hands through her own hair as though it was a relief to have it free, then she replaced the wig and the cap. Why would anyone wear a wig and try to look like a man outside a school?'

This was new evidence, the cap and wig not having been mentioned in the original statement and both policemen felt a fissure of excitement. Both remembered that forensics had found a hair from a wig in the car that had mown down the Nightingales in Seahouses.

'Close your eyes Gloria and imagine you're back there that day. Is there anything else you can see?'

Doing as she had been asked Gloria sat for a minute then added, 'She saw me looking and almost jumped out of her skin, like the rabbits sitting in the field my daddy used to shoot for the pot. I walked on and didn't look back. By the time I went round the track again she had gone. But she was back the next day, the day of the accident.' Loud sobs emanated from their witness, making the cat jump down, an affronted look on its face. The men knew a break was needed.

'Is it O.K. if I make us some coffee? I'll find everything in the kitchen.' Dwayne walked to the door followed by three hopeful cats.

Attempting to lighten the situation, Clive spent the next five minutes (three hundred seconds which seemed infinitely longer) engaging the distressed woman in small talk about her menagerie.

Coffee, cookies and small talk all occupied a frustratingly long time. Eventually Dwayne manoeuvred the conversation back to the day of the hit-and-run, with all the skill of a top politician in full control of the agenda. 'You are being so helpful; we can't thank you enough. Just before we go and leave you with your friends would it be possible for you to tell us what you remember about the actual event, the terrible moment when the car hit them?' He had deliberately made the question as long as possible to give Gloria time to think. 'Would it help if you shut your eyes again? Try to return to where you were as the last of the kids exited the school after the softball practice.'

Her voice became robotic and as she spoke each word seemed to be louder, as though a hidden volume control button was being turned up. 'The kids are coming out. They are running to their cars. Where do they get the energy after so much exercise? Almost the last to leave...it's a man and a boy. I know the man is a teacher at the school and I've seen the boy before but don't know him. It's a different car parked by the mailbox today but when I walked past earlier I saw that it was the same driver, the one pretending to be a man. Oh God, the car is driving at them…so fast…it's going to hit them.'

A long silence. The large ginger tom, asleep by the electric fire which was adding to the almost unbearable stuffiness, stirred and meowed, then sank back, fast asleep. The tension in the room was palpable.

'It's alright, Gloria, you're perfectly safe. Can you tell us what is happening now?' Just when it seemed that there was to be no further information Gloria whispered, 'She is driving straight at them. She means to hurt them. The sound is horrid. Oh no, no, no, they're on the ground, blood everywhere. She must have known she hit them but she's just driven off, so fast, it's all so fast.' Opening her eyes she shrieked, 'There was nothing I could do. She killed them. A mom rang for the police. Nothing I could do.' As Gloria stopped talking tears coursed down her face and she mimed the person using her mobile.

After spending some time calming her they thanked her for the information. Reassuring her that her statements were more important than she realised the two men took their leave and returned to Dwayne's office. Both were satisfied that they had enough new evidence to reopen both investigations, though Clive knew the one in Seahouses would prove far more difficult to resurrect.

Chapter 5

*Don't panic. No new evidence. Just that dratted police-
man again. He's the hound with the proverbial bone.
I don't even know that he can go anywhere with the
American link, but he's posted an entry on his Facebook
page. He must be desperate if he's using a social media
site. He states that the hit-and-run driver might be
a woman. Now where did he come up with that idea?*

It had been as he feared. On returning to work the day
after flying back from the States he had asked to have
a meeting with Toby Mullins, still his superior officer
despite the hopeful rumour that he was being moved
on to a new post.

A request to re-examine the accident in Seahouses
had been denied. 'If it's about that bloody case again,
forget it. Just forget it. I heard that you've been back to
America. This has to stop. There are other crimes that
need investigating and even solving, though that seems
increasingly unlikely if all you can think about are two
incidents separated by thousands of miles. Now do us
all a favour and either enjoy your time off or get back
to proper policing.'

The internet was Clive's next thought and then
perhaps an anonymous item in the local paper. Mullins
would know it was him but if he got his friend at the

paper to insert it, following a tip-off from an unknown source, there would be no proof.

The next day there was a small article on page fourteen, not exactly giving the item the high profile Clive had hoped for.

North East Guardian

New evidence has come to light concerning the hit-and-run in Seahouses in October 2011. The accident resulted in the deaths of a father and son who were well known and highly respected in the town. Joseph and Peter Nightingale were struck by a car which drove off at high speed, leaving the scene of the accident. It was suggested at the time that the driver of the car was a man. However, there is now some evidence to support the theory that the driver may well have been a woman.

If anyone can substantiate this or indeed has any new information regarding this incident, please would they contact DCI Clive Rogers at the police station in Seahouses, telephone number 01665 7788932. Anyone coming forward to assist the police is guaranteed anonymity.

Crank calls by the dozen, his phone line red-hot for two days. This was followed by the usual array of useless calls, people either trying to aid the enquiry or be a nuisance. Any request for help from the public results in a lot of police time being wasted and Clive was on his own with this one.

After a week he doubted whether anything helpful would emerge this side of the Atlantic. Totally frustrated, he knew he had to stop thinking about the case or he would lose his job and, in all likelihood, his marriage. Even Ellis, his best friend, and the man who knew how aggravating it could be to leave a case unsolved, had told him to forget it.

'It's a terrible thing to say but the only way forward will be if there's another similar incident this year: let's watch out for October 15th. I sincerely hope nothing will happen but if it does then maybe that will be the time to rethink and open the others as cold cases. Until then, and as I say it is really the worst case scenario, let it go.' Even Clive had to agree that his friend had given him sound advice.

Chapter 6

It's in the paper. AGAIN! I would love to know how many responses he will get to his request. Could anyone have "new information" at this late date?

I know I'm tired after such a frenetic end to the term but it's all I can do to stay awake, let alone start some serious planning and reading that article has made me do some in-depth thinking.

Two major points: I seem to have got away with it so far – two dads, two offspring, all out of the way. Should I therefore quit whilst I'm winning? However, if a father, and in the next case a daughter, remain there will have been very little to gain from the other demises. Such an attractive word compared to deaths. I know it's a euphemism but it made me smile and I don't have much that makes me do that at the moment. On thinking about it I could have used departures, terminations, annihilations or my favourite, expirations.

To continue or not to continue as the bard might have said. I am far too exhausted to make such a major decision at the moment and such an important one.

Matthew and Natasha enjoyed Christmas in Australia. Natasha was young and rarely asked about her mother and why she wasn't with them. On the rare occasions when she asked why others in her reception class had two parents Matthew responded with the time honoured, 'She loves you very much but sometimes mummies and daddies want to live apart.' Matthew knew that was only half true. There was a time when he had assumed that his wife would be with them for ever, though he had known from the start that she only ever acted the part of a mother and it had never been a BAFTA winning performance. Would she have stayed if she had not met Robin, a successful lawyer, whom she had employed to deal with the legal side of her work?

Would he have known about the affair had she not slipped on the pavement as she walked to work one wet Tuesday morning? Matthew blamed the ridiculous height of her heels; she claimed it was the wet ground. An ambulance was summoned which took her to the local A and E department. She had been unlucky and had sustained several injuries: a broken ankle; dislocated collar bone; and most seriously a rib had been forced out of place and punctured her left lung.

Late nights should have alerted him. He even believed her when she said she had to go to London on business and would be away for three days (and nights). Matthew had thought that she took their marriage vows as seriously as he did, so was totally unprepared when he went to see her in the hospital later that day and found Robin at her bedside. It was obvious that the man was more than a friend. Natasha was with him so a scene was inappropriate. That could wait.

Despite her lack of maternal feelings the thing that had shocked Matthew was the ease with which she left their daughter. Surely a mother wants her child with her? Not this one.

'Yes, I've been having an affair. I thought it might burn itself out, but it's not doing so I think it's better if

I leave,' was her announcement when she came home a week later. Nothing had been said in hospital as their daughter was always at the bedside.

'Is that it? Don't I deserve more of an explanation?'

'There's not really much to say. I met Robin at work and we fell in love.'

'Love? Really? Is that how you dignify a sordid affair?'

The conversation derailed into a slanging match, both attempting to win the hurting game. Only late on when the final insults were being hurled, with more venom than a Scot with his caber, did it emerge that she had no intention of taking Natasha with her. Matthew was exhausted and could hardly fashion any appropriate words.

Following her to the bedroom, where she had already begun to pack, Matthew attempted one last appeal. 'How much do you intend seeing Natasha?'

His wife's reply left him aghast, wandering in an alien world, one bereft of the rules of conduct he had taken for granted. 'It's probably better if I have no contact with her. I'm sure in the long run that will be for the best.'

'Best for whom exactly? Not your daughter, but – oh yes – best for you,' the sarcasm in his voice made her look at him and for the first time since the argument had begun she showed some emotion.

'Believe me it's the best for all concerned. You might not believe it but I am actually thinking of the three of us. Natasha will forget about me and you are a much better father than I am a mother. She will be all right with you.'

Since that night there had been no contact: letters, birthday cards, Christmas cards, presents or phone calls. She had meant it when she said that she was leaving their lives for ever.

Matthew wished his parents lived closer. Melbourne was a long way away. He knew he needed full-time help and contacted an agency claiming to supply the best nannies.

Brenda Collinge was a woman of indeterminate age who had spent her working life looking after other people's children. She arrived on a dull Saturday afternoon a fortnight after Natasha's mother had performed her disappearing act, the one that would have won *Britain's Got Talent* for an aspiring magician. She was dressed in a sober fashion a style Matthew suspected was her normal attire. References spoke of her "exceptional organisational skills, calm demeanour and dependability" but the one that most impressed her future employer was her "love of children and kind, caring nature". During the interview she indicated that she was prepared to commit to the long-term care of Matthew's daughter; a prerequisite for the post.

'As I'm a single father I would need to employ someone who will stay with us when Natasha starts school. My work means that I don't just do nine-to-five and there are times when an emergency demands my attention, either in the evenings or at weekends. Agreeing that she would receive time in lieu (elderly mother to visit) Brenda said she was flexible and the following week she moved in.

Shirley Owen, their home-help, had her hours increased. Matthew knew that the situation could have been worse, even though on numerous occasions this philosophy felt like straws being clutched or indeed dropped. He was grateful that he had enough money to pay for the assistance they needed. Natasha, following an initial black period when she missed her mother and couldn't understand why she didn't come home at night, stopped wetting the bed and behaving like a toddler with daily temper tantrums and began to thrive. She had always been a sociable little girl and after a few weeks of stability with Brenda began to enjoy both her days at home and the three mornings a week she spent at nursery. When the time came she settled easily into the Reception class at Dawson Road Primary School.

Given the circumstances life was as good as could be expected. Matthew had always loved his daughter but over the weeks, months, then years his feelings had grown deeper and he remained adamant that Natasha would be affected as little as possible by her mother's desertion.

Chapter 7

The end of the Christmas holiday arrived and I didn't seem to have done much. No contact with Sophie, thank goodness. Families are such a pain at Christmas and I wasn't in the mood for pretence socialising. Amy was holidaying in the Caribbean. She did ask me if I wanted to go but I needed the fortnight at home.

Made the decision to go ahead with the next "Road Kill". This is my latest catchphrase which I rather like.

Once I'd made up my mind, no easy matter at the best of times, I wanted to make sure they were still at the same address. It's a lovely area: wide streets, tree-lined pavements, typical middle class suburbia. And finally, two weeks into January, I was able to ascertain that Matthew and Natasha are indeed still living at number twenty-three.

Problem: they don't live alone. There is a nanny, a rather serious looking woman, very un-Mary Poppins, though I haven't seen her with an umbrella!

How frustrating that I couldn't determine a schedule with them away for so long. They were out of touch, that word will be used literally one day. I phoned the surgery to try to make an appointment with Matthew to be told that he was on leave until January the tenth. No doubt they flew to Australia to visit his parents. Good to know they probably enjoyed fantastic weather:

might be their last chance. A shame they weren't around when I had so much spare time as it's much easier to watch their activities when I'm not at work. One idea is to throw a "sickie" and go to observe them during the week. I may well succumb to a debilitating bout of a horrible flu-type bug. I might even stretch it to a week as no one will want me anywhere near them with something like that.

January the first: New Year's Day. The Australian beach was crowded and after making yet another sandcastle Matthew was endeavouring to explain the concept of New Year Resolutions, a phrase they had just over-heard. His five year old daughter was not finding his explanation easy to follow.

'A resolution is like a promise to do something over the next year. It should be something good, something that will make you a better person.' He continued, patiently explaining that a long time ago the Romans began each year by making promises to their god, Janus, and that the first month of the year was named after him. Understanding some of what her father said Natasha decided that she wanted to make a promise.

'We both will. We can call them promises or the posh word, resolutions.' The pair spent several minutes suggesting a variety of ideas.

'I will be kinder to Susie but I don't really like her. She pulls my hair and always pushes to the front of the line when we go for dinner.'

'Well, if you can be kind to someone you don't like that will be a wonderful resolution.' Matthew had been told that his daughter was one of the well-behaved pupils at school and probably didn't need to make such a promise. Her teacher had described her as, 'A delightful little girl who makes my job easy. She's so pleasant; invariably has a smile on her face and she tries her best at all aspects of school life. She's just a pleasure to have in the class.'

Brenda Collinge was proving to be an ideal nanny. Hard to believe she had been with them for almost two years. His New Year Resolution would be to tell her more frequently how much he valued her.

Following the break Matthew was inundated with extra patients. The papers hadn't helped by suggesting that a flu epidemic was imminent and people were making appointments for symptoms that could have been dealt with at home. By the end of the first week he was exhausted and longed for a peaceful weekend.

'Can we go to the cinema tomorrow, Daddy? Everyone's been to see *The Dog Who Saved the World* and Tracy says it's brilliant.'

'If Tracy says it's brilliant it must be.' His sarcasm was lost, unlike the planet Earth in the film. If they went he could probably sleep through most of it and decided that there were worse ways of spending Saturday afternoon.

'Sounds like a plan. A pizza first then go to watch the amazing hound which is looking out for us.'

Clara, pleased at having survived another festive break, was happy to be back at school, the busy routine giving little time to worry or think about her next venture. A new pupil had started in Year 5 who needed a great deal of help. Rosie was a sweet child but found anything academic inordinately difficult. Her previous school hadn't put her on the Special Needs Register so there was no extra funding to provide additional support. Fortunately the group Clara worked with was small:

Wayne, Tiffany and Harry. See nothing, hear nothing and speak far too much.

'I've given the new girl a week and it's obvious she can't cope on her own, so sorry but Rosie will have to work with your group Clara. No records from Millington Road yet, but she's being assessed as soon as possible to see if she can get a Statement. I know they are almost nonexistent these days, like a win for the school football team this season, but I think she may be so far behind the others that she will qualify for one. I know you'll do your best with her until then.'

Unfortunately the following week the numeracy topic was multiplication. Her group was called the Pluto Party. Had they been so named because that planet was the smallest and furthest from the illuminating sun? Good job the numeracy sets weren't named after animals or Slumbering Sloths might have been deemed appropriate. They started each lesson with the distinct disadvantage of not knowing their times tables, so each sum became a prolonged manoeuvre involving fingers rather than brains. Instant recall was a distant dream. Each times table was counted up from the beginning starting with one times the number. Even the two and the ten times, supposedly the easiest, were providing a long trek up the digits; on occasion exceedingly long as Harry was in the habit of forgetting which digit he had reached. Most days it would have been quicker to scale Mont Blanc in a blizzard.

Following the final numeracy lesson of the week Clara vented her frustration. She rarely ranted but felt totally frustrated that she had yet again failed to fix the numbers in her charges' heads. 'I've tried every whichway but at the beginning of every lesson we go back to not being able to do two times ten without starting with one times ten! With my lot visiting the tables are like an elderly relative in a care home. She has a vague recollection that she has seen you before but can't find enough points of reference to identify you.'

Katie laughed and said she was sure something had gone in, but then made Clara's day even worse by saying, 'It's fractions, decimals and percentages next week. Have a good weekend!'

Part of most Saturdays was spent observing her next prey. The problem was that they had no fixed routine, each weekend occupied with different activities: roller blading, walking, swimming, clothes shopping, a birthday party at a friend's house and an afternoon at the cinema were all undertaken by half term. Unless the pair began a regular schedule it would be virtually impossible to devise a workable plan. Knowing there was still a lot of time until October Clara decided to curtail her visits to the Lloyds' to once a month. They could become more frequent during the summer holidays.

Chapter 8

February half-term break already. Six weeks have flown. No wonder people who don't work in schools think the holidays come round faster than a race car completing its winning circuit. Teachers can appear to be part-timers, but what the general public isn't aware of is the time spent completing the endless record keeping for the term that has gone, then preparing for the next however many weeks. Holiday: what a misnomer.

Sophie rang last night and, to my amazement, asked if we should celebrate our birthday together this year. The end of February has miserable weather and not much happens in my life so in a moment of madness I said yes.

'Eight o'clock (she knows I hate eating late) at the Omar Khayyam on Chesterfield Street. It's a new res-taurant with the most amazing Middle-Eastern food. It'll just be the two of us and my treat. See you then.' And with that I was left standing with the dialing tone reverberating in my ear. I decided to go as I don't have much of a social life and I like to see her wasting her money. After all, she's got plenty of it to throw around.

Trust Sophie to select a venue that managed to be pretentious, overpriced and the place to be seen. Even I recognised two local footballers and their cloned girlfriends sitting at the next table.

My sister was in high spirits, having in all likelihood downed several beforehand. As we sat down she handed me a small, beautifully wrapped package. We don't do presents so I mumbled something about having left hers at home. It has to be admitted that it was the perfect present: driving gloves in soft crimson leather. Hand-stitched with fancy piping, they shouted "money". Thanking her I assured her they would come in useful!!

After ordering both our meals, 'I've been here a couple of times and know what's delicious,' she regaled me with her latest ventures, all successful and adding to her already considerable wealth. 'New outlets (nothing deemed as common as shops) in Bolton and Coventry and two more are in the pipeline in London.' Was I supposed to be impressed?

My lack of interest didn't deter her and she launched into a detailed description of her next holiday. I had heard enough and interrupted sharply, a pin that I hoped would burst her bubble.

'Do you realise that you have asked nothing, and I mean zilch, about me? What I'm doing, how my job is progressing or where I might be off to this year. As usual it's all about you.' With a flourish that would have pleased Maggie Smith I rose from my expensive seat and stomped out of the restaurant.

So dear Sophie, nothing has changed. You have it all. The good news is that I will be the only twin who will enjoy many more birthdays.

Snow flurries, biting winds and colourless days did little to enhance the North East. Foolhardy walkers fought their way along the Arctic beaches, hooded heads bent forward, faces protected by scarves, and fur-lined anorak collars pulled up as far as they would stretch.

Most endured the inclement environment to walk dogs, whilst a few maintained that they were on holiday and enjoying themselves.

It had been a long-drawn-out winter and only the frozen snowdrops standing bravely to attention, like Napoleon's army at the gates of Moscow, heralded the coming spring.

Favourite walks: most locals have them, the sort less frequented by winter visitors. Beadnell to Low Newton by the Sea was Clive's choice. When he needed time to think this was one of the best places to do it. Four miles of glorious beach, the stretches of sand second to none.

Unless the tide was very high the entire walk was possible along the sand and when the water prevented this, the inland path behind the dunes was equally attractive with stunning views the whole way. The walk began along Beadnell Bay then continued past the wonderfully named Football Hole and finished around Newton Point with its old coastguard's cottage, now owned and let to visitors by the National Trust. A friend had once stayed in the cottage and told Clive all about the bunk beds, outside lavatory and HM Coastguard radio equipment still in use in a separate room.

Tuesday was Clive's only day off in the penultimate week of February. He arrived in Beadnell by eight o'clock, for him, without doubt, the best time of the day. High winds were propelling gigantic sheets of water over the harbour wall. The sea broiled and bubbled, a cold, liquid eruption. He liked to walk along the walls around the small harbour but knew that would have been foolhardy in these conditions. Instead he stood in awe, attempting to predict the force of the next deluge. One boat was moored, probably safe from the storm, a seagull clinging to its mast. Even a bird would surely feel nauseous if it balanced there for too long.

Depression: that most horrific affliction had descended, the unwelcome trespasser invading hours then days and recently weeks. Having never suffered from it before, Clive had been unsure how to cope.

'For goodness sake, go to the doctor. You need help. Ask for pills and a psychiatric assessment. Maybe he or she will help you get over your obsession.' Mari had not meant to sound unsympathetic but she was losing patience with her husband's moods. He was either at work or on the computer searching for hit-and-run accidents. Regular phone calls to North Carolina didn't help. They just added fuel to the fire which was never extinguished: the two cases that remained unsolved.

'I'll get out more. Go for regular walks. Clear my head. That will do the trick. I really don't need any medical intervention. No doctor. Not needed.' His speech had become jumpy, short sentences delivered either at a rapid speed or so measured that every syllable became a monumental effort and sounded to Mari like one of her pupils when they were attempting to master reading.

Half way along the curved beach one of the many wartime pillar boxes, that had once protected the sea-shore, lay collapsed in the sand. Despite having passed the decayed remnant many times before it added to Clive's sense of despair. Given sufficient time everything ended. Even the dune-top wooden chalets, painted in their gaudy colours, were slowly falling down, the sand eroding beneath them leaving each structure unsupported.

Arriving too early to get coffee, or something stronger, at the Ship Inn in Newton, normally one of his favourite haunts, Clive sat on one of the benches outside and looked at the age-old fishermen's cottages that made up three sides of the inhabited square, the pub situated at the top end. How simple life must have been centuries ago: fishing, selling the catch, mending nets, maintaining boats, eating, sleeping, start again. Spectacles, so rose-tinted, took no account of the hardships endured by the men he envied, his imagination lost in the blackness of his mood. With a heavy step he began the return journey which today missed his usual detour to the extensive nature reserve situated behind the beach.

'How was your day, did you enjoy the walk?' Mari asked when she arrived home after a full day at school followed by a protracted staff meeting: new government initiatives discussed ad nauseam.

'I did it – all the way from Beadnell to Low Newton.'

'And back presumably?' her attempt at humour was wasted. Knowing that in all probability there would be no response Mari went to make the evening meal.

Chapter 9

Tidying is utterly rewarding: creating order out of chaos. One of my best moments is when I bake for our monthly cake sale at school, in aid of St. Cuthbert's Children's Hospice this year. All the cakes are either in the oven or sitting in their cases ready to be baked and I look at the devastating mess that obscures every work surface: egg shells, bowls waiting to be licked – a childhood habit I still maintain – and washed. Flour and sugar spillages and the discarded remains of a variety of other ingredients form a war zone requiring my attention. Only I can restore my kitchen to its normal peaceful condition. Bliss.

Kitchen cupboards, the bathroom cabinet and my two wardrobes are sorted on a regular basis but my bedside drawers are rarely opened and I can't remember the last time I looked in the middle one.

Why I decided to "bottom it", a phrase I remember my mother using, remains a mystery. It's a deep space and full of a variety of paraphernalia including old reports from both my schools, piano exams and a whole gamut of dance festivals, none of which I recall enjoying. In the middle of the erstwhile reports was the letter, the one I had surely not kept. But there it was in all its disingenuous glory. Too distressing to write about now: it's late and I am tired. If I spend any longer ruminating, sleep will vanish like words written in invisible ink. If only the letter had that propensity.

Statesville was enjoying an early spring. Most inhabitants loved this time of year when it was pleasantly warm but without the intense heat and humidity of the summer.

Deputy sheriff Dwayne Vanstory had a new case but one that he expected to deal with quickly, then hand over to the prosecutors. At six o'clock the previous evening a man had shot his wife's lover. It was definitely premeditated: he had followed his victim into town; pulled up beside him at the traffic lights; opened fire; job done.

Will Toler, the accused, had then driven to the police station to hand himself in. 'I've just shot Donnie Miller. He was messing with my wife and now the bastard's dead,' was his succinct account of the shooting. Dwayne met him a few minutes later to conduct the interview and take his statement.

Leaning forward, head in hands, the man in the interview room sat weeping, the loud sobs bouncing off the walls like balls on a squash court. Dwayne knew him as a mechanic who worked at the local garage where he took his car for its regular checks and wheel alignments. Will was still wearing his work clothes and the overalls looked as though they hadn't been washed for weeks. He raised red-rimmed eyes as Dwayne entered the room and accepted the proffered box of tissues, a necessary accompaniment for many of the talks the room witnessed.

Without waiting for the interview to begin he launched into his story, desperate to get it over with. 'Sherri met Donnie Miller at the school. They both go in to eat lunch with the kids.' Not particularly interested, Dwayne asked for the name of the school, though the information would almost certainly have no bearing on the case.

'Martin Luther King Elementary, the newly built place out on Wilksboro Highway. My three all go there, a darned good school, just a shame about the moms and dads who think it's a good idea to cheat,' the last words spoken with all the venom of an adder attacking its next meal.

The story continued: a narrative of jealousy and suffering as old as time. 'I know I shouldn't have shot him, but I had to do something. It was him or Sherri and the kids still need their mom.' After getting Will to write and sign his statement Dwayne took him down to the cells. Only then did he allow himself to think about the school, the location of last October's hit-and-run. It was a few weeks since he had made contact with England so the next morning he rang Clive.

'Hi old timer, how's things?' The American was feeling upbeat after a few successful days. Not so the man doing endless paperwork at his desk in England.

'Have been better but how are you? Any news?' Clive longed to hear a positive response and be told that this was why Dwayne was ringing.

'Sorry to disappoint you, nothing about the case. You know I'd be in touch pronto if there were. It's just the school's name came up today and it reminded me that we hadn't spoken for the longest time.'

'The school – as in Martin Luther King Elementary?'

'As in the very same. But nothing to do with our incident, just a gun being used when it shouldn't be. A jealous husband whose kids go to that school killed his wife's lover.'

Once he had ascertained that Dwayne had nothing important to add to their linked cases Clive had stopped listening.

'The story is that there was a liaison between this man's wife and a dad at the school. Get this – they met over spicy tacos in the school canteen. Now that's what I call romantic. Anyways the cuckolded husband decides to deal with the situation and shoots his rival in his car at the traffic lights on Mooresville Road. He even came in to give himself up.'

'No news? Nothing more has emerged?' Clive's needle had stuck, the groove wearing thin, making him unaware of any conversation but the one he wanted to hear.

Sensing Clive's despondency Dwayne tried to encourage him. 'Like you I keep an eye on that internet site but no incidents similar to ours have been reported. Don't despair, I often find something "gives" in the most unyielding of cases, a tiny part of the puzzle fits into place, like filling in the vital number in a difficult Sudoku: one day this conundrum will be complete and make sense.'

Realising that Clive was on the verge of full-blown depression he resolved to ring him on a more regular basis. The conversation, which had been rather one-sided, ended with a promise to keep in touch. On this side of the Atlantic things felt worse than ever. No new information forthcoming on either case. If only he could work out the connection. He knew there was one.

Chapter 10

Birthday meal and rediscovered letter: both would provide gruesome reading in my autobiography.

Showing me the letter was one of Sophie's most despicable actions and done with such malice. No sibling could read it without being hurt which was her one intention. I read it for the first time over three years ago but on Friday evening its contents found their mark once again, a perfect shot: a bull's eye, hitting the target dead centre.

Our father wrote it to my sister a few weeks before he died. He had been ill for almost a year and knew the cancer had spread and that his illness was terminal. In it he tells her of his decision and the reasons behind it. The letter is lengthy – he never used one word when twenty were available – and some sentences were particularly hard to read.

"I know I can trust you, my beloved daughter, to carry on from the point where I have been forced to stop."

"You have been my shining light, my mainstay, a reason to live when your mother died." Had he really forgotten her teenage years when she made Hades look attractive?

"Should you, when the time comes, wish to alter my instructions then so be it. I have added this as a codicil in my Will."

All the evidence I needed. My sister had been given a "Get out of Jail Free" card before he died which she had chosen to ignore. Proof, indisputable proof, that not only was she the favoured one but also the selfish, self-centred bitch I had always known her to be.

I had been the "good girl", the one who worked hard and made a success of each job. Sophie had been irresponsible, lacking the initiative or drive to make a success of her opportunities until she agreed to start in the lowest echelons in the shops. Even then her love life had taken preference. Yes, OK, on occasion mine has been salacious but it has never been allowed to interfere with work.

It remains impossible to write more. He had never been a particularly forgiving man but his favourite daughter could obviously do no wrong. In his eyes I had made one mistake and for that I must pay. Nothing to do with refusing to do demeaning work: no, he used an excuse that only he could inflate to Hindenburg proportions.

I love being a teaching assistant but by now I should be on the Board of Directors of Bedford's Jewellers, our family firm. I use the penultimate word ironically!

Thanks Dad; thanks Sophie.

Completely unfair. That is true of many of life's vagaries, but the injustice done to her hadn't been some random deed, some act perpetrated without due thought or lack of attention. No, it had been signed and sealed by her father then delivered, with a total lack of empathy, by her sister.

Temptation. Oh the temptation to act quickly, get it all over with! Re-reading the letter had upset Clara. Nights were endured, tossing in a tangle of oppressive bedclothes, a maelstrom of disjointed ideas all vying for prominence. Her sister must not be allowed to carry on with the life handed to her on the proverbial plate: the rich, successful life denied to the daughter who had supported their father through the bleak days when he was swamped by dark shadows following his wife's suicide. Sophie had not been the one to make sure he got up in the morning; the one who put him to bed late at night when he was completely inebriated; the one who listened to his irrational rants, blaming the world for his wife's death. Sophie had never denied herself an evening out in order to keep him company.

Was the waiting necessary? Was the date of such paramount importance? Clara realised that October the fifteenth was an indulgence. Delaying the next act until then – enter Matthew and Natasha stage left – meant an excessive postponement and more importantly deferred the final act – exit Sophie, stage right. Only Wagner made his audience wait that long. Why should the date matter? October was eons away. The world had surely evolved in less time. However, the order had to remain: Matthew and Natasha, then finally Sophie. Only at that point would justice be done, parity restored.

Clara spent every weekend watching the Lloyds' house. It had been impossible to restrict herself to her original plan of watching them monthly. If she could become au fait with at least some of their routine she would be able to devise a plan and the pair could be eradicated long before October. This year Clara had decided that the auspicious date would belong solely to her sister. That would provide such an agreeable conclusion. She didn't know why the enchanting idea had only just occurred to her. It was perfect, worthy of patenting, though even she knew that the concept was not for public consumption.

Finding different disguises was becoming tedious. One week she was a young girl in mini skirt and boots, an auburn wig held in place by a wide bandana. The following week she became an old man in cords and anorak, a flat cap and ridiculously large beard hiding her face. Matthew and Natasha never appeared to notice their surroundings and certainly not the people they passed. Occasionally Matthew would greet someone, perhaps a patient, but most of the time they seemed to be happy together and chatted animatedly, unaware that anyone was following them.

It quickly became obvious that almost every time the pair left the house they were on foot. The doctor obviously believed in fresh air and exercise. In reasonable weather there were trips to the park, the route taken meant they crossed one main road. Their stalker knew that this was a possibility. There was a pelican crossing situated near the junction at the top of their road and the duo often walked round the corner then used it to get across the busy road. Easy to park a little way from the corner, watch their house, and as long as she knew how long it took them to arrive at the crossing she could accelerate and *meet* them as they crossed. The difficulty was they didn't always follow the same schedule and it was hard to plan with so many variables.

A few weeks into the new term Clara took a Monday off school, claiming she was suffering from the tummy bug that had decimated the class the previous week. Donning a jogging suit, a ridiculous outfit purchased for the occasion, she set off to observe the Lloyds' weekday schedule. Arriving at half past seven, she began her jogging routine. Although it was a rather damp morning the sky was easing, the dark clouds replaced by those of a lighter hue and Clara didn't look out of place, merely another runner out for her early morning exercise. Anyone watching closely might have wondered why her route consisted of repeated laps of the same avenue. Fortunately for Clara, the people she encountered were far too concerned with their own morning dramas: hurrying to catch the train; parents encouraging their reluctant offspring to the childminder; others stopping at the local shop for a paper or sandwich. She felt confident that no one would be able to supply a description of the girl they had hardly noticed. She was merely another person determined to keep fit.

At eight o'clock Doctor Matthew Lloyd drove away from the house. Half an hour later the door opened again and Natasha emerged, dressed as a dragon, hand in hand with the nanny. The two walked the short distance to the end of their road then, turning left, they continued along Brownlee Avenue, then Crossways Road and finally onto Dawson Road and the school. The whole journey took just under ten minutes and no main roads were crossed. It was a perfectly safe stroll and one they appeared to enjoy, Natasha chatting excitedly the whole way. Feeling bold, their pursuer moved close enough to listen to their conversation. The little girl was excited, looking forward to the Fantasy Day in class.

'Jodi's going as a princess and Marcus is a wizard. I can't wait to see their outfits. Mrs Jones is coming in to help and she's going to be a fairy.'

How innocent it all sounded. Guilt encroached, like mist descending on a mountain top, hiding a spectacular view. Clara knew she couldn't afford feelings for the child but wondered, momentarily, whether she should leave her to enjoy life until October. Sentimental drivel – children die every day and hers would be a quick and, in all probability, a painless end.

It would have to be a weekend as they obviously didn't go out together on weekday mornings and she knew that Matthew stayed at his surgery until six. She would watch the school at home time and expected to see the nanny collect the dragon-attired Natasha.

Matthew Lloyd was oblivious, totally unaware of the impending disaster. He was a kind, caring doctor who took his work seriously. His patients trusted him and were happy when they were able to make an appointment to see him. During his training at The Queen Elizabeth Hospital in Birmingham, one of his tutors had said that although, given sufficient time, a doctor will lose a hundred per cent of his patients it is also the case that every day he will save some lives and alleviate a lot of suffering.

On the day when dragons were meeting witches and wizards Matthew's surgery had been frenetically busy, a not uncommon occurrence. However, he knew from many years of experience that the last patient of the day is just as important as the first. Easy to become careless and either miss something a patient says or, even worse, not ask the relevant questions.

Edward Jefferson walked in, looking as though he would rather be anywhere else. His wife, Joanne, accompanied him, the more confident of the two. Matthew recognised him as one of the bus drivers he saw when he and Natasha ventured into Manchester.

'Good evening Mr Jefferson, I don't often see you here.' In truth he couldn't remember the last time he had seen the man in his surgery but surmised that several years had passed. 'What can I do for you today?'

It is well known that an individual can spend his entire appointment discussing a minor complaint and only as he stands to leave does the real reason for the visit become apparent: men being particularly prone to this delaying tactic.

'I've been having problems sleeping,' Edward began, adopting a muted tone, then continued several decibels lower, 'I drop off quite quickly but wake up at all hours and can't get back to sleep. It's beginning to affect me during the day and Joanne said I should come to see you.'

'Are you aware of anything that might be waking you up once you are sleeping?' Matthew knew there was usually an underlying cause when sleeping patterns were disturbed.

'Most nights the cat jumps on the bed and he's no lightweight. He's a huge ginger tom, been out on the prowl then comes in and wants a comfy spot to curl up.'

Matthew wanted to laugh, knowing if that was the only cause of Edward's insomnia then there was a very easy solution: shut the moggy in the kitchen. Good manners forbade such an inappropriate reply. 'Can you think of anything else?' he asked gently, realising that there was more to this situation than his patient was ready to admit.

'The cat purrs and the wife snores. They're not yet quite good enough to enter *The X Factor*,' his attempt at humour failing to dispel the increasing tension in the room.

'Oh for goodness sake, Ted, tell the doctor the real reason you're here.' Joanne was obviously worried and her voice had become shrill. 'It's his waterworks Doctor Lloyd, he has to go to the loo at least five times every night and it's getting worse.'

Dear, oh dear, Matthew thought, if only men would come to seek help earlier. No wonder women outlived them. The symptoms made him think of prostate cancer and if so it was almost certainly too far advanced to respond to treatment. How many months he wondered before he might be invited to attend his patient's funeral?

Thank goodness his own life wasn't plagued by illness: Natasha was safe and sound and waiting for him at home.

Chapter 11

A weekend it is. It will have to be on the crossing on Brownlea Avenue, all other possibilities (and there are some, for instance near the park) are too unreliable. There is no way of knowing their movements before-hand, the only given is that they invariably start their walks the same way. They go up to the top of their avenue, far too select to be designated a road or street, then turn left and cross the next avenue via the pelican crossing.

At the moment the plan is to park a few doors away from their house and watch as they set off. I have timed the event and know that if I start forty seconds after seeing them walk out of their gate it is possible to accel-erate sufficiently to be round the corner and connect with the pair in the centre of the main road. Resume a normal speed and leave the scene.

Next decision…where to borrow a car? I need to do it some distance away and several days beforehand. This is all too close to home to be comfortable. The car needs very careful thought. Just had a brilliant idea, well I think it's rather good and let's face it no one else can verify my assessment. I'll visit Amy next week, not seen her for ages. Her old garage has an essential piece of equipment, just what I need. Yes: phone her tomorrow; see her this week; say I want to go in the barn for old time's sake; take the necessary and return home.

'How lovely to hear from you Clara, I was thinking about you yesterday and was intending to get in touch.' After several minutes of pleasantries Clara managed to get herself invited to the old farmhouse. 'Wednesday evening will be great and what a pleasure it will be to have someone to cook for. There never seems much point going to a lot of trouble when it's just me. I'll make your favourite, though you've probably developed more mature tastes by now.'

'No, not me. Toad in the hole with your special Yorkshire pudding followed by kiwi and grape cheesecake,' Clara exclaimed, trying to sound more enthusiastic than she felt. Eating was the last thing on her mind.

Wednesday was stressful and felt never ending. The entire day consisted of meetings with parents to discuss their offspring's recent progress (or lack thereof) and set new targets for each individual, small steps being, almost inevitably, the order of the day. Katie was in all the meetings but appreciated her assistant's input as Clara was the adult who worked so closely with the group of Special Needs children. "Steady progress" was Clara's favourite euphemism. She was aware that most of the mothers realised that this indicated that their child's progress was still disappointing and that they remained at the lower end of the ability range. After five hours of tactful comments Clara felt drained.

'Fancy an early tea?' Katie asked. This was their usual wind down after a day of meetings: eat stodge, erupt with laughter and forget school.

'Sorry, going to see my godfather's wife, well widow. When we arranged it for today I had forgotten we had this on.' Agreeing to go out with Katie the following evening Clara left and drove straight to Amy's.

Delicious food was followed by coffee, drunk in the kitchen, the place Clara had sat so many times talking to Henry. When a person dies there is a longing for some element of them to remain in the space where you knew them best. That evening Henry's aura dominated the room and the two women talked about him until long after the time Clara had planned to leave.

'This has been delightful Amy, but if I stay much longer my car will turn into a pumpkin and that might make the journey home a tad tricky.' Promising to keep in touch and meet again soon the pair parted. Having enjoyed the evening Amy went to bed feeling more content than usual.

Clara drove to the ancient barn at the bottom of the paddock. It was an isolated building tumbling into a state of disrepair, but as it was out of sight it was ignored and had been left to become increasingly ramshackle. In Henry's time it had been used as a second garage and its cavernous space had housed many of his rally cars. As Clara entered she could see that it was now used as a general store for junk and unwanted furniture.

Creeping forward, she stepped gingerly past an outmoded wardrobe with fly-blown mirrors and a discarded kitchen table, the one that had been used by generations of Henry's family. It was a valuable piece of furniture: nineteenth century French design, over seven feet long with the overhang longer on one side, a common feature of continental tables allowing the table to be butted against a wall. The one drawer had once held cards and dice and as Clara looked at it she thought of the hours she and Henry had spent playing

games across it and of how adept her godfather had
been at cheating. Once Henry was no longer there the
table had been deemed too large for the single meals
that Amy endured each day. It was now a sorry sight,
an infestation of woodworm spoiling its former glory.

The desired junk was several feet further on but
Clara almost lost her confidence as a large rat scuttled
past her, its horrific shape caught in the powerful beam
of her torch.

Henry had kept every number plate from all the cars
he had ever owned: the motors he had restored, driven,
crashed or taken to the scrap yard. He always maintained that he could remember every car by its number
plate and refused to part with them, even those that
might have been worth a substantial amount of money.

Acting quickly, more afraid of rodent than human
intervention, she selected two pairs of plates. There
would be time to decide which ones would be used.
What, she wondered, would Henry make of the chosen
plates' reincarnation. With the plates in place Henry
would be sitting alongside her and her driving would
be fast, controlled…and deadly.

At home, after a journey completed on autopilot,
the purloined items were hidden at the back of her
garage, behind the lawn mower, covered so meticulously with plastic sheeting and used with such reluc-
tance. Gardening had never been her favourite activity
and the machine was given an outing just a few times
a year when it became a case of cut the grass or borrow
a sheep.

Knowing that sleep would be as elusive as a football
manager's praise for a referee's decisions she sat with
a brandy, the only drink she enjoyed, and attempted
to watch the episode of the latest second-rate ITV

drama she had recorded. The following day she couldn't recall a single scene.

Either set of number plates would suit her purpose. They were from the late sixties and early seventies and any records of the cars to which they had once belonged would have disappeared decades ago. On the day of the next event, should an eye witness be quick enough to remember the numbers, there would be no direct link back to any car that Henry had owned and so no association with her. Most of the time he had, sometimes literally, run the cars into the ground, then sent them to his mate, Billy, a local scrap merchant, who disposed of them. There had been no need to involve the DVLA.

EPL 721K was chosen. Now all that was needed was the car. It would have to possess a powerful engine and, perhaps more importantly, great acceleration. Her "run-up" would be short and she needed immediate access to speed. Google gave her the answers she sought: Mitsubishis, cars she had always liked, were no good, taking a pathetic fourteen seconds to go from zero to sixty. Chevrolets were great at five point one seconds but it was unlikely that she would be able to borrow one when needed. Two cars caught her eye, both reasonably common makes and models. The claim for the BMW 135 was that it could accelerate from zero to sixty in five point two seconds. Her alternative was the Audi A8L, slower by three seconds. Either would do and once borrowed it would be possible to hide the vehicle in the garage until the fateful day. She would start her search soon: the sooner the better. Once she had the car the date could be set, preferably before the summer as no doubt the pair would be going away.

Over the next four weeks visits to a variety of car parks occupied every spare minute. She was confident that her ancient Honda was so innocuous as to be virtually invisible, though she took care to avoid stopping for too long in any one spot or driving too near to the CCTV cameras that had sprung up, like unwanted weeds, in almost every venue. Realising that the day would come when the right car appeared she resorted to walking or catching a tram or local bus. At least when the day arrived she would have a car in which to drive home.

Clara was beginning to think that she would never find the ideal car: correct make, selected model and one that was easy to appropriate, until the day she walked past a BMW parked in Sainsbury's car park, the venue a most satisfactory distance from home. Clara had allowed herself to search for a car within strict parameters: between two and six miles from her house. So many cars were available within this self-imposed boundary that she had been surprised that it had taken so long to finally select the one she wanted.

Parent and Child Space: Short Stay Only. The notice, in bold red letters, dominated the area set aside for busy shoppers who had their offspring in tow. Even better, there was no obvious surveillance camera, though she knew she would be caught on one at some point in the large car park. The car was parked within easy walking distance of the main doors of the supermarket and Clara smiled at the thought that the owner and child would have a lot further to walk when they returned. No one could accuse her of making it easy for little legs and a frustrated parent.

Mothers can be distracted when dealing with young children and this mother, or possibly father, had been careless. Extremely so; the car was unlocked! Had the adult been side-tracked at the last moment by a toddler's cries or had he or she thought it would be safe to leave the vehicle for the short time they would be shopping? Not only was it unlocked but the key fob was hidden behind the sun visor. No originality there, it was the first place anyone would look.

Many years ago part of Henry's tuition had included how to enter a car without keys. He had been thinking of those moments when, for a variety of reasons, one is without the necessary set: they're inside a locked car; dropped down a drain; lost, etc. rather than with car theft in mind. He had also given tuition in how to start an engine minus the aforementioned item. Theory had been followed by months of practise so that from her mid-teens his protégée had been able to enter any car without too much damage or noise and start the engine with minimal fuss. The only thing he had not covered was the necessity of driving away nonchalantly. How fortunate that his goddaughter had become an expert at this and anyone watching would have assumed that she was the proud owner of an almost new, extremely attractive, car.

Twenty-five minutes later, after a frustratingly slow journey through heavy traffic, the new acquisition was housed in Clara's garage.

No one had shown any interest in her new car.
No one had noticed her parking it in the garage.
No one had come knocking at the door.
No one knew that the next part of the plan was in place.

Chapter 12

What fun! What an achievement, another car borrowed – ready for its moment of fame. For some reason this time it feels better than ever. I am seventeen again and passing the test on my birthday.

Once home I sat down with a cup of tea and three chocolate biscuits – large ones – my reward. Half an hour later I was altering the identity of the BMW by replacing its number plates. To begin with I was slightly perturbed as the old plates looked so out of place on such a modern vehicle. They were definitely out of sync. But how many people would notice? They gave the car a "Picassoesque" quality. I love his paintings but most of his efforts are, to say the least, unbalanced.

Great – car ready and waiting. Probably my over-wrought imagination but it sits there as though it's aware of its destiny. It must know it has a mission to complete. Next step, when? Where is now definite. The pelican crossing round the corner from the duo's house.

My outfit is assembled: grey curly wig and sensible hat, the kind my grandma wore – felt with a braid trim. Large black-rimmed glasses and a brown coat complete the ensemble. Not a get-up to grace the cover of Vogue or the latest collection from M and S but I'll be sufficiently old-fashioned to play the part of an elderly lady, the kind who should no longer be behind the wheel of a car.

I opted to be female this time. The change feels right. Hopefully anyone who sees the accident will assume that the old girl lost control and was unable to avoid the two on the crossing. Why she didn't stop will remain a mystery.

Spring arrived late. Weeks of showers and strong winds abated and days of warm sunshine took their place, a welcome change. People took advantage of the lovely weather to start gardening, go for walks by the canal and play with Frisbees in the local park. Unfortunately for Clara the weather meant that her weekends were spent in a hot, stuffy car. Sunday after Saturday she sat in her winter weight clothes, waiting for her moment.

Weekends passed without success. Clara's frustration grew as she observed her targets: Matthew and Natasha accompanied by his friends; the duo walking to a party with a gaggle of little girls all dressed up and clutching birthday presents; Natasha with the nanny; and even the odd occasion when Matthew was on his own.

Finally. Finally, five weeks later, the Saturday morning sojourn proved successful. The duo walked out of their drive: together.

The Sunday papers all reported the accident. The headlines varied from the prosaic to the ghoulish.

Hit-and-Run Accident on Sunny Morning
Slaughter in Sale
Doctor and Daughter Killed on Pelican Crossing
Driver Leaves the Scene of a Fatal Accident
Tragedy Strikes Doctor and His Daughter

Clara drove miles, this time in her own car, as she purchased every paper, each one bought in a different shop. Reading the reports did little to lift her mood and the entire day felt like an anticlimax, an assortment of presents already boring on Boxing Day. Early in the morning she had forced herself to enter the garage and replace the original number plates. She had then driven the BMW back to Sainsbury's and parked it in the exact spot it had occupied six weeks before. Her audacity and foolhardiness in undertaking such an auspicious plan would have amused her had she not been so exhausted, both physically and mentally. As she left the car she experienced great difficulty putting each foot in its appropriate place and the walk to the nearest bus stop was laboured.

BBC reports indicated that the north east of the country was, most unusually, enjoying higher temperatures than the Continent. Families were able to picnic on the beach, the windbreaks, normally so essential, left in car boots. Weekends were particularly busy with all three fish and chip shops in Seahouses happy to see every table occupied. Before the school holidays began, those of more mature years flocked into the area during the week keeping the town full of activity.

In this spell of glorious weather Mari had occupied every spare moment gardening, an activity she normally enjoyed, especially when it was warm enough to venture out without a jacket. How sad that this year she was doing it to escape Clive with his bad temper, sulks and generally irritating disposition. His moods had worsened until it had become impossible to have a reasonable conversation with him and their exchanges now consisted of monosyllabic answers to her increasingly mundane questions about his day at work or what he wanted to eat. Such trivial communications are a common occurrence in most long-term unions but hopefully conducted with slightly more interest and enthusiasm.

To keep her sane she had organised a few days away with a friend and couldn't wait for a week on Tuesday to arrive. Bruges sounded like an outpost of heaven and the guide book she had bought suggested numerous town walks. There were far too many museums to visit in the time available but some were essential: The Flemish Gallery, Contemporary Art Collection, The Lace Centre, Diamond Exhibition and the absolute must – The Chocolate Museum. Boat rides on the canal looked like fun. Judy, her friend and colleague, had also joked that there would be many opportunities to indulge themselves with meals that someone else had cooked and the Chocolate Museum would surely give samples. Five days away from her husband sounded like bliss.

The Sunday Guardian dropped onto the front door mat. Mari picked it up and took it through to the lounge where Clive sat in his usual slumped position, staring at the carpet. Leaving the paper on the coffee table, Mari returned to planting her two new azaleas, one purple, one red.

'Mari, Mari, come and look at this.' Clive opened the window and yelled, his voice the most animated it had been for months and his wife dashed back inside to find her husband clutching the main part of the paper with a look of bewilderment on his face.

'Look, look, I was right. I knew it would happen again. Another hit-and-run. It's just the same – a single father and his daughter…killed by a driver…who didn't stop.' Clive paused, overwhelmed by his thoughts. 'This will prove me right. They've got to take notice now.'

As soon as the time difference allowed Clive was on the phone to America. 'We've got another one, it's happened again. We knew it was just a matter of time. It's in all the newspapers this morning. We were right, absolutely right.' Clive's excitement woke Dwayne and his hopes for a gentle Sunday vamoosed with the speed of an escaping bank robber.

Chapter 13

How do I feel? Weeks now since the accident. A certain elation that it's six down and only my beloved sister left to deal with. But the trouble is that for the first time I'm sorry, really sorry. Not just about Matthew and Natasha but the others as well. I know it's too late for regrets and tears are an indulgence. None of it can be undone. I once read a Buddhist mantra that said something along the lines of "Don't dwell on the past. If at all possible make amends, forgive yourself…move on". Would anyone of that faith think that this superb advice is suitable for me?

The Whit holidays have just started, almost two weeks off, so I don't have the all-consuming distraction of school and I need to do something to take my mind off recent events. As per usual the sunshine vanished as soon as the schools broke up so I might go into the travel agent's tomorrow and see if I can book a last minute break in Spain.

Clive made two phone calls on the Sunday. The call to Manchester had been a lot easier than his one to his boss in Seahouses where his asking for some time off had been greeted with a coldness normally associated with the north east winds that blew along the Northumberland coast in winter.

'More bloody leave! You're becoming a part-timer, Rogers, and not a particularly efficient one at that. When did you last do a proper bit of policing? There are more than enough crimes being committed in our neck of the woods without looking at those in far flung parts of the world.' Toby Mullins puffed out his chest, reminding Clive of the flock of birds he'd been watching on the shore.

As patiently as his temper would allow, Clive explained that he was now absolutely certain that the deaths of Joe and Peter Nightingale were in some way linked to the ones in the States and now to the one in Sale. If he could find the link then he would solve the initial incident in Seahouses.

Superintendent Mullins was almost beyond words but when they came they were delivered like rounds of ammunition from a machine gun. 'My godfathers...ye gods... don't believe what I'm hearing! It's Sale now as well! Another link that one feels is only in your over-fertile imagination. I used to have you down as one of the saner members of my team but I'm beginning to think you're paranoid. I'll be referring you to the police psychiatrist if this carries on. Where will the next so called hit-and-run be? Shanghai?'

'I hope not, sir. I will, of course, take the days I'm away this week as unpaid leave.'

'You're bloody right you will. My budget doesn't stretch to wild goose chases and this is one if ever I saw one. No expenses, you can pay for the hotel out of your own pocket.'

Monday morning, ten o'clock, saw Clive impatiently outside Superintendent Thompson's office. He had arrived over an hour early, desperate to discuss the latest incident. 'Good morning, Chief Inspector

Rogers, how lovely to see you again.' The two had met on various training courses where Reginald Thompson had given lectures. Clive remembered him as an excellent speaker who, unlike some others, managed to give his audience something new and relevant to think about. He had seemed the most appropriate officer to contact.

Mari had warned her husband about *launching in with his obsession*. She had received a stony look for this observation but that had not stopped her reminding him of the need to observe the niceties of a conversation. She would have been relieved to hear him continue with, 'Thank you for seeing me at such short notice.'

'I'm keen to know why you are so interested in our accident and do call me Reg. Not Reginald if you don't mind. I hated the name when I was a child and it's not improved with keeping. My mother could never explain why she chose it. Now Clive, coffee then down to business.' The last thing Clive wanted was a drink but his wife's harangue about good manners and "Festina lente", another of her gems to which he had had no reply, forced him to agree that a drink would be most welcome.

Finally, coffee consumed and small talk exhausted, the two men began their discussion. 'Can you tell me what happened in Sale on Saturday morning? It said in the paper that the victims were a single father and his daughter and that the car didn't stop.'

'It's a strange story. I wouldn't normally have much to do with a traffic accident but after you phoned I looked into it. These days the Serious Collision and Investigation Unit take any cases like this one. Manchester is on the cutting edge of dealing with hit-and-runs. They used to be the domain of the traffic cops but they were deemed to be far too busy dealing with other duties to have the time needed to work on these, often complex, incidents. The general feeling is that it can take months to investigate a collision that at the time took only a few seconds. Unfortunately, in most cases the vital piece of evidence – the car – is missing.'

Clive almost interrupted, 'In the cases that I think may be linked to this one both cars were "borrowed" and then returned.'

Reg continued as though he hadn't heard the interruption. 'Matthew and Natasha Lloyd were crossing Brownlea Avenue at about a quarter past nine on Saturday. It was a clear morning, no rain or mist. It's a fairly busy road on the way to Sale Moor. The crossing where they were hit is just round the corner from the road they lived on. Apparently Matthew died on impact and his daughter in the ambulance on the way to hospital.' Reg was delivering the details in a professional manner but was obviously moved by the deaths.

Unable to stop himself from breaking in again Clive blurted out, 'Was it deliberate? Did anyone see what happened?'

'Two CCTV cameras picked up the car involved. The first shows it accelerating out of Brownlea Road where the Lloyds lived and the second is horrific to watch as it has several stills of the actual event. Unfortunately neither camera was near enough for our experts to be able to produce a good view of the driver. She looks elderly and is wearing a hat but she keeps her head low and I don't think any jury would feel confident saying that a defendant was the same person as the one driving the car.'

Giving his colleague what he hoped was a calming look the superintendent continued. 'We do have one excellent eye witness. Cheryl Harris was taking her dog for his morning stroll and was walking on the other side of the road, near the crossing. She saw the whole thing and has been able to give a fairly detailed account of the entire event. I've got her statement but it would be better for you to read it for yourself then I don't miss anything out.'

Almost grabbing the proffered document Clive read it several times, each time growing more excited. The handwriting wasn't the best and the content was rather disjointed, as though the witness had needed reminding to include all the relevant aspects, but the information was explosive, bonfire night had arrived early.

Statement written by Mrs Cheryl Harris, May 12th 15.30 hours

This morning - Saturday 12th May - I was walking down Brownlea Avenue at just after nine o'clock, taking Sam, my golden retriever for his morning constitutional.

I saw Doctor Lloyd and I know him by sight as he is, sorry was, a doctor at the surgery I go to. I've seen him there and I knew he lived in the area. He was with his little girl and they walked round the corner and approached the pelican crossing. They stopped and looked both ways and as there was nothing coming - at least nothing at that moment - they stepped off the kerb.

As they walked into the road the car, a silver BMW, appeared. The registration number was EPL 721K - I'm sure about that as I have a photographic memory. The car accelerated as it drove out of their road and kept getting faster and faster making no attempt to stop as it approached the crossing. By the time the car was at the crossing the Lloyds were in the middle of the road and the car appeared to swerve towards them, almost as though the driver wanted to knock them down.

Dr Lloyd was hit full on and then the car ran him over as he landed in front of it. The car just kept going. His daughter was swept sideways by the impact and was still alive when I went to see if I could help. Mrs Jennings, a friend of mine who lives at fifty-three Brownlea Avenue, rushed out of her house and said she'd call for an ambulance. She hadn't seen anything but had been in her front room and heard the noise as they were hit and had come out to see what had happened.

The driver made no attempt to stop, though she must have realised she had hit them. The sound was horrendous.

Yes I'm sure it was a woman. She looked elderly. I think she had grey hair but it was hard to tell under her hat and she was wearing a dark coat. But however old you are you know if you've hit two people. The strange thing was she didn't seem to be in a hurry to get away. I was busy going to see if I could do anything for the victims but I don't think she was speeding as she left. I would say she was well within the thirty mile an hour speed limit as she drove away.

I'd say the weather was good with excellent visibility.

I don't think I'd recognise her again as it was all so fast and I was watching Dr Lloyd and his daughter more than her.

I know the car was a BMW as my father-in-law has the same model. It was silver and I'm a hundred per cent sure about the registration, though it's not a very modern one.

It's a terrible thing to say but I do think it was deliberate.

She didn't attempt to miss them, in fact the opposite, she seemed to move towards them.

No, she made absolutely no attempt to stop and just drove off.

Signed: Cheryl Harris

Witnessed: P.C. Mark Howard 348092 Sale Station.

'It's the same. This is what I've been waiting for.' Seeing the other man's face Clive added, 'Apologies, that sounds terrible and I'm really sorry that two people are dead but I have a couple of identical cases, one in Seahouses and one in North Carolina, and so far the powers that be won't countenance a joint enquiry.'

'One happened in Northumbria and the other in America? How can two accidents have any links across the Atlantic?'

'That's been the problem so far. No one, apart from the deputy sheriff in Statesville, a small town in North Carolina, has believed that the two incidents are identical, but they are and now there's a third.' Clive went on to explain about the single fathers and their children and the October the fifteenth date that had first made him believe that the two previous events were more than a coincidence.

Stating the obvious, Reg replied that this latest incident had happened in May.

'That's true, but maybe the killer, and I know that is the most apposite word for this person, grew impatient and for some reason couldn't wait another five months. Perhaps she's got more victims lined up for October.'

'A dreadful thought and one that will encourage us to move quickly,' the superintendent muttered, whilst wondering how much of a case he could make should his superiors intervene and try to stop him. There were, on average nationwide, sixty-eight fatalities a year involving drivers who failed to stop. Both he and his superiors knew that outcomes were often elusive and he would be told to leave the matter to the Serious Collison and Investigation Unit. It was, after all, their domain. However, he had to admit that Clive had got him intrigued.

'The number plate she used this time is interesting, any leads?' Clive asked, thinking that any clue was better than none.

'It's from the early seventies and belonged to a Ford Cortina, registered to a Lawrence Mills who died in 1982. No news about the car after that. No information, nothing about it either being sold on or scrapped. The Authorised Treatment Facility has extensive records but they can't tell us when and if it was scrapped and the Driver and Vehicle Licensing Agency has no knowledge of it being sold on. It disappeared off the radar, into a Mancunian Bermuda Triangle, after Mr Mills purchased it in 1979. It belonged to a Thelma Gordon before that and I'll follow up her details but I doubt she's our "old lady" who enjoys running people down.'

The superintendent paused for a moment before adding, 'Our suspect is probably far too clever to use her own number plates, even if she had kept them all those years.' As Clive had thought, the number plates were of little use, changed almost certainly so that the vehicle couldn't be identified.

The next statement made his body tingle, like an allergic reaction to newly prescribed pills, 'The car has been found. It was returned to a Sainsbury's car park the morning after the accident. Its usual number plates had been refitted. The owner reported it missing weeks ago and thought she'd never see it again. The forensics boys tell us that it was the car used in the accident on Brownlea Avenue. The blood on the front matches the Lloyds.'

'I told you!' Realising he had sounded rude Clive continued more carefully, 'That's identical to the other cases where as I said the cars used were borrowed and returned. If all three are linked we're looking for one incredibly confident assailant.'

Reg smiled, 'I've not come across many villains who return a stolen car after using it. This person is highly organised, sure of themselves and thinks they're in perfect control: a profiler would be in their element. He or she must be thinking they'll always get away with it to exhibit such self-confidence. There's nothing to link her to the vehicle. Johnny, our forensic expert, assures me that, apart from the owners, no fingerprints have been found.'

'Is there any CCTV footage covering the relevant part of the car park?'

'Frustratingly none. There's no camera near the Parent and Child area and the one covering the rest of that section of the car park has been out of use for weeks. Why these things aren't maintained is beyond me. No doubt I'll have something to say about that.'

Hour after hour was spent dissecting the information Clive had brought, all his research carefully organised in a blue folder. The gender of the assailant was now established as female and it had become obvious that she used a different disguise for each event but, most discouragingly, his case wasn't much further on. The only agreeable aspect of the day was that someone else, and someone of higher rank, now believed him. Things might start to move.

When they parted, late in the afternoon, Clive was satisfied that the superintendent was willing to support his application to have all three cases reviewed with added assistance from the North Carolina deputy sheriff.

On returning home, very late in the evening, Mari's reaction to Clive's agitated account of his day was mixed. She was pleased to see her husband more upbeat than he had been for months but the obsession which had smouldered gently had become ignited into a raging inferno. Thank goodness for Bruges.

Chapter 14

It didn't take them long to find the car. Reading the latest article in the Manchester Evening News it appears that the gentleman who collects the trolleys noticed it about a quarter of an hour after I returned it. Thankfully there is no mention of anyone seeing it being parked. I love the paragraph when he says that it was the blood and dints on the front that alerted him to the fact that it wasn't "in pristine condition". No, it wouldn't be after annihilating two people!

The owner had reported it stolen on the day I borrowed it and her words about its return amused me, 'Amazing, I was told it was back exactly where I parked it weeks ago. It's as though I had a dream and when I woke up it had never been gone.' Apart from the red stains and extensive damage. She obviously spends too long with the under-fives.

As I was ultra-careful there is nothing to link me to the car. How I love my new driving gloves! However, the blood and some entrails on the front have been identified as a match to the Lloyds.

Off to Spain tomorrow, using my own passport this time. The Costa del Sol. Hope the emphasis is on the Sol.

Knowing that the longer a case remained unsolved the less likelihood there was of a conviction, Superintendent

Thompson moved quickly. Being the senior officer he would take overall charge of the three cases and the headquarters for the investigation would be situated in Sale. It had been agreed with the SCIU that they would share any information they gathered on the "fail to stop" in Sale and Reg promised to keep them informed if he was able to ascertain anything new. It appeared that the specialist unit was far too busy to wonder why a senior officer was taking such an interest in the case. Clive had agreed to return for a meeting on Thursday and Reg said he would phone North Carolina.

If his American colleague was surprised to hear from one of the top policemen in Greater Manchester he didn't react. 'Sure as hell, I'll be there. It's about time we dealt with this lunatic. There's no saying when, or where, she'll strike again and you can count on me to do my darndest. Be swell to visit England, my folks on my mother's side came from somewhere in the south, not too sure exactly where, and I've always wanted to see what it's like.' Reg stopped the excited flow and said he would organise a car to meet Dwayne at the airport and arrange some hotel accommodation.

'You've got my email address,' less time-consuming than another lengthy conversation, 'so let me know your flight details and we'll look forward to working with you.'

'Sure thing. I'll sort out all the info I've got and bring it with me. We might be going to solve these cases. Clive and I have been like two bears with fuzzy heads since this all kicked off.' Assuring the garrulous American that they all wanted the same thing he said goodbye and got to work selecting a small team to work with the trio.

Thursday morning saw Reg and Clive discussing the two English cases, their similarities and the main difference: the date. Dwayne sat, trying not to think about the jetlag that was affecting his ability to engage in any meaningful way. Overawed by his first trip to England he had not slept on the plane and had landed less than two hours ago. Any suggestion that he might like a few hours in his hotel room had been dismissed but he was finding it hard to remain focused.

'Carry on guys. I've got my Dictaphone on so I can replay every word back tonight and be ready to chip in tomorrow. Sure I'll be fully with it by then.' Hardly the ideal way to begin their investigation but Clive and Reg continued dissecting their incidents, hoping that some crumb of information, some minute detail, would give them the insight they required.

'Any news about Natasha's mother? We made no headway with looking for Peter and Paul's mothers.' Clive was almost certain what the answer would be.

'Absolutely no information. Matthew was an only child and his parents immigrated to Australia about twelve years ago, apparently to be near some relatives who were already there. I spoke to Mrs Lloyd on Saturday and she's giving us an internet interview tomorrow morning, bright and early to fit in with the time difference. We've got it booked for nine o'clock, but no doubt we'll have been working long before then.'

Taking the detailed notes he had made back to his hotel, a rather stark affair near St Peter's Square, Clive knew each of their cases had been scrutinised as thoroughly as humanly possible. Unable to relax he looked through the main points, made in his school-boy handwriting, all loops and curls and as always excessively neat.

Joe and Peter Nightingale.

Single father and his son

October 15th Seahouses, Northumberland

Joe a local business man, well thought of and no known enemies

Peter a school boy, keen on sport. No dealings with the police.

Hit-and-run. Car used was taken from nearby car park and returned, indicating a bold, confident person (or as Dwayne suggested a loop-the-loop) CCTV shows the car being taken and returned but of little help with identifying the thief

Forensics found nothing despite a re-examination of the vehicle

One witness who saw very little said he heard a car revving at the top of Smithfield Road, the site of the accident. He was sure the car was driven back at top speed

Incident occurred on the street where they lived as they returned from a football practice

Victims hit twice: deliberately?

Thought originally to be a male driver and no evidence to the contrary

Parents on Joe's side. They couldn't think of any reason for their son and grandson to be targeted.

No mother on the scene

No photos of her

No news of her whereabouts

No birth certificate in the house: request made to Registrar General

Stewart and Paul Wilson

Single father and his son

October 15^{th,} Statesville, North Carolina

Stewart a teacher at an Elementary school

Paul a pupil at the same school

The pair had immigrated to America several years before, having lived in the Manchester area until then

Stewart's parents had joined them soon after they arrived.

No known enemies

Respected in the close-knit community

No record of any trouble with the police

Car used taken from car park fifteen miles away and returned the same day (see Koplenski's witness statement)

Incident happened on the school car park after a softball practice

No CCTV footage either at the school or in the Wells Fargo car park

Several eyewitnesses including the Gwyneth Paltrow look-alike who says the driver was _definitely_ female (look carefully at her statement – calls herself Gloria)

Deliberate? Hit only once but no room for the car to manoeuvre

Car driven away at a "relaxed speed"

No mother on the scene

No photos of her

No news of her whereabouts

No birth certificate at the house: once again certificate requested

Matthew and Natasha Lloyd

Single father and his daughter

May 12th Sale, Greater Manchester

Pelican crossing near their house. Saturday morning.

Some CCTV footage of the incident but not clear enough to identify the driver

Driver dressed as an old lady, seems to favour disguises

Matthew Lloyd a well-respected local doctor

Natasha in the Reception class at Dawson Road Primary School.

Both spoken of with affection

No known enemies

No record of any dealings with the police

Car involved taken from Sainsbury's car park in Didsbury several weeks before the incident and returned on Sunday morning, the day after the accident. Number plates changed then replaced. No CCTV assistance

Deliberate
Excellent eyewitness (see her detailed statement)
Grandparents are the only known relatives. Live in Australia
Skype interview tomorrow
No mother on the scene
No photos of her
No news of her whereabouts
No birth certificate at the house: certificate requested

Having read his summaries, which were, he knew, merely brief resumes of all that had been discussed during the long day, Clive was excited to realise that although nothing new had transpired, the most obvious clue was beaming at him, a guiding light cutting through the fog. At the time the men had been so engaged with talking circuitously, revisiting the facts ad infinitum, they had become lost for hours in a maze of detail. Clive felt like an archaeologist unearthing a vital piece of evidence. At the time the crux of the matter had not been given sufficient credence. Now it stood out in all its black and white glory: the final four lines of each case. They were identical. No one had realised at the time that each man had ended his information employing the exact same words. The mother, or rather the absence of one, was the vital link. She was the connection. Find her and the case would be solved.

Chapter 15

Lovely holiday. Lots of sun, sand, sangria and yes, I have to admit it, sex. Prosaic, I know but I was so relaxed, so happy, so determined to reward myself for completing the penultimate stage and Carlos (yes it's true I never learn) was extremely dishy in a sultry Spanish style and so attentive. The knowledge that this time it was definitely just a silly holiday romance removed any anxiety. He pretended to be heartbroken when I left but let's face it he is hardly likely to follow me, to want to savour the delights of Manchester, and my contact details were erroneous in the extreme. Adios Carlos, Buenos Dias reality.

Nothing new on the Sale escapade, the papers have all gone quiet. How I would love to be the proverbial fly and position myself on the relevant wall in Sale police station. I could be earwigging (oh dear another insect) any discussions about the demise of the Lloyds. Perhaps it has all died down, pardon the pun, and the investigation has already been designated a "cold case". After all, they really haven't got much to go on.

Lying on the beach one sun-drenched afternoon I wondered what Henry, my much-missed godfather, would think of me. Since returning home I am experiencing some sleepless nights. The Lloyds' deaths are proving so much harder to deal with than either of the *first two pairs and I am aware of a most unwelcome feeling of loss. Is it the fact that Matthew was a doctor, a valued and respected member of the area, and Natasha was sweet and still totally innocent? She was the youngest of my victims and maybe that also comes into the equation.*

In my bleaker moments I know that my wonderful, kind, caring godfather would have been horrified. No excuses would have been accepted. He was a man who lived by Biblical rules. In his eyes I would be a sinner, breaking several, if not most of the Ten Commandments.

I have definitely coveted my sister's money and status: they should be mine – to remain Biblical, my birthright.

I have not kept the Sabbath, though no murder has, so far, been undertaken then.

I have stolen, or borrowed, cars and Sophie's passport and I won't even think about Commandment number six!

As a Christian he would have told me to love Sophie, my enemy. Fat chance of that. Only his opinion has ever mattered to me and I can't avoid dwelling on the fact that I would, to put it mildly, have lost my reputation with him.

And so…six dealt with and only one left. I cannot give in to sentiment now. All that remains is to make plans for Sophie, the cause of it all. I have four and a half months until she takes her final journey. Oh how I enjoy these Victorian epithets. Potentially this final escapade might be the one to fail. It's a given that the police look at family members first in any investigation so I must be squeaky clean. Better stop now before I turn into a walking idiom machine.

Sleeping pill, I need a good night's sleep, as I'm back to my wonderful quartet tomorrow. No doubt they'll come in looking as though they're high on Ecstasy after almost two weeks with parents who can't say no and feed them junk food. Still, only six weeks to the long summer holiday when entire days can be devoted to formulating plans for my sister.

'Good morning Mr and Mrs Lloyd. Please accept our condolences. We are so sorry for your loss and realise that to lose both a son and a young granddaughter is beyond words.' Over his many years in the force, the superintendent had been required to deliver such words on far too many occasions, but he was finding this conversation particularly difficult.

Although thousands of miles separated the Lloyds from the three policemen the Skype system was crystal clear and they could all have been in the same room.

'I'm sorry to have to ask you this,' Reg continued, hating every second of the link, 'I just wondered if you were aware of anyone who might have wanted to hurt your family.'

Bill Lloyd sat stock still and let his wife speak. 'Matthew never mentioned any problems; in fact he seemed so happy. It hasn't been easy since she moved out, Natasha's mother, but he's had reliable help and our granddaughter was flourishing. We saw them at Christmas and they stayed on for the New Year. We've both got health problems and have been told not to fly so we have to rely on them coming to us.' Samantha Lloyd broke down, loud sobs filling the room.

Putting his arm round his wife's shoulder Bill spoke in a surprisingly strong voice, 'Matthew said they'd come to visit us for several weeks in the summer once

Natasha broke up from school. She's only been there since last September but can already read and write. She's a clever little thing, just like her dad.' Neither parent realised they were still using the present tense: that knowledge would come later.

'Can you tell us anything about Matthew's wife?'

'We never met her. Matthew phoned us to say he had got married, not to the girl he'd been engaged to, but to a woman he'd met called Pearl, or he said that was his pet name for her and we never heard him use any other. There were no photos of her, either at the wedding or afterwards. Even when the baby pictures arrived they were of Matthew and his baby daughter, never any with Natasha's mother.'

His wife interrupted, 'We asked him about it once as we thought it strange we'd never seen what she looked like. He told us that she hated having her photo taken and even he didn't have any of her. Not a single one. We never said anything to him but we thought it was peculiar.'

Knowing that this information was vitally important Clive continued the conversation, 'Did Matthew bring Natasha to Australia when she was small?'

Fighting back the tears which threatened to escape like water from a cracked pipe, Samantha whispered so softly the policemen struggled to hear the words, 'Yes, he brought her to see us when she was six months old. She was the most adorable thing we'd ever seen and we loved having them with us. They stayed for two weeks and Matt said his wife was too busy to travel with them. At that time he seemed happy with the relationship and we were shocked when a year later he told us she had walked out. What kind of woman leaves her own child?'

'Do you know if they had much contact afterwards?'

'None. We know Matthew was terribly disappointed about that but he said there was nothing he could do. Apparently when she left she said she would be out of their lives completely and she kept her word. We were so proud of the way Matt coped.' At last Bill was using the past tense.

'Is there anything else you want to add? Any tiny detail you can think of that might help us with our enquiries. We would really like to contact the mother. So far no one seems to know anything about her.' Reg was at his calmest and most persuasive, aware that people could divulge details they didn't know they possessed.

The bereaved parents looked at each other, desperate to be of assistance. Samantha replied softly, 'Maybe one thing: her nickname, Pearl, was something to do with her love of jewellery and we know she had a pearl engagement ring. But that doesn't seem very helpful.'

Each side promised to get in touch if anything new emerged and the link ended. The men sat in silence, exhausted both by the emotional tension of the call and frustration at the lack of progress.

'Have the birth certificates come through?' Clive asked, knowing all three had been requested.

'They should be here by now, I'll go and check. P.C. Withington has been dealing with that.' Reg was already half way out of the door by the time he finished his sentence. Returning a few minutes later he put the required documents on the table. Each man selected one and began to read it.

'The Lloyds were quite correct about the name. The mother is down as Pearl Lloyd, date of birth 24th March 1977, place of birth Manchester. Her maiden name is recorded as Smith: Pearl Amber Smith. The father's details look to be accurate: Matthew George Lloyd, doctor, also from Manchester.' As Dwayne finished speaking he realised that his colleagues were staring at him like fish derived of water, mouths open, gasping for air.

'You're not going to believe this. On Peter Nightingale's certificate the mother is Ruby Smith, place of birth Manchester. Date of birth 24th March 1977. The father is correct: Joe Nightingale, self-employed, born in Seahouses.' Clive turned to look at Reg. 'Your turn.'

'Baby: Paul Wilson, mother: Beryl Smith, and you've guessed it, same date and place of birth. Father Stewart Wilson, teacher from Manchester.'

Reg said he was rather confused by the name Beryl as it didn't appear to fit with the other pseudonyms. Clive spoke excitedly, knowing that this latest information was the breakthrough they had been seeking. 'No, Beryl fits perfectly: it's an important gem material. The famous Beryl is emerald but some are aquamarine. I know all about them as Mari loves them and her engagement ring is an emerald Beryl.'

Poring over the details on the three certificates created more questions than answers. None of them would have felt confident applying to *Mastermind* with their case as the specialist subject. It was Reg who suggested that they start to work more logically and create a data base of their new findings. Clive wrote as his colleague attempted to put the new details into some semblance of order.

'The ephemeral Ms Smith gave birth in 1995, 2005 and 2009. That would make her eighteen when she had Peter, twenty-eight when she gave birth to Paul and thirty-two when Natasha arrived. Ruby/Beryl/Pearl must be thirty-eight by now so there's been time for another one since she left Matthew Lloyd.' Moments later he continued, 'The names she uses are almost certainly fictitious so we can't be sure about the rest of her details. Her first baby, Peter, was born in Reading, the next two in Manchester. Did she come from this city as the certificates claim or were her early years spent down south?' On each certificate there is an honest description of the father – a different man in each case – nothing new these days, so if she was being honest about each dad, why fabricate her details? Did she always intend to abscond? Was motherhood never a big part of her life?' Knowing they had gleaned all they could the men walked downstairs to the canteen. Over lunch the mysterious Ms Smith was the only topic of conversation.

'We should contact Seahouses and Statesville to rein-terview anyone who might have known about the mother. Someone might have found an old photo or a letter she wrote. Surely in both cases there must have been some contact with the mother of their grandchild.' Adjusting the phone to loudspeaker mode Reg rang Evie and Michael Nightingale in Seahouses.

After the usual introductions and pleasantries the Nightingales' disappointment was palpable when they realised that the police weren't contacting them to say they had been able to apprehend anyone for killing Joe and Peter.

'No news, after all these years. Murdering our lovely boys and getting away with it. I know nothing can bring them back but we would love to see someone pay for what they did. We'd also like to know why. That's what we'll never understand.' Michael Nightingale sounded wounded; the hurt evidently hadn't diminished in the intervening years.

'Have you ever seen Peter's birth certificate?' Reg asked carefully.

Following a brief discussion with her husband, Evie sounded perturbed as she replied, 'No, we never saw it. We don't know anything at all about the circumstances of Peter's birth or the woman who gave birth to him. She was never in his life. Never. I think I told you at the time that Joe went to collect his son the day after he was born. He didn't even tell us where his son had been born though he must have had quite a journey there as he was away for almost two days. We never met her and Joe didn't even want to tell us her name.'

'Have you ever heard of a Ruby Smith? We don't know if that is her real name but it's the one on the birth certificate.' The trio were not surprised when the name meant nothing to either grandparent.

Trying one last time, like a boxer attempting to land the vital knockout blow before the final round ended, Reg asked, 'Did she ever make contact? A letter, birthday card, phone call?'

Evie didn't have to think about her response, 'Nothing, absolutely nothing – we were appalled but Joe said it was what he knew would happen as she had informed him that they would never see her again. She'd been all for having a termination until Joe stopped her by promising to bring up the baby alone. He was doing such a grand job, it's all too sad. We still don't sleep and life will never be the same again.'

'Is the birth certificate a new lead? Have you reopened the case?' The hope in Michael's voice was mortifying. He was told that there was some new information and that fresh leads were being investigated but that they couldn't say too much at the moment. He knew that wasn't what the bereaved parents wanted to hear but it was as much as he could tell them.

'That went well,' Clive's exasperation was vented on his colleagues. 'We know no more than we did two years ago.'

'My turn now, it'll be mid-morning in NC, so might as well get on with the call.'

Just like the Nightingales, Dan and Holly Wilson were surprised, and then hopeful, when they heard the deputy sheriff's voice. The ensuing conversation was almost identical to the ones they had recorded that morning. Dan and Holly Wilson knew nothing about the mother. They had never met her, seen photos or spoken to her. Frustratingly, no new information had emerged, the kind that might give the essential break through.

'Stewart and the woman never married and we didn't meet her. There was always some excuse. Even when we were all living in England Stewart came to see us on his own. Later on he brought Paul with him. We know it's unusual but that's how it was and any time we hinted that we would like to meet up he said she was shy with people and preferred to stay at home. We never got an invitation to their place.' Holly's long speech had tired her and Dan took over.

'You say you have the birth certificate. Does it have her details on it?' The couple had no knowledge of the name Beryl Smith as Stewart had always referred to her as Poppet. 'Sorry we can't help, we would love to be able to tell you more but Stewart always clammed up if we ever so much as mentioned Paul's mother.'

Just as the men were about to give up for the day the computer indicated that there was an incoming Skype call. 'Hello Reg, sorry to disturb you but Bill and I have been talking and we don't know if it's important but we have remembered one thing.' Assuring Mrs Lloyd that no detail was too small she was asked to continue.

'When Natasha was born Matthew rang us and he was so excited. He was really pleased that the baby was a girl but when we asked what they were going to call her he said they were still discussing that. We commented afterwards that arguing was probably the more appropriate word. Anyway it was ages before he told us the baby was going to be called Natasha and when I said what a lovely name his comment was that it was a great deal better than Mary. From the odd comment he made it seemed that his wife was a strong character who liked her own way. He once said that at least he had won on the name front. That's probably of no consequence but you did say to contact you if we thought of anything.'

Agreeing silently that the new information was almost certainly useless Reg thanked Samantha for the call but before he cut the link she added, 'He once said that she was keen on her job and earned a lot of money. We know she took a very short maternity leave after Natasha was born and we assumed she worked in some professional capacity, though we know she wasn't a doctor, Matthew would have mentioned that.'

Once the computer had reverted to its lurid screen-saver – a psychedelic world of multicoloured mountains, rainbow coloured cattle and orange rivers – Clive muttered, as though speaking to himself, 'Peter, Paul and Natasha. But it should have been Peter, Paul and Mary.' His colleagues looked confused. 'When I was young my father's favourite pop group was Peter, Paul and Mary. They were a nineteen sixties folk trio, sang some Civil Rights songs like Bob Dylan's *Blowin in The Wind* and *Where Have All The Flowers Gone?*'

'Sure do remember them now,' Dwayne butted in, 'they kept going for almost five decades. I loved *Leaving on a Jet Plane.*'

'*Puff the Magic Dragon* was my favourite as a child, but it brought tears to my mum's eyes,' Clive quipped, attempting and failing to lift the men's spirits.

Having listened to very little apart from classical music Reg was unable to join in with their reminiscences, but was interested in the names. 'So this group was known as Peter, Paul and Mary and you're saying that having had two sons with the appropriate names the mother wanted to complete her trio by calling her daughter Mary?'

'Sounds like it but it doesn't really help much.' Clive's enthusiasm about the group and its well-loved songs had faded as reality reasserted itself, like an alarm clock waking one to face the day. 'Could she have something to do with the music industry? Manchester has always produced a lot of good musicians, some great bands still around. The Bee Gees, Herman's Hermits and The Hollies all began life here and the music scene is still buzzing.' Even Reg admitted that he had heard of those particular groups but thought Clive was so keen to make progress that he was willing to consider any new lead, however tenuous.

'Thank you gentlemen but I think we should leave it there. We're all tired and it would be good to have a rest and return refreshed tomorrow. Shall we say eight o' clock?'

'Just one thing before we leave it for the day. Is there any mileage in putting articles in each of our local papers asking for anyone who knew our victims and more importantly the mothers to come forward? We've asked for eyewitnesses to the hit-and-runs and spoken to each immediate family, but so far we haven't tried spreading our enquiries more broadly.' As he spoke, Clive remembered the trouble his last article had caused but if a new one might uncover anything he was willing to risk another reprimand.

'Let's think about that overnight and discuss it tomorrow. The wording would have to be carefully written, but it's worth thinking about.' Reg had his doubts but he was willing to try anything.

Chapter 16

An article in today's paper asked the question "What is your most precious possession?" The journalist suggested writing down ten things one would want to save in the event of a fire and select the one most cherished. What a waste of time, surely everyone knows what their ultimate one would be without expending any time or thought on it. Why bother committing ten ideas to paper when all most people are going to choose is something prosaic like a photograph album or "You're the best mum in the world" mug.

Mine would be the grandfather clock that Henry left me. It had been in his family for generations and stood in the corner of the hall, marking the quarter hours with a delightful alto chime. It is an impressive timepiece and on almost every visit I would comment on it, admiring its cherry wood case and the face topped by moving pictures which circled at a leisurely pace displaying the sun rising and setting followed by the four phases of the moon. As a child I would stand and gaze at it and, although Amy liked it, Henry promised it to me as it would remind me of the time we spent together.

Strange choice? It's true I couldn't rescue it from the flames, even Superman would have great difficulty salvaging it, but it is, for me, par excellence and definitely my favourite possession. Every week, first thing on a

Sunday morning, I wind it eight times. The key fits in its brass-lined aperture as effortlessly as it did when the clock was made at the end of the eighteenth century and it is a salutary thought that so many hands have completed this action before me. My living room is too modern to do full justice to such a superb antique but as I tend to be the only person who sees it I am thrilled to share my space with it.

That ridiculous article exercised my mind before I discovered the newspaper's bombshell which created more shock waves than any nuclear warhead. Turning to page twelve I sat immobilised and more frightened than I had ever thought possible and, having never suffered from asthma, was alarmed to find myself fighting for breath.

I always read every part of the papers I buy, skimming some sections and examining every word of others. Having glanced at the main news items: Arabs and Israelis still attacking each other; the summer storms bringing motorways to a halt in Cheshire; a spate of armed robberies in central Manchester; the success of the free school meals which have been introduced for all Key Stage One children – I almost dropped the paper when I read:

New Information Sought in Hit-and-Run Incident

Superintendent Reginald Thompson, the officer in charge of the investigation into the recent hit-and-run accident on Brownlea Avenue in Sale, is seeking further information about the incident. A father, Doctor Matthew Lloyd, and his five year old daughter, Natasha, were killed in the accident.

At the time eyewitnesses were able to give valuable assistance regarding the incident itself. Superintendent Thompson is now keen to speak to anyone who may have known Natasha's mother. The lady in question does not appear to have been a major part of Natasha's life but the police are keen to ascertain her present whereabouts.

She was almost certainly living in the Manchester area in 2009 when Natasha was born and went by the name of Pearl Lloyd. At the time she is believed to have been in her early thirties but very little is known about her apart from that.

Anyone who thinks they may have known her, or can give any details as to where she may be living today, is asked to contact Sale police station, telephone number 0161 2266776. All information will be treated as confidential.

Just looked at Statesville's and Seahouse's local papers on the internet and guess what…the same article in them asking about a Beryl Smith and a Ruby Smith respectively. Now which super sleuth linked that trio of long-forgotten individuals?

Googling (oh dear, a verb from the noun – sounds like a transatlantic innovation) the three names given in today's newspaper reports, I found the following item in The Reading Chronicle:

Information Requested on Missing Woman

Manchester police are keen to hear from anyone with information about a woman who went by the name of Ruby Smith. Ms Smith gave birth to a boy in Reading in 1995 but her present whereabouts are unknown. Police are keen to speak to her in relation to an incident in Sale, Greater Manchester, and would like anyone who thinks they may have known her in 1995 or who knows where she may be living today to contact them on 0161 2266776.

It was a very small piece at the bottom of page thirty so may go unnoticed, but it feels as though the walls of the dungeon are closing in, like a scene from an old horror movie. My only comfort is that few people will remember anything: anything at all. Pearl, Ruby and Beryl had short incarnations and have long since departed.

However I must admit that if I was a drinker I'd be downing a bottle of vodka – or five.

Days became weeks and apart from the usual nuisance and idiot calls no one came forward with any useful information. After his moment of euphoria, when it had seemed that real progress was being made, Clive had retreated into his black shell, if anything more despondent than before. Sometimes hope can be so cruel: the "might have been" highlighting the trio's futile efforts with an unwanted clarity. He had to admit that the cases had come to another standstill. 'It's like sitting in a frustrating queue of traffic with no green light in sight.' Clive's terse comment did little to lighten his or Mari's day.

Each summer the couple went away as soon as the schools broke up. Two weeks in Austria their annual escape. They had stayed in Alpbach before and agreed with the comment that it was "Austria's prettiest village". In previous vacations they had rejoiced in the lack of human noise, loving the recuperative value of hearing only nature: birds, waterfalls, the wind and rushing streams. By the seventh day Mari was weary and ready to go home. Each walk had been an endurance test of listening to her husband's incessant murmurings about the unsolved investigations. Normally a keen hiker, Clive lacked the energy to complete even the shortest and least challenging of the walks.

'I'll take the gondola down from the middle station and you can walk the rest of the way. We can meet back at the hotel.'

'If you think for one moment that this is how I want to spend the holiday, you're mistaken Clive Rogers. You've hardly spoken to me since we arrived about anything other than we both know what. And for your information I have not come here to spend time on my own. We either walk together or I'm on the next flight home. For goodness sake, we're miles away from work and I need a break just as much as you do.'

The remainder of the walk was conducted in an uneasy silence, broken only by the sounds of the natural world, which despite their crescendo to double forte went unheard. On arriving at their hotel Clive was told he'd got a message recorded on the telephone in the room.

'Hello Clive, Reg here, hope all is well and that the holiday is relaxing. I know you're away and enjoying yourself but I thought you'd want to hear the latest development. We've had a lady come forward from Reading with some information. There's too much to say and I don't want you to miss anything so I'll send an email attachment of her statement. I assume you've got your iPad with you. No need to respond, we can meet up when you return. It's nothing earth-shattering but there are a couple of small leads in what she says. Do hope the sun is shining, it's pouring here, and that the scenery and food are great. Best wishes to your wife. Bye.'

Fingers shaking so much that he had to put his identity number in three times, the machine was finally up and running and the email opened.

Information received from Mrs Shirley Pullis. 11.20 July 30th 2014. Telephone call transcribed by P.C. Anthony Jenkins.

Hello, I'm ringing in response to the newspaper article in the Reading Chronicle in late May. Sorry to have taken so long to get in touch but I was away at the time and although my daughter buys all the local papers it's taken me ages to read them as I've not been well.

I'm contacting you about the lady called Ruby Smith. You said anyone with any information should phone you. I can't remember much but I think I delivered her baby.

In 1995 I'd just qualified as a midwife and I'm pretty sure she was one of my first ladies. I remember her as she had a long and difficult labour and I was nervous as I was still inexperienced. She was very young, maybe late teens, and there was no father with her, though they didn't always want to be present at the birth in those days. I'm pretty sure her name was Ruby Smith but the strange thing was, and it's the reason her case sticks in my mind, she didn't want anything to do with the baby. He was a lovely little boy but she never held him or so much as glanced his way.

She should have stayed in hospital for at least forty-eight hours after such a tricky delivery but discharged herself later that day, against medical advice, leaving the baby behind. I seem to recall that an older woman came to collect Ruby, probably her mother.

The dad came for his son the following day. She had given us his name and details, sorry I can't remember them, and he arrived and showed us some identity then left with the baby. That wouldn't happen today, Social Services would be all over it. She was the talk of the unit for weeks. We'd never had a mother do that.

I seem to think that she was blond with shoulder-length hair, but I wouldn't recognise her now. I was too busy dealing with the other end!

Yes, I am willing to be interviewed but I rather doubt that I would be able to add any more. I will be in touch again if I think of anything else. I still work on the unit and I'll speak to Jenna, one of our senior nurses. We started together and are still friends. I think she was with me on Maternity that day.

I'll ask her and see if she can come up with anything I've forgotten. She's got a far better memory than me, so you never know.

Having read the email for the nth time Clive relayed its contents to Mari. 'I don't know what to make of it, whether it's useful or not.'

Knowing when she was beaten, Mari spoke calmly. 'It does confirm that the mother was in absentia from the beginning: if, of course, it's the same woman.'

'If it is we've not got much of a description…"Blond shoulder-length hair". That could have changed twenty times since then.'

'Can you ask your superintendent if he's going to get in touch with the other nurse, Jenna? She might be more informative especially if she wasn't too involved in the actual birth. She might be able to furnish a better description of the mother. Also, there must have been someone who signed the voluntary discharge papers. Hospitals need to cover their backs when someone leaves against a doctor's advice. The hospital should have a record of that.'

Realising that his wife was not only being sympathetic but also helpful, he rushed over to hug her. His impulsive gesture was the first for longer than either of them was willing to acknowledge.

'I'll just phone Reg and suggest both ideas then we'll get ready for dinner. The evening is yours. Sorry I've been such a bore.'

For the remainder of the holiday, unfortunately only a few days, Clive made a monumental effort to relax and enjoy the scenery and his wife's company. Neither ever liked arriving home, the knowledge that once they walked through their front door normal life would encroach with an immediacy that always surprised them. As they went into the living room the telephone's red light indicated missed calls: three of them.

'I know you're away and won't get this today and it will keep until you get back but we've had some worthwhile stuff, sorry what a word, but not sure whether it's real identification or someone's hazy memories. You'll understand when you hear them. Give me a ring when you're home and we can arrange a time to interview our two – yes two – women who say they remember something. One is about Ruby Smith and the other Beryl Smith. Speak to you soon. Oh, hope the rest of your break was good.'

Priorities prevailed. Suitcases stood unopened in the hall, rucksacks were abandoned at the bottom of the stairs. Mari was dispatched to the kitchen to make a cup of tea, the first decent one for almost two weeks, and Clive picked up the phone. A meeting was arranged for the end of the week with Clive left feeling frustrated at how little his colleague had wanted to divulge. 'Wait and hear what the ladies have to say. I'd like your reaction to be untainted.' Feeling like a child who has been told there are three more sleeps before Father Christmas pays his annual visit he tried valiantly to fill the days with the work that accumulated during his absence. Somehow dealing with the drunk and disorderly couple or the habitual petty thief did little to exercise his mind. What would Friday bring?

Chapter 17

Summer holidays – always too long. Unfortunately my time away is already over. I spent it rally driving in Finland. There are British breaks involving driving rally cars but they tend to be just two or three nights and I've done a couple of them before, both in South Wales, and although I enjoyed them I fancied something longer and more challenging. I went for the self-drive option as the escorted tour sounded too easy. Five days of the most exhilarating driving on rough gravel roads with jumps that hurtle driver and car for forty to fifty metres through the air. Wonderful and all on the wrong side of the road! Thought I'd hone my skills before the October denouement.

Sophie – the when is a given. The how goes without saying. Only the where is unknown. My brain feels frayed, like paper at the wrong end of a shredder. The more I ponder the less confident I feel about the location. She lives in a gated community with coded entries and surveillance cameras: totally inappropriate. Her working life covers several venues, none of which is appropriate, all in the centre of busy towns. Perhaps I will have to be more sociable and suggest some weekend outings. The final one might just have to include October 15th.

Transcript of the Interview with Jenna Franklin
August 11th 2014 D.C.I. Clive Rogers and
Superintendent Reginald Thompson present.

'Thank you for attending today Mrs Franklin. We believe you may have come into contact with a Ruby Smith in 1995. We understand that it is a long time ago but anything you can recall about her would be most helpful. Take your time and just say anything that you remember.'

'I was a young nurse and knew I wanted to work on Maternity. I'd been on that ward at The Royal Hospital in Reading for about two months and was really enjoying it. I was allowed to be in the delivery room to assist but at the time I wasn't a midwife and so didn't play a direct role in the actual birth. I was there to pass the appropriate equipment. Fetch and carry if you will.

Well, this particular day a very young girl came in, her labour already quite advanced. She was a screamer and let the whole hospital know she was in pain. It was a very long birth and when the baby, a gorgeous little boy – I do recall that as it was one of the things that made what happened afterwards so surprising – arrived, I assumed she didn't want to hold him because she was tired. Shirley, Mrs Pullis, was the midwife who delivered him and when she told the mum that she had a little boy her reply was, 'Good. A son will make it easier for him.'

Wanting to gain new information, Reg interrupted the flow, 'Can you give us a description of the woman?'

'It was a long time ago but I remember her being very pretty. Longish blond hair and I think blue eyes though I might be imagining that. She was above average height and I could tell she was normally a slim lady. She had a northern accent, though not very broad. I'm not good with accents and I can't say exactly where the accent came from.'

Transcript of the Interview with
Teresa Blackall August 11th 2014

In the paper it asked anyone who might have known Pearl Lloyd to contact the police. I'm sorry I haven't come forward sooner but my husband said I shouldn't interfere.

We used to live next door to the Lloyds. When they were first married, I think it was in 2007, they moved into the detached house next to ours on Sutton Lane in Urmston. They're big houses and we wondered how they could afford one. They both worked or, maybe like us, they'd inherited some money. We'd been there for a year before they arrived and it was good to see new people move in. They were always pleasant but made it obvious that there would be no socialising, so we never got further than passing the time of day over the communal fence.

We knew he was a doctor but she never said what she did. It must have been something professional as each morning, and even sometimes at the weekends, she was out of the house before eight, dressed in a smart suit, and she was never home until the evening. When Natasha was born Mrs Lloyd was only home for about six weeks before she returned to work. It's a terrible thing to say but we weren't surprised when she left as she didn't seem to enjoy being a mum, never took the baby out much or talked about her. The baby must have been about eighteen months by the time the mother went.

Once she left, Matthew seemed to cope well on his own and looked after Natasha with help from a full-time nanny. She was a lovely woman and so good with Natasha; they didn't stay long after Mrs Lloyd departed and moved away within a few months.

Sorry, I've no idea where the mother went and I only know about him from the newspapers.

She was a very attractive woman – think Cliff, that's my husband, fancied her! Blond hair cut short, about five foot eight and with a good figure. Her voice was more refined than a lot of the locals but she did have a slight accent. Most people would have known she came from the Manchester area.

Clive was disappointed. 'Neither lady gave us too much to go on.'

'At least the descriptions tally, though what we've heard could cover about twenty per cent of the female population.'

'The same woman – where the devil is she and what is she doing now? I'm totally convinced that if we find her we can solve our cases.'

Clive said that they ought to inform Dwayne of the latest developments. 'If we tell him what our witnesses said it might trigger something.' Even to his ears this had an air of desperation.

Was the mother involved in their cases? If so, why would any mother murder her children? Abandoning them was bad enough but to kill them was incomprehensible.

Although pleased to be kept up to date, Dwayne had to agree that they weren't much further forward. Hearing the latest theory that the driver in each case might be the mother of all three children resulted in several moments of transatlantic silence.

'Dwayne, are you still there?'

'Yes, just lost for words...See this is the thing, we know the assailant in Statesville was over here for several days before the incident. Miss Loopy saw her outside the school on several occasions before the fateful day. We also know she was wearing some sort of disguise and hardly left her car. However, as we've said before, someone must have seen her dressed normally. On many occasions we've agreed she must have been a visitor and we don't rightly get too many of those in our little bit of NC. She must have stayed somewhere and if she's English she has to have arrived at an airport some time before the accident. You will remember that I checked British females entering the United States for the week leading up to October 15th and those leaving the following week. I also have the passport details of visitors staying in all the local hotels.'

'And nothing relevant came to light,' Reg said, adding, 'remind me which airports you tried.'

'The ones most people staying in NC come through: Charleston, Raleigh and Greensboro.'

'Might be worth extending the search: more airports, even those some distance away and any hotels you might have missed.' Reg knew he was giving his friend a huge amount of extra work.

'You're right. There's nothing to say she stayed in Statesville or Wilksboro. I'll try Daviston and Salisbury. They've both got tourist hotels.'

'Good luck and keep us informed,' Reg said before realising he was talking to the dialling tone. 'He's excited, didn't even say goodbye. Not much point feeling too eager. Let's face it this might not lead anywhere.'

After sandwiches were purchased from the canteen, lunch was eaten in the local park. The day threatened rain but the men were too animated to notice. Remaining indoors had not been an option. Both had taken their mobile phones and sat staring at their screens hopeful that some telepathic input might speed Dwayne's response.

'Why are we sitting waiting for him to contact us so soon?' It could take days or even weeks for him to access the necessary information. There are so many other airports she could have used. Who's to say she didn't enter America via New York or Washington and travel down to Statesville? Widening the net to such an extent is going to involve a tremendous amount of work even before he has a chance to get the records from all the hotels in the area. And if you think about it there must be a lot of those within striking distance. Sorry, no pun intended.'

Agreeing that they probably wouldn't hear from their American counterpart for some days Clive accepted a lift to Piccadilly station.

'I'll email Dwayne later and say we'll be in touch every seventy-two hours. He'll be stressed enough without us harassing him too often.' Clive had to pretend to be satisfied with Reg's timescale though all he wanted to do was take a taxi to Manchester airport and get on the next plane to America.

Chapter 18

If Sophie has been surprised by my sudden interest in her she hasn't shown it. But then she's always been a consummate actress. The times Dad believed her when she claimed to have been at a girlfriend's house completing some homework became almost comical.

Fortunately she isn't involved with a man at the moment: most unusual. So far we've been out for another meal – cheap pizza this time, much more my style; spent an afternoon shopping – for her, she's off to some swanky dinner dance at the end of the month; and seen a show, Dancing on Ice, *clever but boring.*

My next suggestion is a day in The Lakes. That could be the dummy run I need. If I drive this time I can say how much I love the quiet roads in that area, as long as one avoids Ambleside, Grasmere and Bowness, and suggest we do it again in the autumn. The colours can be quite spectacular. Maybe think about mid-October!

School is back next week and I won't be sorry to return to the all-consuming routine. Going in today to get ready for the onslaught was cathartic. Katie was there and we had a good catch up. Obviously I sanitised some of my thinking and planning activities. Names needed writing on exercise books, pencils, pens and rulers placing on every child's desk (we're old-fashioned and have retained double desks) and the many display

*boards needing backing with a glorious array of
rainbow-hued paper ready for the first exhibits. Our
room has been painted a light lemon, and everything
looks fresh and ready for action. Can't wait.*

*Strange to think that by the start of next half-term
I will no longer have a sister. It's all going too well.
Sophie cannot possibly be this easy. Strangely, and
comfortingly, it's gone quiet on the newspaper front,
no more items asking for witnesses. How very frustrating for my pursuers. Will they link the accident in
Cumbria to the others? Probably, especially should it
occur on the "oh so special" date.*

Millions of women had entered the United States during
the relevant weeks. The U.S. Customs and Border
Control, which monitors the numerous points of entry,
was happy to supply the information but Dwayne's
team were amazed to learn that more than a million
people enter the United States legally every day. (No one
dared mention the unauthorised contingent.)

Dwayne had queried that figure, but Jon Delways,
the Border Control official with whom he had had
several conversations, was certain that the average
number is about the million mark.

'There are three hundred and seventeen entry points
into the States. People come in by air, land and sea. We
can't cover them all so will have to go for the more
obvious airports.' Dwayne addressed his newly assembled team sounding almost as overwhelmed as he felt.
'It's highly unlikely that the woman we are seeking
entered by sea or indeed by crossing a land border.
Even restricting ourselves to the airports will be a
monumental task.'

Dwayne informed his team that they were looking for a woman, in theory halving the incomers, and he told them to concentrate on females between the ages of twenty and forty. Unfortunately no airport which received flights directly from Europe could be excluded, after all why might she not have used Chicago, Atlanta or any of the other hubs then flown, driven, taken a Greyhound bus or travelled by Amtrak to North Carolina?

By working sixteen-hour days each female's credentials was checked and double-checked. Although the person they sought was believed to come from the Manchester area this didn't mean she had flown from that airport.

'She's one clever dame so there nothing to say she didn't arrive via Amsterdam, Paris or Frankfurt, all common routes and often less expensive.' Dwayne's comment did little to encourage his team. As Jed Spruce, an experienced policeman and committed Baptist announced, 'It's like separating the Biblical wheat from the chaff.'

Almost three weeks after initiating the search Dwayne called a meeting. 'I think we're going at this cock-a-hoop. The dame must have stayed near enough to drive to the school on at least two occasions before the day of the hit-and-run, so it stands to reason she was staying somewhere close. Let's forget the point of entry and concentrate on where she stayed. We have the info from last time from local motels so first off we recheck them then widen our enquiries. We know she had a car – Jerry, check car hire outlets – though she probably hired one at whichever airport she used, then we go to every goddam place with a bed for the night.'

All venues claimed to have reliable records: passport details married to length of stay. However, the police were aware that some guests slipped through the rigorous checks. The geographical area initially covered was extended to include the many small towns in the vicinity which advertised motels, guest houses and European style B and B's.

'Did she use her own name? Was she travelling under a false passport? Could she have stayed somewhere that wasn't too careful about requesting her ID?' These and similar thoughts invaded the enquiry headquarters, like the swarm of hornets that had put the town in a recent panic.

Day followed day of labour-intensive scrutinising. Names were highlighted then deleted. Lists were formulated and cross-matched with airport details. One of the last motels to be visited was The Easy Way Inn. It was not on the official list of accommodation and had been missed the first time. Situated off a quiet side street in Wilksboro it had a rather dilapidated façade which would not entice many visitors. The motel's side rooms overlooked the Wells Fargo car park: the scene of the disappearing car. The police officer couldn't hide his frustration when he realised that this establishment didn't bother observing the State's rule on guest registration. No records were available for the period in question.

The receptionist looked too young to be at work and was still suffering the teenage embarrassment of uncontrolled acne. 'I seem to recall that we did have an English lady staying about that time: lovely accent and so polite. She was definitely here during the Fall Festival which was the same week as that terrible accident. We all thought she'd have chosen one of the other motels, as she seemed kinda out of place here. Paid in cash. She hadn't booked beforehand and I remember she just turned up and liked the second room she saw which overlooks the car park. I'm no good on older people but I'd guess she was about thirty. She was a bit of a looker: a bit of a Barbie, blond hair, great figure and above average height. She was definitely English. Strange thing is that she claimed to be sightseeing. There's not too much to see in these parts.'

It was late when Brandon Mead reported back. Exhaustion exacerbated the disappointment experienced by the team. They had been so confident that one motel's records would provide more than the youth's brief description.

Later that night, after a meal swallowed but untasted, and several much needed drinks, Dwayne phoned England. Having found Clive more straightforward to talk to and despite the Geordie accent easier to understand, he dialled the Northumbrian number.

'Sorry, not much to report. Our lady probably stayed at one of our less salubrious watering holes, the kind you and I wouldn't set foot in let alone spend the night. The only thing we've got is a description of her which matches the ones given by Gloria and the ladies at your end but I don't feel we're much further forward.' Promising to continue the search Dwayne ended the call. That night neither man enjoyed much rest.

Chapter 19

Living on my own has generally been my preferred modus operandi. On the few occasions when I have had a partner, I've missed the independence that a solitary existence allows. So why am I now starting to consider looking for someone when this is over? Could it be as a result of the large feather which sat in the middle of my bedroom carpet for many days? Having walked around it for the best part of a week, I finally bent down and picked it up. Either I did it or it stayed where it was and the realisation hit me that the rest of my life was laid out: everything was down to me, nobody else. There's absolutely nobody to see or care about any aspect of my life.

It is fortuitous that Sophie is on her own at the moment as it means that nobody is aware of her recent outings. During the week she spends long hours working but is available to go on jaunts at weekends. We've been up to the Lake District twice. As she's not keen on driving in the countryside I act as chauffeur. For someone who drives as little as she does it surprises me that she invariably has the latest model of top quality car. This season it's a red Mercedes SL Class, a real beauty. Journeys are a pleasure and the vehicle reminds me of a pampered pussy as it purrs along. Thankfully it is has old-fashioned gears, though nothing else about this particular car is out of date. I have never found automatics to have the same acceleration but I love the fact that this model can zoom from zero to sixty-two in three point eight seconds. That should suit my purpose nicely. I have found my next weapon.

Visiting The Today Store, a newly opened and extremely popular venue on the outskirts of Windermere, was the turning point in my planning which I must admit has been on the back-burner (such an appropriate phrase to employ when thinking about an outlet that sells everything one could want for a kitchen and a million other things for one's house or garden one didn't know one needed!). The place is an impulse purchaser's idea of Paradise and I was delighted to see that it is situated three-quarters of a mile from the railway station. All the ingredients were there, staring at me – and I'm not talking about food! All I had to do was combine them into the desired dish.

The superstore has only been opened for a few months and it still has that brand new look and smell. The front wall with its mosaic-like steel structure supports the most enormous sheets of glass I've ever seen. We both went mad on our first visit and bought everything from A to Z. Sophie's A was "Amaretto bis-cuits: a taste of Italy" and I purchased the more prosaic Z: "Zip-sealed freezer bags in four sizes". The "Eatery", on the first floor, and far too refined to be called a café, has wonderful views over the lake, which is surely not intended to detain the avid shopper. We cer-tainly enjoyed lunch watching the steamers moving sedately across the water. After a very rich dessert a walk sounded like a good idea. I had forgotten that my sister doesn't do exercise. How she remains so slim is a mystery.

Suggesting a stroll around Rydal Water was a bad idea. I prefer the route that is the reverse of the one in the guidebook so we parked by Wordsworth's cottage, a house we visited as children, crossed the main road and then walked over a footbridge. The river was surprisingly fast flowing, frightening Sophie. 'Thank goodness we've got to the other side, I hate bridges. This is hard work, the path is very uneven,' were her first moans.

'Might have helped if you'd worn more sensible shoes,' I replied thinking that she probably didn't own any, Jimmy Choo being her preferred choice.

'Do we have to climb up to an old slate mine? This is getting worse.'

Glorious views went unnoticed, thick woodland unappreciated, and the Old Coffin Route only suited her when we rested on the Coffin Stone as so many bearers had surely done before us.

'Remind me not to do this again,' she muttered as we staggered back to the car. That afternoon there were moments when I was tempted not to wait for October.

For the most part we both enjoyed the outings and for the first time since that unforgettable afternoon when "it" happened, the "it" that has led to so many deaths, we were able to enjoy each other's company.

But, and it is a huge but, it remains obvious that my beloved sister has absolutely no idea what she has done to me, what she has made me suffer, or indeed what she has forced me to do. She continues to act as though everything she did was a fait accompli and beyond her control. I know differently.

Has it ever entered my mind to alter my plans?
No.
Have I had a moment's hesitation that what I am going to do is wrong?

Not many.

Despite our recent, and I have to admit rather enjoy-able, rapprochement, could she be forgiven?

No, never.

Was October 15th still the day?

Yes, definitely.

Superintendent Thompson had always hated being beaten by any investigation. His very first case as a senior officer had remained unsolved and twelve years on it still rankled. There were times when the details of it cavorted around in his mind like a maelstrom, a violent turmoil of ideas drowning without resolution. The abduction and murder of a college student is abhorrent and, most frustratingly, this particular crime had long since been relegated to the Cold Case files: a dozen years of failure.

Following this disappointment there had been numerous occasions when cases had seemed impossible to solve, only for some snippet of information to be dropped, like manna from heaven, to reveal the way forward. How he longed for another such moment.

'Good morning Clive, hope you are well.' Spending many minutes revisiting the sparse information they had, both men felt utterly dejected. 'All in all we've got almost nothing. A common date for two of the hit-and-runs, three single fathers and their offspring killed, almost certainly murdered, and in each case an absentee mother who we think is the same person but about whom we basically know sod all.'

If Clive was surprised to hear the superintendent swear he didn't comment. Instead he reminded his colleague that all the people who claimed to know the woman they sought gave very similar descriptions of her. 'The only thing I can suggest is an identikit photo to put in the various newspapers and hopefully on the internet. Our expert who does those is excellent. He'll need more facial clues so we can ask our witnesses for any other details they remember: shape of face, eye colour and whether she had any distinguishing features like a hairy mole, protruding teeth or a gigantic nose.'

'Ha, ha, those last features would make the job easier. It's a good idea. I'll contact the former neighbour and see if Dwayne can ask the goofy Gloria. Hopefully get back to you by the end of the week.'

Clara was revelling in finalising all the details. Each element of the day must be planned meticulously: a military campaign that would result in a single death. This time, more than any other, there was so much room for error. The car was ideal but it was Sophie's so instantly identifiable. October 15th was a Saturday and the venue would be packed with people: families with young children as well as the usual hotchpotch of retirees. Three visits, without Sophie, had been undertaken and on each occasion the car park had been almost full. In all probability the entire area would be overrun with possible witnesses. Hopefully, immediately after the "bump", the vast majority would be looking in the direction of the stricken Sophie.

Anyone watching Clara might have wondered at the woman who, time after time, stepped out of her car and calculated how long it took to walk from The Today Store's main car park up the steep hill to the railway station. Fourteen minutes and twenty-two seconds. If however, she was able to complete the dismissal of her sister in the favoured spot, on the far side of the car park and well away from the busy shop doors, it was a lot nearer to the main exit and would reduce the walk by almost a minute. Sixty seconds less to be seen.

In the 1970s, Windermere station had been reduced to a single track, belying its former glory of four platforms and a large roof. A Booth's supermarket had been built on the site of the original station, imitating the initial building with its ornate canopy. Especially in the holiday season it remains a popular entry to Windermere and the Lakes. In October, and especially if the weather was kind, the whole locality would be teeming with late season holiday makers.

During her penultimate visit Clara had coincided with a hiking group, a huge assembly of senior citizens, who were disembarking armed with walking sticks, boots, maps and rucksacks. A very enthusiastic leader had barked orders managing to outshout the piercing announcement that the next train for Oxenholme was about to depart. How she would hate to meet such a party on the 15th.

Next problem – how long would it take to purchase a ticket? It depended on the number and type of people in the queue. On her final visit two Germans had taken an age to select and pay for a Five Day Advanced Ticket. Her ticket could be purchased beforehand but if she did it online it would be traceable and ordering it at another station might look suspicious. No, it would have to be on the day. The average queue meant a wait of just less than two minutes.

The first ticket to be purchased would be a one-way single to Lancaster. The trains left roughly once an hour, but she needed to study the timetable: 11: 15, 12: 34, 13:44 or 14:58. She would be leaving on one of these, hopefully one of the earlier ones. Train times from Carnforth, Lancaster and Preston needed checking as her journey home shouldn't be too straightforward. No direct route that day.

On her final saunter, slower this time just in case she was caught up in the almost inevitable melee that follows any sort of incident, she made a careful note of the CCTV cameras. There were three at various points in the car park, but as long as she was able to park in one of her preferred spots she would not be seen by any of them. There was one on the station platform. Head down, she counted five steps where she would be under surveillance. Big Brother would be watching so it would be imperative not to look up. Footage could provide such irrefutable evidence.

No difficulty was envisaged getting Sophie into the shop. She loved spending money. The emporium, too vast and upmarket to be called a shop, would keep her interested for ages. The next part of the plan was tricky as timing was of the essence. Exiting the building and the subsequent actions must fit in with the train timetable. The last thing Clara wanted was to arrive on the platform as a train disappeared.

Clara would insist that they arrived early on the 15th, which meant leaving Manchester at an hour Sophie didn't know existed on a Saturday. Some excuse about allowing sufficient time to shop before catching a lunchtime steamer might convince her sister. Early birds would catch the appropriate parking place.

At least half an hour would need to be allocated for the inevitable coffee break – with cake – Sophie couldn't be denied her final treat. The rucksack must be placed on the back seat, readily available. Making a list of the rucksack's contents she realised that a new one was needed. The old dark blue one at the back of the cupboard was far too small. Should Sophie comment on its presence Clara would merely mumble about all-weather gear, this being Cumbria in the autumn.

Most people know that horrible moment when, despite one's best endeavours, one is aware something may have been overlooked, the best laid plans and all that. The most competent cook can miss a vital ingredient rendering the cake inedible, nightwear can remain in the airing cupboard after the suitcase is locked, and who hasn't double-checked they have their passport as they arrive at the airport? Clara was having such a moment. What had she overlooked?

Jonty Hetherside had compiled an identikit photograph from the information received. The picture was ready to be placed in the papers and everyone seemed satisfied that it matched the details supplied. The woman looked rather attractive. However, Reg remarked that she could be any one of the dozen females one might pass in the street on the way home from work.

'Fingers crossed, it will only take one person, just one, to recognise her and be able to tell us her whereabouts.' Clive knew he sounded more hopeful than he felt.

Permission had been granted for the photo to appear in the dailies as well as the relevant local papers: it was useful to have a more senior policeman involved. 'I'm also seeing if *Crime Watch* has a slot. They're getting back to me early next week,' had been his parting shot at their last meeting.

Hiding his frustration at yet another delay, Clive had to admit that it was the sort of coverage he hadn't even dreamt of a few months ago.

Dwayne had managed to persuade *In Touch with North Carolina*, broadcast on Channel Eight on the hour every hour, to show the picture and run the story with as much detail as they could fit into the one minute forty second slot it had been allocated. Three days of coverage had been promised.

Someone somewhere not only knew the woman but could also tell them exactly where she was. What was her present persona? Where was she living? Was she still confident that she would avoid detection?

Most importantly was she planning the next hit-and-run?

October the 15th was only a few weeks away.

Pleased that they had done as much as possible the three policemen turned their attention to more mundane matters. Everyday crimes continued to need solving.

Chapter 20

Hilarious, totally hilarious. Who came up with that photo? It's in all the papers today and the blurb says there's going to be a piece about it on Crime Watch. *I must make sure the television is set to record for that gem.*

Some of the sentences are so amusing: "Has anyone seen this woman?" Well yes, everyone in the entire country has seen someone like her: the look is so utterly generic. The identikit is absolutely devoid of character; she could be any one of the sulky models who adorn the Sunday supplements.

"Police wish to ascertain her whereabouts." I bet they do.

"The woman is known to have used the aliases Ruby Smith and Beryl Smith and was last known as Pearl Lloyd." My, my, most of that is such ancient history that it will prove useless. Who is likely to remember any of those personas?

"The lady in question is believed to have lived in Reading and more recently in the Manchester area. Superintendent Reginald Thompson, of the Greater Manchester police, believes that she has a northern accent and may well have returned to the North West after living in the Reading area when she was young."

Pure supposition, it just happens to be true. He shot that bull's eye blindfolded!

"The police would like to question her about a series of accidents." Accidents...what a superb understatement.

"Any information will be treated in the strictest confidence." Why bother adding that. It's not as if MI6 is involved, though the FBI might become concerned if the sheriff gets his way.

I haven't laughed as much in ages. It would be a lark to phone with some spurious info but that might be a tad silly. I'm too near my goal to risk straying from the good old straight and narrow, though some might say I left that particular path a long time ago.

Thousands of calls were received from people claiming to recognise the woman. Overtime bills soared as every piece of information was followed up. Calls were recorded then returned, house visits made and hundreds of statements taken. Trying to be helpful people sent a present-day photograph of the woman they believed matched the identikit. Each one needed careful scrutiny. Some appeared to match the picture published in the papers but on further investigation all the women highlighted were rejected: the wrong age, living abroad with no re-entry stamps on their passports or with solid alibis for the relevant dates. Several times it looked as though there might be the vital clue as to her present identity and whereabouts. Frustratingly, all the information proved to be spurious and after many fourteen-hour shifts the latest search had provided nothing new.

'So many people claim to know this female that she must be extremely popular. Trouble is she's living in

Glasgow, Crewe, Wolverhampton and Birmingham, all at the same time.' Clive sounded exasperated.

'We've heard that she's a nurse, doctor, electrician and bus driver,' Reg replied. 'We've discovered zilch. It's been a monumental waste of time.'

'Have you heard from Dwayne?'

'Same story, only in America she's now called Brooke, Kylie or Melody and is supposed to be living in most of the fifty-two states. Hell, where do we go from here?'

School occupied Clara's days. The end of September meant the traditional Harvest Festival, the children bringing their time-honoured gifts of fruit, vegetables and tins to decorate the school hall. Clara and Katie had the job of displaying the various items.

After a few minutes Katie burst out laughing. 'I was just thinking about when I was little. My brother and I always argued over everything, we must have driven our parents mad. Mum always claims that the final straw came when she made up boxes of fruit for us to take along to church for the Sunday Harvest Festival service. On the way I noticed that the bunch of grapes in his shoe box, decorated beautifully with red tissue paper and covered in cling film, looked bigger than mine. We stopped in the church porch, took the covering paper off both boxes and counted the grapes. He had six more than me so I went for him! I kicked him then thumped his chest and just as the vicar appeared I spat, a wonderful aim landing on my brother's left cheek. Boy, were we in trouble.'

'Well,' replied Clara, 'my grandfather was one of four brothers and he once told me that they used to count the peas on their plate. If one had more than the others there was hell to pay. Can you imagine my poor great-grandmother making sure that each quota of peas was identical? Bad enough living with four boys before you start counting peas.'

By the time they had finished the hall looked wonderful, the harvest colours bringing the space to life. The following morning the service began straight after registration. Family and friends had been invited and the hall was full. Clara's job was to make sure the children who had poems to read went up to the front at the appropriate time. Just as the final boy took his place a sudden attack of nerves struck without warning, a deluge that her internal weather station had failed to forecast. Clara fled pretending to feel sick.

Sitting in the staff room, listening to a rousing rendition of *Cauliflowers Fluffy*, she was amazed to realise that her entire body was shaking uncontrollably and for the first time she really understood what a panic attack felt like.

What had caused such an onslaught of mind-numbing fear? Was it the innocence of the children, reading their own work, the words so fervently thanking the god in whom they still believed for His bountiful harvest? Or was it the knowledge that if she was to complete her programme another killing was necessary? Both were true. One reason was so good, the other so bad. Bad, bad, bad. She was only too aware that what she was about to do was unforgiveable. Bad, she was bad. It was a shocking word. A word she had never used before. Unfortunately she was only too aware that it was most apposite.

'Breathe deeply. In, out, in, out. That's good but you don't look well. I think you'd be better off at home. You've looked a bit peaky for a few days and as usual you've been very busy.' Mrs Greenwood, the school secretary and the motherly type, had seen Clara leave the hall in some distress. 'I'll run you home and you can go to bed. Just wait here a second, I'll let the Head know what's happening.'

Realising that the last thing she needed was to be alone, Clara assured Josie that she would be all right in a minute. The usual remedy was supplied and after two cups Clara returned to the classroom, still shaken but back in control.

That night she studied her planning, the sheets of writing that would be destroyed before the day. No one could help. Not another soul knew about her part in the six already dispatched or the one next in line. Dividing a piece of paper in half she wrote two headings: Reasons to continue / Reasons not to do so.

The former won the day, like a horse romping home several lengths ahead of its nearest rival. Just over a fortnight to what she kept referring to as "the finale". Not long to keep her nerve. So many battles must have been lost, or not even fought, due to fear and doubts. Hers would not add to the total.

Part 4: Sophie and Clara

Chapter 1

Almost there, the final lap. If I were a long distance runner I'd be putting on a last spurt ready to breast the finishing line to rapturous applause.

Instead loneliness, that most debilitating of human conditions, rules my life. Monday to Friday I am surrounded by people, but school is proving to be the most desolate environment. Children chatter, giggle inanely and occasionally concentrate on their work. I exaggerate, but my mind is elsewhere for so much of the time that I am failing to ensure that my group are staying on the tasks they have been set. Poor Katie was very disappointed by their writing last week and asked if the work had been too hard for them. No, I'd said, I think we were all very hot and found it hard to concentrate. "Must improve" would be writ large on my school report.

Sleep rarely arrives and the night hours tick-tock by pedantically, their metronomic setting almost at a standstill. The hours of darkness pass more slowly than I would have thought possible. If each night were a piece of music the tempo would be lento or more accurately molto lento. Will they return to presto after the event?

The new rucksack has been purchased. It's black with a blue trim, very ordinary and hopefully innocuous but it's the perfect size. I've had a dummy run filling it with the necessary garb.

For some reason I've found it hard to decide what to wear at the beginning of the day. Blending in with the crowd is essential but it wouldn't do to look so humdrum that my sister comments, though as she remains totally self-absorbed others are noticed only rarely and commented upon even less frequently. Her radar is set within an impregnable half metre range: most mirrors allow for this!

The wig I intend to wear will hardly merit a mention and she will accept my excuse of sore eyes that require the relief provided by my extremely dark glasses. The driving gloves she gave me are of course de rigueur. Not much of a disguise but, in the circumstances, it will have to do.

Everything ended up on the bed in a sorry tangle of jumpers, tops and trousers. I must have tried a dozen outfits before deciding on my brown cords and beige top. Yes, I know, such a plebeian outfit to take so long to select. It has to be acknowledged that the final choice is reasonably smart but is not the sort of outfit that would grace the pages of a fashion magazine. Hopefully I won't stand out. Miss Anonymous will suit me just fine. I was going to wear a raincoat but if I have my anorak in the rucksack I can assure Sophie that I am prepared for all eventualities. Oh how I hope that is true.

So…all organised. Sophie agreed with my agenda. A return trip to Cumbria: shopping, coffee, a lunch-time cruise on Lake Windermere and dinner somewhere on the way back. Shame she will only enjoy the first part of the agenda.

I'm not laughing as the nerves I am experiencing would be at least a seven on the Richter scale. Even

Shona, Year Five, and marooned in her own world most of the time, commented that my hand was shaking as I gave out the Numeracy worksheets on Friday morning.

Am I sufficiently determined to see the day through? What if I waver at the last moment? Will she still be around to enjoy everything on the itinerary?

Superintendent Thompson was dealing with the familiar aftermath of a Saturday night in the centre of Manchester. The city had suffered its usual catalogue of crimes. Having imbibed too much alcohol several people had enjoyed a night in the cells and would have to wait for Monday morning to have their moment in the Magistrates' Courthouse. Three houses in Hale had been burgled, almost certainly by the same person, and a shop window on Deansgate had been kicked in. As usual, the most depressing cases involved domestic violence, a particularly unpleasant crime that seemed to be on the increase. The last thing on anyone's mind was the elusive driver.

'Sorry to bother you, sir, but you asked to be informed of any hit-and-runs yesterday.' The large room appeared to shrink to such a degree that Reg wondered whether he had disappeared down Alice's rabbit hole.

Not realising how loudly he was shouting Reg bawled at the poor PC. He was aware that this might be the news that he both wanted and yet dreaded hearing. 'Well Marian, what do you want to tell me?'

'There's a report of an incident in Cumbria, yesterday morning in a car park. A hit-and-run – one casualty.'

After extracting as many details as he could from the young woman Reg was straight on the phone to Clive. 'Have you seen the news? There was a hit-and-run in the Today Store car park in Windermere yesterday morning. A single victim, young woman in her thirties, but it's worth following up. Same date so we need to see if it was deliberate and if it might have any bearing on our cases.'

Clive was less than impressed. 'Same date but no child involved. Do we know if she was a single mother? This one could have been a pure accident. Do we know what any witnesses have said? Did it appear to be deliberate?' Reg allowed his colleague to complete his barrage of questions then had to acknowledge that he had few facts.

'Who was the victim?'

'Sophie Bedford. Apparently she lived in the Manchester area. She's got a sister and I imagine she's been informed but it might be worth one of us going to see her. There might be some link to our cases but I can hang fire if you want us to go together. I'm sure we can wait one day. In the meantime I'll get onto the Cumbrian police and ask for all the details they have.'

The completion of a long planned event can result in a sense of anticlimax. Anticipated events often fail to live up to their billing. Not so for Clara who revelled in the days following her final triumph. The end game had been magnificent. The tournament was hers. Now all she had to do was claim her prize.

She had undertaken a most convoluted route home, extending her original plans which were more straightforward and therefore traceable. She embarked on two journeys through the most delightful countryside, at least some of which was appreciated. The first train took her from Windermere to Oxenholme where she changed for Carlisle. This was followed by the

delightful run from Carlisle to Carnforth, with afternoon tea in the station café watching sections of *Brief
Encounter*, parts of which had been filmed at the
station. Carnforth to Lancaster proved a pretty run
with glimpses of Morecambe Bay. After several minutes
on Lancaster platform she caught the fast London
bound train, alighting at Preston where she changed
for the final leg of the journey to Manchester.

Getting off the trains at each station had added to
the journey's length but had, hopefully, made her home-
bound travels difficult to track. Should anyone have
noticed her they would have seen another hiker on her
way home. The rucksack was lighter, containing as it
now did her morning's attire which had been superseded by anorak, bobble hat, scarf, boots and walking
stick, all swapped in the Ladies on Windermere station.

Neither outfit had attracted much attention. Or that
was her fervent hope. Her timing had been perfect:
emerging in her new outfit just as the Windermere to
Oxenholme train pulled into the station.

'Good evening Miss Bedford, sorry to disturb you. May
we come in for a minute?' Her blood became a slow-
moving glacier as the two officers were invited into the
living room.

'I'm Sergeant Trevor Leander and my colleague is PC
Jan Cobblestone. I'm afraid we've come with some very
bad news.' The middle-aged man had delivered such
words on many occasions and sounded quite matter-
of-fact. 'It's about your sister, Sophie. I'm very sorry
to have to tell you that there was an accident earlier
today. She was hit by a car and unfortunately died of
her injuries.'

Knowing this moment had been inevitable Clara had practised her response. Crying uncontrollably had been deemed inappropriate; receiving the words calmly too unfeeling; asking if they wanted a drink too friendly. Calm, but not too calm, had been her chosen option: the sibling who cared, but not one who was about to fall apart.

Using a stunned voice she asked for details.

What she hadn't prepared for were the bubbles of mirth that threatened to surface as raucous guffaws. The policeman's account of the morning was hilarious. Her sister had been knocked down by her own car, almost certainly by someone trying to steal it. The driver had gone by the time the first people were on the scene. A doctor had tried, unsuccessfully, to help her. That's rather obvious or she wouldn't be dead, skittered across Clara's mind, creating more gurgles, which she controlled with even greater difficulty. My goodness, she thought, even the best champagne can't boast such fizziness.

Sophie had been hit with considerable force and died at the scene. 'Has the driver been found?' Clara asked, just managing to maintain a subdued demeanour.

'Not as far as we're aware. As I said, the driver had gone before anyone really knew what had happened.'

'You've not said where this was.' She was finding it hard not to let her delight show. It didn't sound as though there were any immediate witnesses. Parking in the most remote spot had been successful. The many people in the main car park had obviously moved slowly, perhaps not sure what they had heard.

'Your sister, Sophie,' (yes I know her name thought Clara fighting the temptation to giggle), 'was in the car park of the Today Store which is situated half a mile up the main road out of Windermere.'

'Windermere?' As she repeated the word, with an upward inflection, she realised she had to maintain some modicum of self-control. 'What on earth was Sophie doing up there? I'm just surprised as she didn't really like driving, though she did have a wonderful car... maybe she wanted to give it a spin.' Clara paused, attempting to give the impression of a caring relative trying to control her emotions. 'Is there anything else you can tell me?' How agreeable it would be to be able to tell them that she knew far more than they did.

'Apparently your sister went back into the shop to retrieve a package she'd left. The incident occurred after she'd collected it when she was returning to her car. She'd parked at the far side of the car park, well away from the shop entrance. That section was almost deserted and no one saw the actual incident.'

The second officer had remained silent, watching Clara's reaction. She was trained in Family Liaison and ready to assist if a relative took tragic news badly. New to the role she cleared her throat rather self-consciously before speaking. 'This may seem a strange question, Miss Bedford, but do you know if your sister was in the habit of leaving the car unlocked? Would she have left the keys in the ignition? You see we believe that no damage was done as the car was entered. It doesn't look as though the person attempting to take the car had to break in.'

'You said she went back to the shop to collect something. Maybe she thought the car would be safe for the few minutes that would take. Otherwise she was very safety conscious and I know she was extremely proud of her car. It was quite new and very expensive. In ordinary circumstances I'm sure she would have locked it.'

'Quite so, Miss Bedford, she must have been in a hurry to retrieve her purchases.'

After a prolonged pause, one that encouraged Clara to think that the pair was ready to leave, Trevor Leander spoke so quietly that Clara had to strain to hear him.

'I'm afraid we will have to ask you to come to the mortuary at some point to identify the body.'

'You seem to be sure it's Sophie, so is that necessary?'

'Yes, I'm afraid it is. She had credit cards and her driver's licence in her purse with her name on so we are certain that the victim is Sophie Bedford. The car involved was registered to her but we do need a formal identification. Someone has to identity the deceased.'

'Is she there already, at the mortuary?' Clara made the final word into a sob.

'We believe Sophie's body has left the Crime Scene and been taken to Manchester Royal Infirmary's mortuary. We can take you there whenever you feel able to go.'

Viewing her sister left Clara unmoved. She had expected to experience something: satisfaction, happiness or a sense of triumph. The body merely confirmed that the denouement had proved successful.

'It is my sister, Sophie Bedford.'

Over the years Sergeant Leander had witnessed every emotion when a relative is asked to do the unthinkable and identify the body of a loved one. The fact that Clara was so calm came as no surprise: he believed that the full extent of her loss would strike later.

After taking her home, the officers assured Clara that they would keep in touch and would let her know of any developments. 'Sophie looks very peaceful. She wouldn't have known much about it. It was all very quick.' This last utterance came from PC Cobblestone speaking in Family Liaison mode.

Had they been told to say that? Were their instructions to make the grieving relatives content that their loved ones had not had to endure too much suffering? That they were merely dead!

In this case Clara knew that the impact had indeed resulted in instantaneous death. No suffering, no agony, but what they couldn't possibly know about were the moments leading up to the collision.

Clara sat and recalled eleven o'clock that morning: Saturday the 15th of October. Right on schedule Sophie had walked back after collecting the bag Clara had left behind the till. She looked surprised that the car had been moved but almost certainly assumed that Clara was merely manoeuvring ready to set off. She had beamed, a rather silly smile, and mouthed that she was coming. As she approached she tapped her watch to show that the joke continued that they were on a strict timetable. Just a few minutes before Sophie had made a comment that Clara spent too much of her life ruled by the school bell.

An instant can be locked in the brain, the key discarded. The moment Sophie realised what her sister was planning would live with Clara for ever. Initially there was a look of utter bewilderment, superseded almost immediately by one of total panic. Clara would always find it strange that the person in front of her didn't move: that there was absolutely no attempt to get out of the way. But then zero to sixty in less than three seconds doesn't allow much time to escape. And Sophie hadn't escaped. The final moment had been magnificent. Now all Clara had to do was claim what was rightfully hers. She knew it would keep. It wasn't going anywhere.

Manchester City was playing at home on the Sunday, a four o'clock kick-off to fit in with Sky's demanding agenda. Katie and her partner were season ticket holders and went to every home match. Stephen was away that weekend and Clara, who normally hated anything to do with football, had been invited to take his place.

'It's not like watching it on the television; far more exciting than that. I bet you'll love it. You might even end up buying a scarf.' Clara doubted the last two statements but had agreed to accompany Katie to the afternoon match. The experience would prove at worst a noisy distraction or, more hopefully, a euphoric celebration. Either way shouting raucously along with fifty thousand other lunatics might be just what was required.

Having slept like the dead, a phrase Clara found amusing but which she admitted was a rather dubious notion, she met her friend outside the ground an hour before kick-off.

'I'm sorry to say this, as you no doubt think it's gorgeous, but the stadium reminds me of a spacecraft: one that was travelling at the speed of light, intending to visit some amazing planet it had spied on its intergalactic telescope. Tragedy struck and it lost its way and ended up crash-landing in Manchester. The aliens are probably on the substitutes' bench this afternoon!'

'Wait until you see the inside. That will make you change your mind. And no more comparing our players to aliens – that's the Everton lot.'

Clara had to agree, that once inside, the Etihad was indeed rather spectacular. Their seats in the Colin Bell stand, named after one of their all-time great players, were on the halfway line which according to Katie gave the best view.

'You look a lot better,' Katie said as they sat down, 'I've been worried about you, well everyone has.

Even David asked how you were the other day and he's normally got limited interests: Year Six, beer and cricket.'

'Sorry to have caused any concern. I've been a bit down recently but I thought it was time to start making more of an effort.'

'Man trouble?'

'No. Nothing like that.'

By tomorrow Katie, and the whole of Greater Manchester, would have heard about her sister, *Look North* revelling in another tragic death. Her excuse for not mentioning the accident today would be that she hadn't wanted to spoil the match. The "more of an effort" could be explained as Sophie's death making her realise that life is short and that every day is precious and to be enjoyed. Katie was such a good person that she would believe her and be nothing but sympathetic.

The swell of emotion that greeted the teams as they walked onto the pitch staggered Clara. How could adults behave with such abandon over men in shorts who were about to kick hell out of a ball and, almost certainly, each other? However, she had to admit that some of them were rather appealing and City's new forward, ('He signed from Inter Milan last season,') was positively gorgeous and even she could see that he was a fantastic player scoring a hat-trick before half-time.

'Three nil up and forty-five minutes still to go, isn't it wonderful?' Katie yelled attempting to be heard above the applause that enveloped the ground, the ultimate stereo experience. As the players walked or ran down the tunnel (where did they get their energy?) Clara wondered if they were about to be rewarded with cups of tea, revitalising drinks or slices of orange.

'Katie, aren't you worried? If City can score three during the first half then Everton can do the same in the second.'

'No chance, they don't call the Etihad a fortress for nothing.' Clara didn't like to point out that even Jericho's defences had been breached.

By the time goal number five hit the back of the net, a powerful header from a well-taken corner, Katie was ecstatic and from the first goal Clara had become one of the faithful, jumping up and raising her arms to the heavens. She was amused to think that had there been a further goal she might have heard herself joining in with the decidedly unmelodic rendition of the City anthem *Blue Moon* that permeated almost every corner of the arena. The away fans had long since given up on their songs and been reduced to a disbelieving silence.

'I think you enjoyed that,' Katie said as they walked back along the canal path into town. Clara had indeed loved the experience but not for the reasons the City fanatic thought. Yes she knew it had been a good match, for one side at least, and the excitement had been palpable. But for her the afternoon had meant a situation where she could legitimately release the emotions yesterday had engendered. To roar with an abandon not permitted elsewhere, to show utter bias, again not a habit that was socially acceptable, and to clap, wave one's arms like a mad woman and generally behave in a manner only seen exhibited by fanatics had been perfect.

What a weekend! And the document still waiting to be read and then acted upon – at some time in the very near future.

Chapter 2

Even my SEN group noticed me today. I often think they regard me as the helpful woman who works with them, reiterating everything Katie has said. Sometimes I even wonder if they know my name, they use it so seldom. In the past I've worked with children who are more inclined to interact and who talk a lot about themselves and ask about me. But until today this could not have been said of this year's quiet quintet.

'You're buzzing today,' was Jem's unexpected comment halfway through the Literacy lesson. 'You went to watch City with Miss didn't you?' I hate it when they call the teacher by such an impersonal title. It makes it sound as though they can't be bothered to use her surname. It's both impolite and very lazy. Trying to re-educate my little troupe in this faux pas has had as much success as suggesting to the rain that it stops falling quite so frequently in Manchester.

'She told us you were a new fan,' he continued, adding, 'you should support Liverpool, they're miles better than City.'

Oodles, a word my mother loved, of sympathy smothered me in the staff room. I was hugged, cuddled, enveloped in David's bear-like grip and cried over by Susanna, a fellow TA, whose capacity for empathy was a wonder of the modern world.

'Oh, you poor dear what a terrible thing to happen – such a tragedy,' Josie Greenwood was back in mother hen mode. It was when she added, 'She's in heaven now with the angels and will be looking down and taking care of you,' I almost lost my serene demeanour (practised in the bedroom) and informed her that that particular scenario was an impossibility. Indeed had my dear twin been watching me it would have been to make sure that the thunderbolts she was hurling my way hit their target.

Arriving home that first Monday, Clara felt utterly exhausted. All the energy and bravado that had swept her through the weekend had evaporated faster than the steam in Katie's science experiment – had that lesson really taken place just that afternoon?

Time was blurring and she couldn't recall when Sophie had met her end. Collapsing onto the settee every part of her ached and even breathing seemed to require an effort that was so gargantuan she wondered if each breath would be her last. How ironic that would be: to become reunited with her sister quite so soon.

'Actions have consequences, girls.' The adage delivered in so many of Miss Wainwright's assemblies ricocheted violently around her brain. Why, so many years later, was she assaulted by words that had meant so little at the time? As a teenager the warning had hardly impacted, especially as it had been uttered by a middle-aged woman whose entire wardrobe consisted of a selection of the most boring dark grey suits, woollen tights and sensible brogues. Hardly a woman whom teenagers would imagine had anything of consequence to impart.

Most of the fifteen-year-old girls, trapped on a daily basis in the school hall, would have been too preoccupied with daydreams of the latest boy bands to even hear the diatribe, let alone pay it any heed, and only a few would have been involved in any behaviour wicked enough to merit an outcome of any significance. In any case, youth believes itself to be invincible and an old fogey like Miss W. surely knew nothing.

How different was today's situation. For over three years Clara had avoided self-recrimination. Obfuscation had ruled: she had convinced herself that she was not guilty.

Was she dreaming or daydreaming? Memories surfaced that most of the time she was able to keep submerged. Miss Wainwright mutated into her father, the man who blamed her, the years never dulling his wrath. That was the link. He maintained, until the day he died, that her actions had been responsible for the direst of consequences. That one horrendous scene – worthy of inclusion in a Chekov play – and ...no her mind slammed down the portcullis. She would not return to that evening so long ago, a matter of hours before the final scene. He blamed her but the faults were all his. Knowing he had been forced to maintain his charade, as anything else would have been unbearable, did not make Clara feel better.

Through the fog of a thumping head, aching joints and a mind in disarray, Clara had one last thought before tumbling into a nightmare-ridden sleep. Her recent actions were a direct consequence of her father's final decision. Her father acted because he maintained she was culpable. If she was not to blame, and at the time at least two psychiatrists had assured her that the tragedy was not of her making, then how could she be guilty? No. Not her.

Reginald Thompson was keen to read the Cumbrian police report on the incident in Windermere. There wasn't as much detail as he would have liked and after requesting a second report he rang Windermere to get further details.

'Superintendent Thompson here. Good morning Sergeant Norton and thank you for your time. I'm very keen to know as much as possible about the hit-and-run in Windermere at the weekend. It may be linked to similar cases I'm involved with and I hope that was made clear when I asked for a second look at the accident report. Didn't intend to usurp your enquiry but this incident may be of great interest to me. Has anything new come to light?'

'As requested the forensic team have gone all, and I do mean all, over it again with the proverbial tooth-comb. There were fingerprints from the deceased in all the places one would expect and some others on the passenger side but none that we have on the data base. The car was meticulously tidy, no chocolate wrappers or empty drink cartons. We then decided to perform an Accident Reconstruction.'

'Before you tell me about that, have any more eye-witnesses come forward?'

'No, unfortunately by the time the first people were on the scene the driver had fled the area, leaving the car with its door open and engine running.'

'Damn and blast. A busy car park, a popular Lake District venue, a Saturday morning and no one saw anything. It's almost as though the driver had planned it, though it has all the hallmarks of a tragic and fatal accident. Sorry, you were going to tell me about the AR.'

'The car has to have been going at an excessive speed when it hit the victim. She was hit head-on with a terrific force. It doesn't appear that the driver made any attempt to miss her and must have been accelerating to strike her so hard. That part of the car park is quite wide and there were no other cars in the immediate vicinity. There were no skid marks which would have indicated that the car was trying to swerve around the body. He or she could have driven off, nothing to obstruct their exit, but they must have run away, leaving the car in situ.'

'No one even saw a person moving away at speed?'

'That part of the car park is a long way from the shop entrance. It's almost like an overflow area, but was open and in use as they expected Saturday to be busy. It took some time for the first person to arrive on the scene. One thing that has struck me as odd is why Miss Bedford chose to park there.'

'If I had a top of the range Mercedes I might not want it amongst the common herd!'

'True, and she was a fit young woman, the elderly or those with children wouldn't park there, but it's still a part of the case that I find unusual. However, it's still listed officially as an attempted theft that went tragically wrong. The report says that the young woman, Sophie Bedford, had returned to the shop to collect a purchase, almost certainly leaving the car unlocked and the key in the ignition. On returning, probably sooner than anticipated, the person caught in the act of taking the car had panicked and in his, or her, desire to get away had hit her then left the scene before any witnesses appeared.'

Thanking the officer for his time Reg ended the call. Almost immediately the phone rang.

The voice on the other end launched straight in. 'The date still intrigues me. We've always said we'd be more than interested in any such events on October 15th and we've got one here.' Clive wanted some follow-up but was finding Reg hard to persuade. 'We should, at the very least, go to see the sister. Manchester isn't too far for me and she lives on your doorstep. It'll only take a few hours.'

Reluctantly, Reg agreed to phone the sister and make an appointment. Should she appear surprised at being asked to talk to more policemen the excuse would be that there was a new initiative which meant that all road deaths were being investigated by senior officers.

School had insisted that Clara take a few days off. When she arrived on the Tuesday morning she had been sent straight home. As she walked through her front door the intrusive ringing of the phone made her jump. Believing that any strange behaviour would be put down to the sudden loss of her sister, Clara agreed to meet the two policemen later that week. Telling herself that they knew very little and, more importantly, had nothing to link her to last Saturday she prepared her story.

'We were twins. We had some years when we didn't have much to do with each other but we'd become quite close recently. *Stick to the truth as much as possible.* Our parents are both dead and there were just the two of us.'

'She did say she was going up to the Lakes on Saturday. We've been to the Today Store before and she really liked it.'

'I was tired on Saturday so didn't go with her as planned. *I was there but nobody saw us together: we went our separate ways around the store; Sophie had coffee on her own. I claimed a "funny tummy" and went to leave my purchases by the till.*

At this point tears were needed. 'I keep thinking that if I had been there she would probably still be alive.' More tears accompanied by loud sobs.

'Do you know what happened? The police who came with the news on Saturday said they thought someone was trying to take the car.'

'She loved her cars and was especially proud of this new one. She would have tried to stop anyone from stealing it.'

'What did I do on Saturday? I stayed in, watched some television, read, oh and in the afternoon as I was feeling a bit better, *how true*, I cleaned the house. Then the two police officers arrived to tell me the awful news.'

'Enemies? Sophie? I don't think so. She was a very successful business woman so I suppose she might have upset someone but she never said anything.' *Again, best to stick to the truth.*

'Are you thinking this might be more than an accident?' *Absolutely no reaction from them – how amusing, such self-control.*

'No, October 15th doesn't mean anything special. *Absolutely not true, good job I'm not taking a lie-detector test.* No one's birthday or anniversary, *pause for effect*, at least as far as I'm aware.'

'Is the date important?' *Was it too bold to become the inquisitor? Neither man gave the slightest indication that their query about the date was anything other than routine.*

'Yes, we were identical twins and people couldn't tell us apart but we started to dress individually and have very different hair styles once we reached our teens. That's many years ago now.'

'I suppose someone might have thought Sophie was me. But anyone who does know me is aware that I drive a Honda not a Mercedes. My wages wouldn't stretch to that.' *Stop talking.*

'I could have borrowed it and often drove it when we were together, *wished I'd not said anything about my driving*, but as far as I'm aware I don't have any enemies who would want to kill me. You don't think it was a case of mistaken identity?' *Now that was a novel idea!*

'I'll be in touch if I think of anything. She was such a wonderful person. W*as I over-doing it?* I can only believe that someone hit her by accident. I hope you catch the person.' Y*es, definitely too much.*

'That was a monumental waste of time. Perhaps we have to accept that last Saturday's incident was an everyday occurrence. Some bastard caught in the act, panicking and running off: just another hit-and-run. Not one of ours.' Clive felt as frustrated as he sounded.

Chapter 3

I deserve the Actress of the Year award. They made it very easy. The questions were exactly what I had expected and there weren't any that could possibly trap me into making inappropriate statements. Once or twice I think I said too much but nothing to incriminate me. When they mentioned the date and asked if it meant anything to me I was able to say that it would in the future as it had become the day on which Sophie died. I was rather pleased with that half-truth.

As I opened the door to them I was a little non-plussed as they looked so familiar. It was almost like meeting friends one hasn't seen for ages. I've looked at their photos in the papers and on the internet so often I know every contour, mole and wrinkle. And there was that never-to-be-forgotten moment when I came face to face with Clive in Seahouses. If he recognised me he gave no sign. Poor Clive is looking older and extremely stressed.

After they left I removed the document from its safe house, no witness needing police protection has ever been more carefully secreted. Over the years I have refrained from looking at it, knowing the pain it would cause. Now I knew the moment had arrived: the contents would have lost their ability to destroy me. A shame it had taken seven other destructions to arrive at this juncture.

How strange to realise that I had been afraid the vital clause might have dematerialised, as if it had been written in the ink that Sophie and I loved as children, the sort that writes on the paper then vanishes like the disappearing lady. As I removed the paper from its hiding place, in the vanity unit in the spare bedroom, my hands were shaking and my knees so feeble I was forced to sit down.

The all-important sentence would still be where it had first been deposited: the penultimate instruction. There was no need to read the final one. I knew it by heart and it was no longer of any significance. That one had been dealt with.

Thinking that in all probability the penultimate one would never be carried out the author had nevertheless made his request plain. It was now up to me to see that this particular directive was realised.

Autumn had arrived in Statesville in all its technicolour glory. Reds fought with yellows and oranges to gain supremacy. Fire-hued leaves brought the countryside to life: hard to believe that these were nature's death throes. The Blue Ridge Parkway was overflowing with tourists, cameras clicking. Shot after shot was recorded to show the folks at home and keep as screen savers. The Fall also brought the annual fogs, disappointing the visitors whose views were shrouded by the thick mist. Seasonal accidents became all too common. Most were the less serious fender benders, but occasionally the euphemistically named car wrecks resulted in fatalities or life-changing injuries.

Dwayne hated this aspect of what was otherwise his favourite time of the year: the summer heat having long since departed and the winter snows some months away. Almost every day he and his team were called to the scene of yet another collision. The latest one involved a couple in a pickup truck who had been hit, head on, by a young driver going too fast for the conditions. His passenger, an extremely immature girlfriend, appeared to find the accident amusing, until she was informed that the elderly couple in the truck they had hit had not survived. How typical Dwayne thought, the guilty party, showing off to his partner, walks away with minor injuries and the occupants of the other vehicle lose their lives, their devastated family affected for ever.

'Name?' he asked the girl, who was by now sitting at the side of the road sobbing uncontrollably. She had realised, finally, that her boyfriend would be held responsible and would face time in prison.

'Sophie Wyatt and my boyfriend is Chase Compton. We live in Mooresville and I wanted to see the colours. We thought the mist would clear, it often does in the afternoon.' The sheriff had stopped listening. It was the name that was bothering him. Sophie: why did that name wake his tired brain, like a clarion call preparing the troops for battle?

Once back at the station, having dealt with the inevitable paper work the accident had hurled his way, he sat and thought. Sophie? Sophie? What was it about that name that was suddenly so important?

'Hi Clive, it's just me. Sorry to interrupt your day but the name Sophie came up today and it sure did ring a bell. I know it was the name of your last hit-and-run victim, but at the time you said you and Reg had looked into it and didn't think that incident was linked to our cases.'

Clive made the appropriate noises and waited, as always, for Dwayne to get to the point. 'I looked at our lists of people entering America at the relevant time and guess what? A Sophie Bedford arrived from Manchester a week before the hit-and-run incident in Statesville and, listen to this, she'd been into the US twice before. The strange thing is there's absolutely no record of where she stayed on any of her visits. To me that sure sounds like she wanted to remain under the radar. She came, she went, but where she was in the interim is anybody's guess.'

'Our victim was Sophie Bedford, a business woman, seemingly very respectable. There must be other women with the same name. Can you fax a photo of your Miss Bedford from the immigration records and we'll see if matches our lady?'

Ending the call from America, Clive rang Reg and informed him of Dwayne's latest information.

'When you receive the fax, send me a copy and we'll take it from there. But as you say both Sophie and Bedford are reasonably common names so I don't think we should get our hopes up just yet.'

Two hours later the fax arrived. Clive did a double take. Goosebumps swathed his arms and the room swam. He could have been looking at Clara Bedford, the other sister. The hair styles were different but apart from that the two young women were inter-changeable. Clara was in the picture then Sophie. Clara had said she and her twin were identical and he had the proof in front of him. Something told him it was the breakthrough they needed.

Shortly after forwarding the photograph to Manchester, he received the expected call from Reg. 'Good heavens, Sophie and Clara, Clara and Sophie.

We need to visit the remaining one again. Someone has got some explaining to do.'

'I'm still not sure exactly what is going on but there's something. It's all too much of a coincidence. Sophie in America at the time of the accident there, then Sophie killed in a copycat incident. We'll see what Clara has to say.'

'She might not know anything. Her sister's death could be a reprisal, someone who knew about Statesville.'

'And Sale. And Seahouses? Let's face it, it's more than odd. You must agree that a part of the story is still a mystery. Three hit-and-runs of single fathers and their children then a young woman killed using the same method. Not sure this is the answer to our prayers but it definitely needs some follow up. We'll start by revisiting the remaining Miss Bedford. When are you free?'

Chapter 4

Mr Jackson, never Edward, has been the family solicitor for as long as I can remember. He must be nearing retirement age but looks just the same as he did when I was first involved with him, following Mum's death, over two decades ago. He has remained slim and kept a head of thick hair, touches of grey the only sign of ageing. Invariably well dressed in a selection of three piece suits, he sits in old-fashioned splendour behind his large mahogany desk, the kind that makes one feel inferior, like being sent to a dictatorial headmistress for some minor misdemeanour. Cravats complete his look which yells authority and professionalism.

Following Father's death I was summoned for the reading of the Will, the infamous "Document" that I purloined that day, knowing that the time would come when its final codicils would be fulfilled: mine the ultimate word.

October 15th all those years ago was a bright, blustery autumn day, the leaves clinging valiantly to the old trees outside Mr Jackson's windows. Unable to look at anyone in the overheated room I got to know the shape and size of every leaf. Just as the final sentence was read – in a suitably sonorous tone – a leaf descended slowly, its time over, of no further use. At that moment I knew exactly how it felt.

That portentous day he was kind. Edward the only one to acknowledge the injustice that had been done to me. He asked me to stay behind after Sophie and her paramour of the month had left and spoke at length, sounding more like a friend than a legal adviser.

Father's penultimate codicil read, "Sophie Bedford is my sole heir. However, should she wish to make a bequest to her sister, Clara, or to appoint her as a joint Trustee of Bedford Jewellers she is entitled so to do. It is not my wish but it may be hers."

'Wills are often questioned and the person's mistakes rectified. We cannot know your late father's state of mind when he recorded his wishes and it is most interesting that he gave Sophie the power to alter the contents to a quite remarkable degree.' The relief of another person recognising that father had not only got it wrong but had also given Sophie, and therefore me, an escape clause was immeasurable. I almost kissed him!

Over the next days and weeks, far too many to recall as I didn't easily give up, I followed his words of advice: to contest the document. Sophie was, as ever, the immovable object personified. No querying or rectifying for her. No money or elevated position was to be forthcoming. Her only offer was for me to manage one of the shops. A shop worker! I'd already declined that particular offer and wasn't going to change my mind to appease her.

Prowling the living room has become my modus operandi as I have awaited the call. I know how Vladimir and Estragon felt but my Godot made contact finally last week. At long last the justice that has taken seven annihilations will be done.

Déjà vu: same office, identical weather, equivalent month – same cast minus Sophie and whoever the lucky chap was who accompanied her last time.

'Miss Bedford, Clara, how lovely to see you again. Such unhappy circumstances, I was very sorry to hear about your sister's accident.' Small talk dispensed with, the solicitor turned his attention to the day's agenda.

'I see you have your father's Will with you. I remember it well. As far as I am aware Sophie didn't make any alterations to it during her lifetime. It is also my belief that she failed to make a Will of her own. It therefore becomes necessary to revert to Mr Bedford's final wishes. As you know there is a great deal of money and property under consideration. I intend to read the important codicil, the final one, and we shall discuss its implementation.'

Knowing the words by heart, Clara mouthed them, like a child joining in with a well-loved bedtime story.

'Should my beloved daughter, Sophie, predecease her sister, Clara, then it is my wish that the estate should pass to the aforementioned Miss Clara Bedford. However, should Miss Sophie Benson have any children then the estate, in its entirety, should pass directly to them. To any son, daughter, or in the case of more than one child, children, all monies and properties should be divided equally amongst them.'

A long silence followed the solicitor's reading. 'Your sister didn't have any children did she?'

'No, I don't think she was the maternal type, so no offspring.'

'That makes the matter very straightforward. If there had been a child I would have been duty bound to see that he or she inherited the Bedford estate. As there were none you are about to become an extremely wealthy young woman.'

No one else had known about Sophie's children. For years Robert Bedford and his daughter had worked together on a strictly professional basis, no socialising or friendly chats. This situation suited them both. Robert was delighted that the shops were doing better than ever and felt confident in his daughter's ability to launch new ones. He relied on her to broker advantageous land deals and inaugurate bright, lively advertising campaigns, aimed at the younger end of the market – those with spare cash to spend on an ever-expanding array of jewellery.

Sophie adored the freedom her father gave her. She worked hard and for relaxation enjoyed her regular dalliances, some more serious than others. She didn't regret having the children but wanted nothing to do with them. Fortunately for them, on all three occasions, the father had been happy to become the sole carer.

Peter had been born during her "year out" when she lived with Aunt Hannah in Reading. Paul followed several years later and although Sophie was by this time working in the family business her "women's problems" explained the weeks of advanced pregnancy when she avoided all contact with Robert who would have found it impossible to ask any embarrassing questions. By the time Natasha arrived her father was too ill to leave his house and Sophie had been left in overall charge of the shops.

Clara had been informed about each baby. For some inexplicable reason Sophie had appeared to view her production of offspring as a way to highlight her superiority. So strange as she then abandoned them.

'You don't like babies and haven't stuck with the first two,' was the only possible retort when she was informed of Natasha's imminent arrival.

'It's different this time. I'm happily married and more ready for a family.'

'So are you finally going to let Dad in on the little secret that he's a grandfather?'

'No, it's nothing to do with him and if I told him about Natasha I would have to let on about the others.'

'The others? Is that how you think about them? They've got names and little personalities. They are both gorgeous children and you don't know what you're missing.'

'And how do you know so much about them?' Backtracking, Clara mumbled general comments about being sure they were being raised well.

Realising she had been revisiting the past Clara's thoughts were interrupted by the solicitor who had been speaking, mostly to himself, for several minutes.

'My word, Miss Bedford, you don't look very happy considering you are now a multimillionaire. I know how sorry you were when Sophie refused to act on Robert's suggestion that you be included in the business but it's all yours now. Sad circumstances but I'm sure you'll do them both proud. The Bedford emporium will go from strength to strength with you in charge.'

Edward Jackson sat still, wondering if he should mention the aspect of the Will that had perplexed him since he had first been privy to it.

'Just one more thing Clara, and I hope you don't mind my asking, but have you any idea why your father cut you out of his will? It was, to say the least, a very strange thing for a father to do.'

'I don't mind the question and to my father it wasn't strange at all. He always blamed me for my mother's death. As you know she committed suicide and I was the one who found her.'

'Did he think you might have saved her?'

'No, she was already dead by the time I arrived home, though he did make comments about the fact that if I'd arrived earlier it might have made a difference. The truth was I always got home at the same time after hockey practice. But that wasn't the real reason.'

After stopping to organise her thoughts she continued. 'The night before she died, my mother walked into the kitchen when Dad and I were having an argument... in truth it was a slanging match...I had seen him with another woman. They were coming out of a local pub one evening...and it was obvious that they were a great deal more than mere friends...I was telling him what I'd seen...I accused him of being blatant...not even bothering to go out of town with his lover. He wasn't denying it...just telling me to keep my nose out of his affairs. Just as I yelled at him that he had used the most appropriate word Mum walked in. We could both tell that she had heard every word, indeed the noise we were making it would have been almost impossible not to do so. And the following day she was dead. Sophie had been with me the evening we saw him but she refused to say anything to Father. He knew that and from that moment my dear sister could do no wrong.'

'Cutting you out of his will still appears a rather malicious act, sorry to use such a strong word.'

'Once crossed, never forgiven. I have always suspected that it was easier for my father to blame me than to accept the blame himself. Faithfulness was not his strong point and over the years I think my mother had looked away on many occasions rather than face him with his infidelities. On this occasion she had heard him acknowledge it and even worse Sophie and I knew. Poor mum, she felt the shame even if he didn't.'

'Thank you for telling me, it can't be easy to talk about.'

'No, I've never told anyone else, but it all seems a long time ago. Now I have the opportunity for a new life.' Walking out of the office she wondered what had possessed her. It had been the truth, but the fewer people who knew the better. She determined to be more circumspect in the future.

It was all hers: multimillions, more than she could spend in several lifetimes, a mansion that a premiership footballer would be proud to own, and jewellery shops with her name emblazoned on the door. She had lost count of how many there were. Strange to feel so calm, to drive home as if it was a normal Thursday. Where was the euphoria? Her universe was back on track, all wrongs righted.

She was determined to revel in her new life: sell Sophie's house and purchase an even grander one; buy several cars, the sports variety that had always made her drool; and travel the world, first class. And then her ultimate plan: to sell the shops, the cause of all the anguish. If only her father and dear sister could be around to see the dissolution of their precious empire.

Chapter 5

So, I wasn't exactly doing a Highland fling as I arrived home, but I was reasonably relaxed, as far as anyone could be who has just inherited a fortune and told an old man one of their darkest secrets.

Waiting on the doorstep, yes literally standing on the brown doormat, were my two policemen, the last people in the world I wanted to see at that, or any other, moment. Dressed in formal grey suits (had they shopped together and found an impossible to resist two-for-one offer?) they looked rather incongruous beneath the Virginia creeper which was in all its red-hot glory.

The plan had been to enjoy a long hot bath, full of the expensive bubbles I bought last week, (no more cheap supermarket bargains for me) heat up a micro-wave meal and watch television all evening. OK maybe not what most people would do after they had just become richer than Bill Gates – well almost! The spending would begin. Just not yet.

Honda parked, door locked, I walked up the path attempting the look of an innocent girl recently bereaved. They smiled and apologised for bothering me again. Bothering was putting it mildly. Did the next hour go well? That is, almost literally, the multi-million pound question.

Neither officer had been quite sure how to approach the afternoon. Was it a chat or an interview? No appointment had been made. They had agreed that her answers would be more helpful, and hopefully truthful, if she wasn't given time to prepare.

Small talk dispensed with, apologies for disturbing her accepted, Reg said that some new information had been obtained and he wondered how much Clara knew about her sister's travels.

'We didn't really see much of each other until recently.' *Cue downcast eyes*. 'For many years there was very little contact between us. Like many siblings we didn't always get on. So sad that just as things had improved she had to die.' *As Clara clutched her tissue she wondered whether she was overdoing it*.

'I asked if you knew whether Sophie ever went abroad as we believe she visited America on three occasions in the years leading up to her death.'

'As I said we weren't in that kind of contact. I do know she used to travel a lot to launch new shops and she did like her holidays.'

'This might come as a shock, but on one of the occasions when Miss Bedford was in America there was a hit-and-run accident which resulted in a father and his son being killed. The driver didn't stop and the incident is, in some ways, similar to the accident that killed your sister.'

Hands clutched tightly to stop them shaking, Clara felt unable to respond. She assumed they had linked the incidents by the common date but the leap from that to include a Bedford in America was like vaulting Niagara Falls.

'We asked you last time if you knew of any enemies who might have wished your sister harm. A slight change of direction, but are you aware of anyone *she* might have wanted to hurt?'

Repeating that she hadn't known much about Sophie's life prior to their recent reunion, Clara longed for the conversation to be over.

'Did your sister know anyone in Statesville? It's a small town in North Carolina.'

How often would they make her say she knew little of Sophie's life?

'There was a similar incident on school grounds outside Statesville during the time Sophie was in the States.'

Clara knew she had to phrase her answers carefully and took a few moments to orchestrate the words, a conductor in sole charge of a duet of players. 'I don't know too much about it but I assume that hit-and-runs are not too unusual. Why are you linking my sister's death with an accident that happened in a town I've never heard of in America?'

Clive spoke for the first time. 'The two incidents occurred on the same date, October 15th, and whilst we would have to agree that hit-and-runs are not uncommon, the similarities between these two have made us suspect they may be linked.'

'Linked? Just because of the date?'

'It's more the fact that Sophie arrived in North Carolina just before the fatal accident there and exactly a year later is killed in a similar incident.'

Reg almost interrupted his partner, 'Did your family have any links with Northumberland, Miss Bedford?' The tone of the conversation had altered, like an unexpected transposition to a minor key.

Clara knew she had to speak in her normal voice but her mouth failed to cooperate. Reg was amused to think that if Dwayne were here he would describe the last question as "One heck of a curve ball. This dame sure ain't going to reach first base."

'You appear upset, take your time, we know it must be hard to talk about her life so soon after losing her.' Clive knew they had worried the woman who sat, eyes down, unable to make eye contact. He just didn't know why.

Cups of tea were made and drunk, allowing Clara to regain some composure.

'Feeling better?' Reg spoke kindly then paused, making sure he appeared to care about her answer, 'I was asking about Northumberland, in particular a seaside town there called Seahouses.'

As he spoke Reg watched her reaction. This time she showed no emotion on hearing the new names and he was cross that she had been given time to plan her response. He knew they should have pressed home their earlier advantage. 'Did your sister have any connections with the area?'

'We went there on holiday as children. It was one of my parents' favourite places. We used to stay in caravans or holiday homes and we knew Seahouses, Beadnell and Craster very well. I don't know if Sophie went back recently. She may well have done as we had such happy memories of the beaches, ruined castles and wonderful walks.'

'Could she have kept in contact with anyone from the area?'

'As I keep saying, for many years Sophie and I led totally separate lives and even after we got back together we never met each other's friends. Why is that part of the world relevant?' As she spoke Clara wondered how innocent she was managing to sound.

Clive explained that he was from the Northumbria force and was based in Seahouses. 'On October 15th three years ago there was a hit-and-run in Seahouses in which a father and son were killed. Last year in Statesville a father and son were also killed on October 15th in an incident where the driver failed to stop. Both incidents, in Seahouses and Statesville, appear to have been deliberate. Now this year your sister is mown down on the same date. Two events on the same date may be a coincidence but three start to look suspicious.'

Feeling that no response was expected the woman remained silent.

The room was becoming stuffy and Clive asked permission to open a window. Hoping Clara had been distracted he enquired again whether she had any enemies.

'You were identical twins so is there any possibility it might have been mistaken identity?'

'Very unlikely, I can't think of any reason why anyone should wish me harm. But then I still think the same about Sophie.'

Knowing that they hadn't made much progress the men thanked Clara for her time and stood to leave. Remembering how successful Columbo had been with his penchant for asking the vital question just as the interview appeared to be over, Reg tried a similar tack.

'Do you know who your sister's doctor was? There may be no connection but a dad and his five-year-old daughter were killed in similar circumstances in May this year. It was in Sale, not far from here and where Sophie lived. Once again the driver didn't stop and once again it doesn't appear to have been an accident.'

'I recall reading about that, a terrible thing to happen. As far as I know Sophie never went to the doctor, but I imagine she was registered with one.'

The men knew this, and that it hadn't been Doctor Lloyd, but the question had once again disconcerted their lady. That would be worth discussing later.

Later was to arrive as soon as they returned to the station. Neither man was convinced they had made much progress but both knew Clara had been disturbed when the other fatalities had been mentioned.

'Might just be hearing about similar incidents. She must be raw having just lost her twin.'

Clive wasn't so sure and said that he had been surprised by her evident desire for self-control. 'It was as though she was afraid to say anything for fear of saying the wrong thing. I think she knows a lot more than she's letting on.'

'You still think Sophie was murdered in some sort of reprisal? That would mean she committed the other three murders, or should that be six?'

Sending out for pizzas the men knew they had a long night ahead as they went over every one of Clara's answers. Both knew she had said things that would aid their investigation. Unfortunately it might take all night, or even longer, to find them.

Chapter 6

Did the hour go well? Impossible to say. My evening was most definitely ruined, all thought of enjoying my moment of triumph gone faster than the land speed record which had been broken the previous day by a young Norwegian.

I expect my interrogators (this had been far more than a friendly chat) spent the evening doing exactly the same as me: dissecting every question and answer.

Had I said too much?

Which of my responses had been ill-advised?

Had any of their questions made me believe that they were anywhere near the truth?

My mood swung from frantic worry to a serene calm. They knew a lot, but not everything, and the vital clues were evading them: the children's mother and Robert Bedford's Will.

Having convinced myself that my responses had led them up the path with the disappearing breadcrumbs I fell asleep, only to endure nightmares where I was the one being pursued by a car with Clive in the driving seat.

Weeks passed with no progress. Dwayne had been informed of the latest line of enquiry, his two English colleagues convinced that Clara knew more than she had admitted.

'If I recall Clara Bedford is Sophie's twin sister. In my experience most siblings know a lot about each other, often more than they want to say. You said that at times Clara seemed uncomfortable. Which questions bothered her?

'She didn't react much to the American angle but we definitely struck a nerve when Northumberland was mentioned. We asked about family connections to the region and she said they went there a lot as kids.'

'So Statesville didn't mean anything?'

'No, and maybe Northumberland just brought back memories of happier times when the family was all together. She's the only one left now, both parents are dead and now her sister.'

A long silence ensued, interrupted by laboured breathing, always an indication that Dwayne was deep in thought.

'This is probably way off the mark but if she's the sole survivor of the family does she inherit much? I seem to recall that her sister ran a business of some sort.'

'You're not inferring that she killed her sister to gain her money? Or maybe you think she employed a hit man. This is the north of England, not the Bronx! And even if she was in some way involved in her sister's demise, we'd be left with absolutely no link to our dads and their offspring.'

Laughing at the thought of hit men in Windermere, a town with its hills and beautiful lake that he had recently researched, Dwayne said that he thought that when money, and in all probability a substantial amount, was involved in a crime it was worth further investigation.

'People kill for cents over here and I don't rightly think it's so different on your side of the pond.'

'Pennies here but I get your drift. Only last week a young girl was mugged and her purse containing less than two pounds was taken. Money and evil remain the closest of companions. I'll get in touch with the family solicitor and see if he can tell me just how much is involved and whether Clara is the sole beneficiary.'

Edward Jackson was not pleased to be visited by the police. As a young man finishing his law degree he had been tempted to become a defence lawyer. His tutor, a brilliant lecturer called Sidney Simmons, had encouraged him to experience all types of law before deciding the route he wanted to follow. Corporate law had not appealed and he chose family law in preference to the criminal variety following some extremely dubious cases he had endured in the local Magistrates' Courthouse where some police behaviour and sections of the evidence had been as suspect as the people in the dock. Ever since then he had found it hard to trust them.

Three decades on he knew he had made the right decision, to specialise in the type of work he found both interesting and satisfying and which provided endless variety. Family issues took up the bulk of his time, from divorce to Wills to Powers of Attorney. He also dealt with trusts and estates, one of the largest being the Bedford's. Employment issues and bankruptcy were the areas he never liked: so heartbreaking for those involved, often far more so than divorce.

Long hours had never bothered him and it was late in the day when the police arrived to find him still behind his desk.

They were polite but insistent. What could he tell them about the estate left by Miss Sophie Bedford?

Half an hour later Reg and Clive left, having ascertained that Clara was indeed the sole beneficiary and that she had inherited both the Bedford Jewellery emporium and all her sister's assets. The solicitor had been reluctant to furnish many details until he was informed that the police might be investigating a murder.

'Murder? I thought Sophie was killed by an assailant attempting to steal her car.'

'We're just following another line of enquiry, sir. We'd be grateful if you didn't mention this to anyone.'

Chapter 7

Damocles' sword has been resurrected and is hovering menacingly over my house. Every day I await the fatal knock on the door. Whenever the classroom phone rings, an irritating innovation installed recently, several heartbeats become mislaid. My nights are a juxtaposition of lying awake feeling terrified and a montage of foul dreams that spoil any moments when I manage to sleep.

Katie understood my request for a lot to do. 'As much extra as you can find. The cupboards all need a good tidy but I can do those at the end of the day. Tell me which wall displays need replacing and I'm sure the library could do with some reorganisation.'

I have been arriving at school at seven each morning and leaving when Janice, the cleaner, throws me out hours after the rest of the staff has left.

'I know how you feel,' Katie said, though that was doubtful in the extreme. 'I found great solace in work when my parents got divorced. I was in my final year at uni and it's quite ironic to think that my excellent degree owes a lot to their separation. As you know only too well, it's always possible to swamp you with a huge range of tasks but try to be kind to yourself and please say if it becomes too arduous.'

Too arduous? No. The only time I am able to cope is when both my mind and body are occupied. Physical work stops me thinking and our classroom has never looked as organised or as clean. Bookcases tidied and labelled, the Space and Beyond *display a thing of wonder and every file organised alphabetically. Even the windows have been polished, using my grandmother's technique of a liberal dousing in vinegar followed by a newspaper assault. Every desk shines so brightly that Jemma said she could see her face in hers.*

Four weeks have passed since the visit. Almost a month endured and an extremely elongated one, a piece of elastic that kept stretching. I have promised myself that if I hear no more by Christmas I will stop worrying.

Three men, none of whom were feeling particularly wise, were forced to concentrate on their day-to-day crimes. No new evidence had been forthcoming on the "Daddy Deaths" as Dwayne had once called the incidents, a vain attempt to alleviate the mood of his British colleagues.

December saw Clive dealing with a particularly unpleasant set of burglaries. Seven houses were involved, one every three days. All had been left looking as though a tornado had passed through. In each case many valuables had been taken, from TV's and iPads to jewellery and money, but it was the chaos that greeted the homeowners that was so upsetting. Greg Harrison spoke for them all when he said he felt violated. Furniture was broken, fabrics slashed and curtains and pictures thrown onto the floor. Bathrooms and kitchens remained saturated after being flooded.

The thief had entered each house during the day when the owners were out at work. No clues were left, not a single fingerprint came to light. The police didn't know of any miscreant who enjoyed creating such deplorable havoc.

Three weeks into the investigation Jimmy Rangle made the mistake of entering a large detached house, number eight on his list, unaware that the owner was upstairs having taken the day off to get over a hangover.

'We've got him. He's from Newcastle and I phoned Ellis who knows him rather well, says he's already spent a lot of his life in prison. It gave me great delight to inform Mr Rangle that he'll be enjoying board and lodging at our expense for the foreseeable future.'

Although it had been a most unsavoury case Mari was pleased that her husband had been kept so busy.

Mid-winter in Northumberland was definitely not Mari's favourite time of year, the days still short and, even on the coast, the temperature remaining below zero. The only redeeming feature was the sea which broiled and bubbled, spilling dramatically over the sea walls. Clive had once joked that when the water was so sensational it reminded him of a film he had once seen where the gods had stirred the ocean with such ferocity that an entire enemy fleet had been submerged.

Neither had enjoyed the Christmas break, Clive finding it difficult to relax and Mari shattered after a particularly busy term. Christmas Day had been spent with Mari's family, a noisy affair with her sister's three under-fives the centre of attention. Although the house in Alnwick was only fifteen miles from home Clive insisted that they leave early, the excuse being that a heavy fall of snow was forecast.

'That was worse than ever,' was his opening gambit as they escaped, 'those children are out of control.'

'It is Christmas and they were very excited.'

'There's excitement and there's bad behaviour. They are totally indulged. Did you see the number of presents they received? Not a thank you from any of them and I'm convinced they've never heard the word "no".'

'I have to admit that I hope Tamsin is a better dentist than she is a mother. Just imagine being one of her victims and making an appointment for a scale and polish only to walk out with two deep root canal fillings and an extraction!' For the first time that day Clive heard himself laugh.

Both were relieved to arrive home. Della and Fluffy, now fully grown cats, met them and explained in their very direct way that they wanted feeding. *Sixth Sense*, one of Mari's favourite films, was on the television, a most unusual choice for the festive season, but they both loved every minute.

Clive was working between Christmas and New Year. More snow was heralded, the weathermen making it sound almost as life-changing as the message the Christmas angels had once delivered. Mari and Clive delayed their trip to Newcastle until the afternoon of New Year's Eve, having been invited to spend the New Year with Ellis and Barbara.

Any mention of "dratted police talk" was banned in the house but the two men caught up on their twice daily walks with Brandy, the family's chocolate brown Labrador, an animal devoid of any common sense but whose lively personality kept the men amused. As always Ellis listened patiently as Clive revisited every detail of all four cases that he assured his friend were related.

'Tomorrow is a new year, a time for optimism. I'm sure the breakthrough you seek will come.' Clive realised that was all the help he was going to get.

Several weeks later Mari returned home after a particularly difficult day. Incessant rain had resulted in frustrated children trapped in the classroom, like animals at an old fashioned zoo, unable to escape at breaktime and run off their abundant energy. To add to the misery the day had culminated with an extended staff meeting to discuss the government's latest initiatives. Mari was exhausted and upset to see the house in darkness. She knew that Clive should have been home hours ago, Tuesday afternoon taken as extra time off following a week of overtime.

'Why on earth are you sitting in the dark?' Knowing she had said the wrong thing Mari put on the lamps and sat beside her husband who was sitting slouched on the settee. To her horror she realised that he was crying, hot tears running down his face. The doctor had advised her that when he became particularly low all she could do was be a quiet presence.

'Failed, we've all failed. There is a way to solve these murders but none of us can see it.' This was the longest sentence she had heard Clive say for several days and the effort had left him shattered. He slumped even lower. Mari wasn't sure this was the time to put forward her idea, but she knew that she couldn't make the situation worse.

'Clive, you know I always say that when a child in my class can't understand the concept I'm trying to teach him I decide to have one final go. If that fails I have to accept that he won't get it. I tell myself that either he'll have another chance to understand it later in the year or he will revisit it when he moves up to Year Four and Mrs Collins can weave her magic. Sometimes a child just isn't ready for the ideas that he is being asked to consider and children these days have so many each term I wonder sometimes how they cope at all.'

Mari wasn't sure Clive was listening and paused for a moment.

'I was thinking...Why not give one of the cases a final try: just one case. Really concentrate on it. You've got some leave due so you could afford to give it your full attention. With children we have to go back to the stage where they last grasped a concept and only then can we take them forward: build on what they know. If I were you I would look at one of the cases from the very beginning, as though you'd never seen it before, and take it from there. Step by step.'

'But you've said I should forget it all. It was making me ill.'

'Yes, and it is, but this might be the way to resolve the matter. You would have to agree that should there be no further progress that would be the end of the matter. You would have given it one last try.'

'I suppose as they're all linked if I solved one the others would follow.'

'Do it on your own, no need to involve Reg or Dwayne. You've often boasted that you're good at working solo.'

Leaving to cook the dinner, a task that would normally have irritated her, the unspoken agreement having long been established that the first one to arrive home started the meal, Mari left Clive to consider her suggestion.

'I'll do it. Not one of the fathers and children but Sophie Bedford. The Cumbria police were most helpful at the time and I'm sure they wouldn't mind if I asked to go over everything they've got on the incident. I know you laugh at my gut feelings but there's something about that case that makes me convinced it's linked to the others. Not just the date, though that's vital, but something else: something sitting, waiting for me to find.'

Two weeks later Clive was ensconced in a tiny room deep inside Windermere police station. The lack of windows was no loss as even Wordsworth would have found great difficulty writing anything poetic about the rain-sodden landscape. It had poured incessantly since he had arrived early the previous afternoon and his initial enthusiasm was beginning to vanish, the work starting to imitate the weather.

No progress so far. Everything he read was familiar. The blinding light had failed to materialise, no Road to Damascus moment imminent. He sat over his third coffee of the morning and almost envied the hikers he had seen setting off earlier from the inappropriately named Fell View Inn. Fortunately they had been clad in full waterproofs but within seconds of leaving the hotel had looked as though they were immersed in a slow wash cycle. How he longed to escape, to join them on a long walk, however inclement the weather.

'Excuse me, sir, have you got a minute?' Rosie Cullen, a young PC, stood uncertainly in the doorway. She was moving from foot to foot, an uneasy dance. Clive couldn't work out whether she was excited or nervous. He had been told, on numerous occasions, that he put the fear of God into new recruits but as she was the one officer assigned to help him he thought it prudent to be welcoming.

'Come in PC Cullen, I won't bark and I don't bite.'

Thanking him, Rosie walked in and stood nervously by his desk. Determined to impress the senior officer she had spent a long time over her appearance. Her uniform was pressed, shoes polished and a liberal amount of make-up applied. Clive saw none of this.

Realising that the girl would not open the conversation Clive asked her to sit down and tell him what she had come to say.

For as long as she could remember Rosie had wanted to be a police officer. Today she knew she was about to become one; she was about to make a difference.

'Sir, you may remember that you asked me to look at all the CCTV footage from the Windermere area for the morning of October 15th.' After what felt like a long pause she continued. 'When I was young I loved a game called *Picture Me*. The idea is to match a person with their disguised self.' Clive looked puzzled and attempted to hide his irritation. He had no idea where this was leading.

'Bear with me Sir, there is a point to this.'

Assuring her that he knew there would be he asked her to carry on.

'The *Picture Me* game was easy to begin with: one picture and a choice of two disguises and you had to say which matched the original. The game got harder until there was an original and a selection of twenty disguises. As it was computer generated none of the disguises was ever repeated. I loved the game so much that I played and played it until I was quite the expert. It got to the stage where I could beat my brother at it every time.

'All quite fascinating but I assume you've not just come to share childhood reminiscences.' Realising he had sounded brusque Clive asked the young woman to continue.

'Well, I looked at all the CCTV images for the morning in question and was concentrating on the people who left packages at the desk of The Today Store. Several women left their items behind the desk but not Sophie Bedford. As you know she was above average height and I read in the notes that on the morning she died she was wearing a rather distinctive red coat. The only one of that height who asked to leave a bag was female but was dressed very soberly in brown and beige... definitely not Sophie.'

'Not Sophie? Are you sure?'

'No, she definitely didn't leave anything but about three-quarters of an hour later the camera shows Sophie Bedford, in her red coat – it was pillar box red with unusual black buttons – rush in and collect the package. She had to show her receipt and then almost ran out of the shop, large package in hand.'

'Did you identify the woman who left the goods?'

'No...not at first. She was very careful not to look up, almost as though she knew the camera was there. So at that point I couldn't identify her.'

Feeling there was more to come Clive sat very still and waited.

'I then looked at the images from further afield. I knew what Sophie Benson looked like from the photograph on the front of the case file and I had seen her in the shop. I also knew the time she was killed: ten fifty. As I was looking at the footage from Windermere railway station I did a double take: Sophie was walking down the platform fifteen minutes after she died.'

Stomach on a trampoline, hands shaking, Clive asked her to repeat what she had just said.

After doing so Rosie added, 'I went back to Sophie in the red coat collecting her goods and compared the picture with the allegedly "dead woman" in an anorak walking down the platform. It wasn't the same woman! Ms Red Coat had a small mole on her left cheek. Ms Anorak didn't. It was that kind of minute detail that made me so good at *Picture Me*.'

A double forte silence filled the room. Both knew that Sophie had a twin sister. Both knew it was the breakthrough they had sought.

'The next thing I did was to look again at the woman who had left the package. They're usually left if the person wants to go for coffee in the upstairs café. When she left her purchases she was dressed differently from the woman on the platform but I'd swear it was the same woman. The first time she had on what looked like a wig and indoor clothes, the second time she was dressed like a walker in hat, scarf and anorak. I'm absolutely certain it was the same person: same height, same build, same style of walking.'

Speaking so softly that Rosie had to ask him to repeat it, Clive muttered, 'Clara claims that Sophie went up to the Lakes on her own that day. I wonder how she will explain being on Windermere station a few minutes after her sister died.'

Chapter 8

Christmas arrived and as promised I stopped worrying. By now all the cases would be relegated, like the unfortunate teams gaining the fewest points in the various football leagues. As far as I was concerned each case would now be colder than the weather. I reasoned that, as there had been no further contact, I was safe. Nothing had linked me to the various deceased. Yes, my sister had been killed but in all probability by some criminal attempting to steal her valuable car. If they couldn't link me to her death the others couldn't follow.

All my newly acquired shops were proving successful, highly skilled managers in each one. I appointed a new General Director, at exorbitant but necessary expense, so have had very little to do with the business. The day to day nitty-gritty of earning money can be so boring. The plan remains to ditch them - for an exorbitant amount.

To celebrate my final achievement I booked a last minute holiday in the Caribbean. There is nothing like escaping a Manchester winter. I reasoned that there is no point having all this money if I don't start to enjoy it. The Caribbean has over seven hundred islands. They're not all vacation destinations and by the time I booked, two days before departure, my choice was limited to Barbados or Saint Lucia. The travel agent, a surprisingly helpful young man, suggested Barbados as the better choice for the single traveller. He said that at this time of year Saint Lucia would be full of Americans on honeymoon. No further information was needed!

A blissful week: I returned home utterly relaxed.

With what speed the new term got under way. Once back one's feet hit the ground as if one is in training for the next major athletics' event. As usual by break on the first day everyone agreed that the holidays were a distant memory.

Three weeks in and everyone is talking about the next break.

My one dilemma is whether or not I should continue with the job that I do enjoy or think of an entirely different way to occupy my time. After all, I never have to do another day's work in my life. To work or not to work? Oh, what a conundrum!

Vets are now of the opinion that cats should not be given cream but Clive and Rosie stood by the fax machine looking like a pair of moggies who had just shared a litre of the double variety.

Within minutes of Rosie's revelation Clive had phoned Dwayne to ask him to fax his photos of the Miss Bedford who had entered America. Immigration had supplied three: one for each visit.

'No mole. It's Clara, not Sophie! She was the sister who entered the States each time. We've got her. We've bloody well got her.' Grabbing Rosie he waltzed her round the room, a dance that matched Fred and Ginger for sheer exuberance if not style.

The time had come to share the breakthrough. 'Slow down Clive, you're not making any sense. Moles? Wrong sister? Start from the beginning.' Hardly capable of putting words in the right order Clive said he would be on the next train to Manchester.

Shortly after he arrived the two men were on their way to have another chat with Edward Jackson. The lawyer was not pleased to be asked to stop what he was doing and speak to the police a second time.

Dispensing with any niceties Superintendent Thompson launched straight in, 'Sophie Benson's death is now being treated as a murder enquiry and we need to ask you a few more questions about the Bedford Estate.'

From long experience Edward had learnt to hide his feelings and sat quietly, secretly intrigued by the situation.

'Clara Bedford inherited all her sister's assets. When we last spoke you told us that in their father's Will, everything was left to Sophie, nothing for Clara. Do you know why he favoured one twin?'

Taking his time the solicitor explained, as thoroughly as possible, the content of the first Will and the reason Clara had given him for being disinherited five years ago. 'At the time she was extremely bitter about it. I have to admit that justice now appears to have been done, though one would not have wished Sophie dead.'

'Were there any codicils to their father's Will?'

'Yes, two: Sophie could, should she so wish, make any alterations she saw fit, including sharing the assets with Clara…'

Reg interrupted, 'But she chose not to.'

'Indeed, at the time that was my understanding. I know Clara asked her several times for a fair share but Sophie was adamant that she wanted to stick to the content of the Will and uphold their father's wishes.'

'And what was the second codicil?'

'Should Sophie predecease Clara then Clara would inherit it all, unless Sophie had any children in which case the estate, in its entirety, would be shared amongst the offspring.

'That would mean that Clara would be bypassed once again.'

'Yes indeed, but as Sophie died childless Clara inherited everything. And everything is in the millions.'

Thanking the solicitor for his time and assuring him that he had been extremely helpful the two officers left.

Returning to the station Reg said that the next step was obvious. 'I'm ahead of you,' Clive said, 'show a picture of Sophie to anyone who remembers the mother of Peter, Paul and Natasha.'

Chapter 9

Decision made: notice handed in. Some colleagues were surprised; others said they would do the same in my position. A week in Beauty is Yours, a residential pampering and well-being centre in the Cotswolds, is booked over Easter. Their brochure describes their numerous treatments as "essential grooming" but I doubt whether most of the world's population would see gel nails, pedicures, Hollywood lashes and waxing as necessities. No doubt by the end of the week I will be looking my best, ready for my month in Tibet, a country I have always wanted to visit. (Yes, I know, who will be looking at me when they have the Himalayas?) On returning home I will look at the list of places on my "must see" list and book my next adventure.

Will I grow tired of travelling? Will the allure of a life of indolence wane? When and if it does I will do something else. At last I am the mistress of my own destiny.

'Hi guys, just checking in with an update. Miss Loopy, the gorgeous Gloria, has agreed that the photo of Miss Bedford, who we now know to be of the Clara variety, looks very like the woman she saw at the school. Being her she couldn't be a hundred per cent sure but she picked Clara's photo out of the selection we showed her.'

Clive thanked the American and said that he had been about to call Statesville as he and Reg had enjoyed great results following their recent enquiries. 'The midwives from Reading, Shirley Pullis and Jenna Franklin, both thought Sophie's picture could have been the girl they knew as Ruby Smith, the one who gave birth in 1995, but it was a long time ago and people's appearance can change and they saw her for a very short time.

However, hold onto that Stetson. Teresa Blackall who lived next door to the Lloyds, and remembered Natasha's mother as Pearl Lloyd, is adamant that Sophie Bedford and Pearl Lloyd are one and the same. We now believe that Sophie Bedford was a mother and I'd bet my pension that she gave birth to all three children.'

'So, dear Clara had to eliminate them in order to inherit her sister's fortune. She's one hell of a dame. I think y'all agree we've got a slam dunk!' Dwayne enjoyed Clive's attempt at a southern drawl.

'We're going back to the school, Central High, where Stuart Wilson taught in Manchester before he moved to North Carolina. Some teachers stay at the same school for years and someone might remember meeting Stuart's partner. She might have attended a school do or maybe someone socialised with the pair. She was Beryl Smith at the time and we'll see if that name means anything and we've got the photo ID kit ready. The Head has invited us in to talk at the staff meeting tomorrow and we'll let you know how we get on.'

A surprising number of staff had remained at the school, some gaining internal promotion and others happy to see their careers out in the establishment they knew well. Most said that Stuart's partner seldom attended school functions but a few recalled the barn dance in the school hall, organised by the social committee, when she had accompanied him.

'She was quite a looker and could really dance. I was one of the people who organised that evening. My band played for the event but I love dancing and go on the floor when I get the chance. I seem to remember partnering Beryl for the Alabama Jubilee and the Cincinnati Reel.' Adam Walker, Senior Master in charge of exams, agreed to look at the selection of photographs.

'That's her, that's Beryl. As I said she was good in the looks department. We teased Stuart the next day and told him we weren't surprised he kept her hidden.'

None of the other members of staff was confident enough to identify her but the policemen were satisfied that Mr Walker's testimony would suffice. Beryl Smith and Sophie Bedford: the same person.

'Crown Prosecution Service, here we come.'

Clive smiled, 'Even the pernickety CPS must agree we've got more than enough to charge Clara with murder. We'll start with the annihilation of her sister and go from there. Sophie: then the other six.'

Chapter 10

I hate the February break. The weather is appalling, the days are short and there's nothing I want to do. I did go for lunch with Katie which is always very pleasant but it's now early afternoon and I'm scrolling through the million and one programmes on an array of television channels no one wants to watch.

Four days remain...then six weeks at school...after that...my life begins.

Dwayne had been told the time. Three o'clock in the afternoon in England, ten in the morning in Statesville. He sat in his office, coffee in hand, watching the four-way stop – and imagined the scene.

Clara's road was deserted. Most people were at work and everyone else was hiding from the bitter wind that the weatherman had said was blowing straight from the Arctic.

No dog walkers.

No children playing out.

Two policemen – parking carefully by the kerb.

Two policemen – walking up to Clara's front door.

Lightning Source UK Ltd.
Milton Keynes UK
UKOW02f2359230117

292732UK00001B/34/P